Praise For The Skulldiggery Series

"DM Gritzmacher weaves an uncomfortable tale of terror. His spooky subterranean passageways into cryptic fiction is like a building crescendo of despair and anguish with a backdrop of brutality. The claustrophobic tension and clever blindsides will become memorable moments for the reader. What Peter Benchley did for the ocean and aquatic life, DM Gritzmacher has done for quarries and archeological relicts."
- Horror Bookworm Reviews

"I really love how this series is coming together! It's a great blend of history, horror, and paranormal. Highly recommend!"
- Spooky Little Book Nerd-Amazon

"...historical horror that moves seamlessly from past to present with incredible world building and addictive storytelling."
- Sharron-Amazon UK

"... contains so many lines that are both poetic and heartbreaking. I greatly enjoyed the descriptions... Somehow the words come together to illustrate such horrible things but in such beautiful prose."
- Review Cat-Goodreads

THE SHRINE

SKULLDIGGERY BOOK 6

DM GRITZMACHER

PIQUED PUBLISHING

Book Cover by Matt Seff Barnes

Library of Congress Control Number: 2025915136

The Shrine – Print - 979-8-9914556-4-0

The Shrine – ePub – 979-8-9914556-3-3

First edition 2025

Gritzmonster.com

CONTENT WARNING

The Shrine contains graphic depictions of violence and gore that may not be suitable for some readers.

SHRINE

Shrine-1: A case, box, or receptacle in which sacred relics (such as the bones of a holy person) are deposited. 1b: a place in which devotion forms an object of religious veneration and pilgrimage. 1c: a niche containing a religious image. 2: a receptacle (such as a tomb) for the dead. 3: a place or object hallowed by its associations.

III

THE BARREN STRETCH OF ground was well-hidden from prying eyes. A bleak field of wispy weeds and hardpacked earth pocked in various places by drifting sand and eruptions of twisted foliage. A near desert where only the hardiest of living things survived. Yet, this desolate plot of land had seemed to call to the man who now trod unceremoniously across it. Pulling him in deeper until the very vastness of the abandoned and unkept field concealed him.

The man shuffled his sandaled feet as he descended a small hill that led him to a trickling stream of gurgling, discolored water. The sandy soil under his step giving way as he stumbled toward a nearby cluster of sturdy-looking trees. The tallest of them supporting several thick branches that had caught his eye as suitable. He laid his deeply tanned hand on the surface of the tree, his fingers absentmindedly exploring the rutted bark as his eyes scrutinized each limb. Satisfied with the choice, he began to unwind the coiled rope at his shoulder before tossing one end of it up and over the branch. He let the remainder of the slack rope fall to the ground as he grabbed the dangling lead. Hunched over, with the setting sun at his back, he worked the thick, rough-textured line. Tying and twisting the end until he was satisfied with the result.

A noose.

When he was done, the man hurried to secure the opposite end of the rope, winding it several times around the thickest part of the tree trunk before tying it off. He tugged and pulled hard until he was sure the knot would hold. When he was finished, he cast his eyes back the direction he'd come. His hands began to tremble as he spied the outline of two stationary figures observing his actions from afar. The man all but leapt for the tree beside him, quickly shinning up it until he sat on the thick branch where his rope swayed in the warm breeze. Without a second backward glance, he fitted the crafted noose over his own head.

Mumbling to himself with a wry smile, the man pulled a handful of silver, tarnish coins from his pocket. "Who wants to live forever?" said the man before softly closing his eyes as he slipped off the top of the branch. Plummeting head-long towards the ground below before the rope snapped tight. The force of the long drop instantly severing the head from his body. As the decapitated torso hit the hardened, cracked and dried earth under the tree, it burst asunder and all of his bowels gushed out. The gore and splatter mixing with the clinking coins.

Blood money.

The deep red moon had risen, and the ominous sky above suddenly seemed awash in blood. A forbidding crimson hue that pricked the eyes and bruised the hearts of all those bearing witness to the executions. The three crucified men – framed against this prematurely darkening sky – each hung limply. Only one figure yet stirred, and he labored painfully through the last of his agonizing breaths. Beneath him, as he sagged one final time, the ground began to rumble and shake. The two crude and misshapen wooden beams he'd been barbarically nailed to swayed slightly in the emerging chaos but remained upright.

Below the crucifixions, staring stoically across the increasingly panicked and scattering masses, a lone woman stood apart from the commotion. Her features and expression unreadable under the fine cloth covering she wore loosely about her face and head. Though her piercing eyes never wavered from the scene of the crucifixions, she didn't move against the soldiers tasked with the grim retrieval of the bodies. The young military men stripping the corpses and casting lots for the clothing and meager belongings of the three.

Behind her, struggling gamely to crest the top of what was known locally as the Place of the Skull, a badly hobbled and disfigured leper girl slowly approached the woman. A tightly folded package of cloth held reverently in her hands. They both wore similar garments of the highest quality, and though the young newcomer's speech was marred by her deformed mouth, she greeted the woman with obvious familiarity. "I've brought what you asked, Madeleine. Do you want me to take it over?" The girl's claw-like fingers pointing to a small group of weeping men who stood nearby.

Pursing her lips together, the woman replied in a hushed tone. "Remember, you need to keep calling me Mary until we leave this place," she said, frowning in mild reproach. "But, no. I want to have a word with Joseph before I give him the shroud." The girl handed the woman the thick, iridescent cloth. The neatly folded material at first appearing grey, or perhaps silver, before slowly becoming more beige or brown as it was passed. The color undeterminable in the strange scarlet glow of the blood moon above.

After conversing briefly with them, the peculiar cloth was passed to the men and Madeleine strode back. Muttering to herself with a wan smile, "Three down, one to go." The girl, nearly a young woman, asked shyly if everything had went as hoped and expected.

Madeleine turned with a wink. "Certainly," she replied. "Sure as the kiss of Judas."

CHAPTER ONE
GERMANY-16TH CENTURY

THE WOODEN WHEELS, BOGGED down with clinging muck, half-turned and half-slid along the sloppy ground they crossed. The driver cursing to himself as he struggled to keep the horsedrawn wagon moving forward amidst the swirling wind and somber darkness of the late hour. The murky spray kicked up by the churning hooves and burdened wheels speckled and dulled the swaying lantern at his head. Though he periodically wiped at the smudged glass with a soiled sleeve, the burning candle inside barely illuminated the crude lane the two men nervously traversed.

On both sides of their route, ancient, gnarled trees of dripping foliage sagged and pressed down on them. The budding branches occasionally fingering their heads as if trying to dissuade them from the clandestine journey. Both driver and passenger peering intensely at the surrounding timber with unwavering eyes. The men hope to pass unnoticed and watching closely for anything that seems out of place. Unnatural. Somewhere unseen, the howling wolves serenading their travel were suddenly joined by a chorus of nearby baying hounds. The combination made for a frightful clamor that echoed in their ears as they knowingly crossed the border into the field of the dead.

The slow rolling cart came to a halting stop, and the skittish horse who pulled it was quickly secured. Freed from the tree cover that had hid the troubled sky for much of their ride, the passenger was grateful to see the lingering flashes of light erupting overhead were now far in the distance. Most of their upcoming work, it seemed, would be as hoped - cloaked in the obscurity of darkness. The last of the lightening from the dissipating storm only briefly filling the black night and ominous rolling clouds above with contradiction. Long seconds later, the thunder that followed rumbled weakly as the storm continued its hasty retreat. Satisfied with their timing, the men pulled aside the soggy tarp that hid the digging tools they'd brought and unhooked their lantern. Holding it high, they crossed the cemetery, careful to keep their footing as they converged on the boneyard's newest resident. The passenger taking charge and leading the driver deeper into the burial grounds.

The deluge of spring rain had softened the recently turned earth. The dark soil clumping together in large globs near the surface. But the passenger didn't mind. After all, the sodden roads and flooding plains only helped further mask these ghastly forays into the local graveyards. Afterwards, should anyone notice the disturbed patches of dirt above the cemetery plots, the raging storms would likely be blamed for the motley appearance. Besides, he reasoned, with his family's storehouse currently packed with the previous winter's haul of ice – chiseled straight from their lake and insulated with straw and sawdust – now was the best time to maximize every possible opportunity. Well before the relentless heat of summer descended and made this work much less palatable.

So, despite the earlier tempest, and though the wind still howled and shrieked at times like the mad, he'd come to claim what he already considered his property. The man's body, a young farmer gored and killed by an enraged bull, would provide the raw material needed for the next stage of his experiments. Though he personally had, of course, never actually spoken to the simple peasant, he'd been vaguely aware of the man.

His untimely passing had proven, ironically, most timely.

Working together in the shallow trench, the passenger, Dr. Herbert Chanet and his faithful assistant, Hans, swept the last of the dirt from the cover of the pine box. The casket – if one could call the crude coffin one – remained underground where it had been interred just the day before. Only the thin wooden lid was pried from the box and tossed from the earthen hole by Hans's quick work. Though the ashen corpse of the unfortunate villager was mere days into its inevitable rot, the punctured and torn abdomen was already expelling the stench of growing decay.

Herbert, with a silken handkerchief covering his nose and mouth, reached for the flaming lantern resting on the rim of the disturbed grave. He lowered it, the soft glow filling the new hole and exposing the dead within. Satisfied with the condition, the unfortunate young man's body was soon liberated from the dirt cavity where it had been laid to rest. Hastily, the two men deposited the corpse in the back of their horse-drawn wagon and covered the remains before returning to the hole. Quickly refilling the empty grave and masking their tracks as best they could. For good measure, they toppled several of the newer headstones and smaller grave markers in various spots around the cemetery. Hoping the minor vandalism would be blamed on the violence of the earlier storms and deflect attention away from the tomb they'd robbed. Keep the local gravedigger busy in the morning and his mind occupied. No reason to tempt fate, as is often said.

With this newest addition to his collection now safely in hand, Herbert allowed himself to relax for the first time that night. As Hans guided their horsedrawn cart back toward the family estate, his mind began to wander. He, Doctor Herbert Chanet, was now on the cusp of his greatest experiment and achievement to date. The alchemy he had developed was a mixture of ancient wisdom, abstract reasoning, quantitative thought, astrology, and the most modern of the 16th century sciences. With the constant refinement and development of his own scientific method, he'd come up with an elixir. A potent batch that would help crown him king of the emerging Scientific Revolution of the 1550s.

The conqueror of death!

Herbert chuckled to himself at the bold proclamation. Ignoring Hans's questioning, sidelong glance. He knew it was premature to say the disease of death was so soon to be fully cured. However, after years of painstaking research and countless failures, his most recent successes had emboldened him. Indeed, the vast lands and dark forests of his ancestral estate contained some of his greatest victories. (And, he admitted only to himself, several blasphemous failures he hoped to never lay eyes upon again). But bringing more four-legged creatures back to life was never the ultimate goal. Or the endgame. Nor was simply creating new life from the varied bounty provided by nature's endless resources. For if Herbert was to be recognized as the genius he truly was, he must fully defeat death among the highest of beings.

Man must rise from the dead. Not of their own bequest, but of Herbert's.

The doctor twisted slightly on the softly swaying wagon seat and looked longingly at what they'd exhumed. He was near giddy with anticipation. In the sky overhead, the windswept clouds thinned and the wavering beams of the moon illuminated the German countryside their cart hurried across. The easing wind and rhythmic creaking of the wooden wheels turning, coupled with the soft *clop-clop* of the horse's hooves in the sloppy mud of the lane, all that was heard.

"Do you hear that, Hans?" Herbert, his voice a hushed whisper, querying his most loyal servant as the wagon driver wearily dragged a soggy sleeve across his mud-speckled features. "I wonder if we should, perhaps, hasten our pace."

"I hear nothing, My Lord." Hans cocked an ear to one side briefly before shaking his head. "What troubles you?"

"Exactly that. The sound of nothing." Herbert swiveling his head while his eyes combed through the trees that lined both sides of the lane. "What silences the brazen wolves that prowl the riverside, moors, and the bogs?"

Hans answered without speaking. His eyes widening in obvious recognition as he hastily snapped the leather reins in his hands - urging the horse to a trot. The suffocating stillness loosening his bowels while, at the same time, an uncomfortable tightness began to expand inside his chest. Hans knew that if more of the doctor's earlier experiments had survived the most recent and harsh winter, he had no desire to cross paths with them. His eyes forever dimmed by all he'd witnessed, his ears forever pricked by the tortured wailing, and his mind forever seared by his sullied hands. Hans shuddered involuntarily as he recalled their previous work.

And what they'd fed those... things.

Ahead of them, looming out of the thickly forested area that surrounded much of the home, stood the noble House of Chanet. A massive, five-story estate surrounded by a cluster of barns, stables, servant's quarters, and long fences. Crossing a bridge of thick timbers that extended across a wide, meandering river, Hans confidently guided the horsedrawn wagon to one side of the opulent home, avoiding the main entryway.

Despite the impressive beauty of the grand manor, Herbert's favorite room, and the intended destination for the cargo they now hauled, was one few had ever seen. A long-forgotten, underground portion of basement that had been walled up with crude bricks and cordoned off from the rest of the cellar sometime in the distant past. When Hans had first uncovered the clandestine space, Herbert immediately commandeered it for his own. Resealing the interior wall and having an outside doorway installed that he alone held the key for. Inside, crafting his own laboratory where he could toil away undisturbed within his home whenever it pleased him. The secret chamber now held what had taken him years to develop and perfect. His most prized possession and near lifelong obsession.

The key to resurrection and eternal life.

Pulling the leather reins in tandem with a softly muttered *woah*, the cart gradually came to rest. Stopping beside a wooden doorway heavily padlocked and secured. Herbert quickly jumped down – his finely crafted leather boots splashing the muddy water they landed in – unlocked and opened the sturdy door. Above their heads, no light was visible from the many windows that overlooked the miles of rugged timber that stretched between the home and the border of France at the two men's backs. Though many of the live-in servants had been employed by the Chanet family for generations, Herbert trusted no one with his secrets. As is often said, one could never be too careful.

He helped Hans unload their cargo and carry it down the handful of steps that led to his hidden workspace. Herbert then secured the cadaver in a make-shift cold chamber they'd created to house the raw materials he worked with. The near airtight compartment, he'd discovered, helped keep the vermin and bugs at bay until his work could begin. The two men labored together in near silence before finally locking away their latest prize and returning outside. The early morning sky above was clearing and beginning to brighten, but still remained a dark, murky color. The stormy, black night begrudgingly giving way to the emerging sun and new day.

Herbert wearily watched the slow retreat of the wagon, Hans unhooking and tending to the horse they'd used. Satisfied with the macabre retrieval and their night of clandestine work, Herbert turned and began to discreetly make his way back inside the home. Rubbing at his tired eyes with balled up fists before slipping in a side door from one of the manor's many patios. Failing to notice the flutter of drapes at the lone, lighted window of the estate - the master bedroom. A soft, yellow glow fading from view as Herbert quietly closed the door behind him.

Chapter Two
France-Present Day

Its gawdy, blinking lights beckoning the lonely, Beth swerved to the curb and parked several blocks from the venue. She discreetly watched as, like doomed moths daring the flame, men and women in near equal measure swarmed the entrance of the bar. Unable, as she well understood, to resist the allure of the flashing beacon in the emerging moonlight.

For a brief moment, questioning her own decisions, Beth nearly pulled back onto the street before finally killing the engine with a slight sigh. Afterall, thinking to herself, she was here now and this was her very last night in Caen. The drive from her hotel – the lodging her employer had secured while she worked in this part of France – had been less than fifteen minutes. Fighting the butterflies swirling inside her stomach, she tilted the rearview mirror and rechecked her hair and makeup.

Her green eyes nearly all she recognized of herself.

Though she'd had plenty of practice in the past faking it, and knew she could easily pass for one of those "girly-girls" as her current lover described most women other than themselves, Beth rarely even bothered anymore. It was just simpler to throw her Carhart work jacket over a baggy t-shirt and slip on some comfortable jeans. Tuck her short blonde hair under a cap, blend in, and forget about trying to impress anyone. Especially men.

The inviting encounters they hungerly promised – is there any nicer guy than a dude who hasn't slept with you yet, Beth often wondered? – rarely worth her time or effort. Still, despite the generally blunted and mostly disappointing endings, every so often, as her lovers all knew, she still craved the enthusiasm of their desperation and raw physicality men so mindlessly provided. Building inside her, at times, like an irresistible itch of a scratch nearly impossible to reach without help. So, here she was. Wearing the most makeup she'd likely put on in years, and wearing the least amount of clothes she was sure she had ever worn on a first date.

Not that this was really a date, Beth reminded herself.

She was simply meeting a few work colleagues whom she'd recently gotten friendly with. The men had, like herself, all been engaged at the same worksite when that terrible tragedy had occurred. The ensuing inquiry into the collapsing tunnels by the local authorities had involved multiple agencies, individual interviews, as well as lengthy group meetings with everyone who had been working that day. The misfortune pretty much halting all the onsite work. Though the exact cause of the unexpected and near catastrophic accident was still under investigation, several lives had been lost.

As a certified and veteran electrician with a specialty in running power and data lines deep underground, Beth had, unfortunately, seen these kinds of tragedies happen before. Understanding that, even once the authorities do finally find and retrieve the missing bodies of those unfortunate souls caught in the collapse, it would likely be months before any work would resume. By the time that happens, Beth hoped she'd be far away from those creepy tunnels and disturbing catacombs riddling the ground under the little backwards town of Vieux, France.

And its godforsaken quarry.

Sighing, Beth pulled herself out of the vehicle to the rhythmic *thumpthumpthump* that poured from the bar with every swing of its front door. She automatically pulled out her phone and made a show of swiping and reading as she walked along the sidewalk. Out of the corner of one eye, she could see some nudges and quick second glances from various dudes crowding the entrance as she approached. The weight of their ravenous stares so heavy it made lifting her feet and continuing nearly impossible.

Ordinarily, she hated walking alone through crowds and would have skirted around the milling patrons. Or, simply left and avoided the entire chaotic scene. But, as of late, she'd not been feeling or acting much like her normal self. Ever since starting this job, it had seemed like something inside was constantly questioning her decision-making and influencing her behavior. At times, leaving Beth feeling like an outsider in her own skin. As if she was watching her actions from somewhere afar. How else could she explain the way she'd done her makeup? The short, tight, black dress she'd purchased for tonight, and the near hour she'd spent on her hair? Not to mention that she'd even accepted this invitation – from an older man, no less – and had ventured out alone.

What was she thinking!

The live music that originated from inside the bar streamed into the bustling street. Beth shifted the thin, leather strap that split her chest and secured the petite bag at her hip. The bulge of the stiletto she always carried inside weighty and comforting. The antique blade, a gift from a dear friend, helping steel her resolve. She reached for the handle of the front door but someone beat her to it. A grinning young man, easily more than ten years her junior, grandiosely bowing as he yanked it open for her. She nodded her thanks with a brief smile while his greedy eyes unabashedly roamed up and down her long legs and exposed thighs. Well-practiced at ignoring, she ducked through the open door, waited briefly for her turn, and paid the small cover charge.

Inside, Beth waited for her eyes to adjust within the darkness before trying to locate anyone she recognized. Melting into a little nook and cranny near the entrance that decades earlier likely housed a payphone. Discreetly deploying her own phone like a shield to avoid making direct eye contact with anyone, she surveyed the scene.

The venue's stage dominated the middle of what may have once been a small theatre. The roughly four-foot high platform jutting out from the backwall and commandeering much of the room's space. Many of the tavern's patrons crowded both sides of the stage and were jubilantly talking, laughing, and dancing. A multitude of heads bobbing and swaying in-time with the music. Two separate bars were located just behind the gyrating masses and lined both walls from front to back. Overhead, a railed mezzanine with clusters of tiny tables stretched from one end to the other. Outside of the usual assortment of beer and alcohol signs, the only décor that Beth could make out in the dim light was all music related. Faded posters from past shows, a mosaic of old concert tickets, dog-eared album covers, and dusty, stringless guitars making up the bulk of the memorabilia.

"Hey! Hey, Beth! There you are!" She turned, the deep, booming voice unfamiliar as it warred with the band for her attention. The energetic musicians sweating through a heated version of the old *Foo Fighters* song *"Best of You"* that thumped from the nearby amplifiers. She lost sight of her caller, unsure if the greeting was actually meant for her until she felt the touch at her elbow. Twisting her head, she recognized one of the men from the jobsite grinning under his thick, white moustache as he slid in beside her. She couldn't recall the dude's first name because she wasn't sure she'd heard anyone call him by anything other than his last name.

Stander.

"I told you this band was going to fucking rock!" His smile was so genuine and infectious that Beth found herself wanting to agree without knowing why. She made a show of cupping one ear with her hand as the music continued.

"...needed somewhere to hang my head, without your noose..."

After a few moments, she nodded an approval aside her most radiant smile. The singer was good, the crowd seemed fun, and today had been her last day on a job that she'd come to loathe. Beth glanced over at Stander as he, in turn, gleefully watched the action on the stage. She resisted the urge to let her eyes wander down to his swaying hips. Instead, inconspicuously surveying the many colorful images that ran up and down each of his thick arms before eventually turning back to watch the band.

Earlier in the week, back at the worksite, Stander had overheard (or maybe butted-in, she wasn't so sure...) a conversation between herself and another coworker. The discussion centering around how it was almost their last night in town and that they should commemorate their impending escape in some way. Stander had immediately invited them to join him and his small team here tonight. Telling them both he'd heard the band was supposed to be very talented, sang mostly in English, and a big draw with the tourists. "You two should tag along," he'd said casually. "The more the merrier."

Beth had heard herself quickly agreeing. The surprise on the begging-off coworker's face likely a mirror of her own shock. The man, a fellow electrician and peer at the company she worked for, was well aware of Beth's girlfriend back where she'd been living. But, this wasn't a date, she remembered thinking. Her eyes at the time like tiny processors recording data she'd found herself later reviewing. Late at night, alone in her bed. And in the shower the following morning. Stander being a stocky six feet of badass tats, rippling muscles and thickness in all the right places had nothing to do with it.

The itch.

He leaned toward her with a grin. "Well, anyway, cheers! Glad you were able…" He suddenly stopped talking. A troubled look pushing aside the joy and leaving a grimace in its place.

Already feeling very self-conscious, Beth looked down briefly at the front of her dress before asking, "What? Do I have something on my face? Did someone spill a drink on me?" Recovering, Stander's smile gradually blossomed and grew bright once more.

"No, no… sorry. You just… just look like someone I used to know." He swiped once at his bushy moustache before using the same hand to brush aside the longish grey hair that spilled over his forehead. The returning grin slightly bemused or maybe embarrassed. "I hadn't really noticed that before. Maybe it's just the funky lighting in this old bar?" He shrugged.

"Please don't tell me some lame story about me looking like an old college girlfriend." Beth felt herself smiling and the giddy beginnings of flirting stirring something deep down inside of her. "I'm pretty sure I've heard that one before." Beth surprised herself by letting out a throaty laugh. She *was* flirting!

"No?" Stander seemed to reflect momentarily, his adorable blue eyes growing distant. "How about grade school?"

"Grade school!" Beth felt herself relaxing. There was something about the man so familiar and comforting that all her usual apprehensions and anxieties seemed to fade like a storm exhausting all its bluster. "No offense, but I'm pretty sure you were long-gone from grade school before I was old enough to even start kindergarten." Beth was instantly mortified by the words coming out of her mouth. Had she just insulted the one dude she actually came here to see? Afterall, she was only a few years from the big 4-0 herself. This guy was likely only ten years or so older than her. Trying to pull the proverbial foot out of her own mouth, Beth quickly added, "Or is it my body? I know I'm kind of skinny and flat chested, but I didn't think I was..."

"No, no, no!" Laughing, he held his fully-tatted arms out to his side as a sign of complete surrender. "I think we maybe got off on the wrong foot here. How about I go get us a drink? I was just headed over to the bar when I saw you. We'll go upstairs where the others already have a table and start over. Wait here and I'll be right back with a... a what? Glass of wine, maybe?"

"Yes. Sounds good," Beth shouted back. Normally, she'd have preferred a gin and tonic. It had only been during this most recent work trip that she'd found herself suddenly craving a good red wine with her dinners. Somehow, he'd nailed that recent change in taste. Returning with a full cup for her in one hand and what looked like a couple shots of whiskey balanced in the other. Beth snagged the offered drink with a smile and took a small sip. She let him grab her hand as he steered them both across the crowded dance floor and up the stairway. Making a bee-line for a table of familiar faces where he pulled a chair out for her before settling into the one next to it.

"Except for Tommy, who must be in the bathroom right now, I know you've already met these guys before. But, since none of these fuckers are very memorable, I'll go around the table anyway and reintroduce you to everyone." Smiling, he first pointed to the man right beside him.

"This guy I've known since I was a kid, and he's one of my oldest friends." Stander switched to a lousy English accent right out of a James Bond film. "Mr. Redhair over there is Bond, Christopher Bond."

The pale, lanky man with thinning red hair wagged a couple fingers her way with a shy smile. "Double shot of Seven-Up, at your...er my service!" He may have used an even lamer English accent than Stander before lifting the bubbling soft drink to his lips and taking a sip. He moved his head stiffly and Beth could see the end of a bandage protruding out from under his collar. "Please, just call me Chris," he added without the fake inflection. His true accent an American one. Beth raised her glass in greeting while his eyes seemed to slowly narrow. Studying her features before glancing over at Stander with a strange look on his face. Beth felt herself redden before hastily raising her drink for a quick swallow while turning to the next man.

"Hopefully, you remember Lucas Chanet, Beth. Our resident brainiac and the lead archeologist of our little project." Beth smiled and waved across the table at the familiar face. She had been introduced to Lucas early on when she'd first began working on the site. She remembered he was local to Caen and taught at the Caen-Normandy University campus which was only a few miles from where they now sat. Or, Beth tried to remember, had he recently quit his teaching gig? She couldn't recall what he'd told her.

Lucas appeared close to Beth's own age and the youngest of the seated men. He had a Band-Aid over one eyebrow that Beth knew covered fresh stitches. Lucas, like Chris, fortunate to have come out of the recent cavern collapse needing only bandages instead of a body bag. His wire-rimmed glasses and thick, black ponytail made him look more like the students he taught than a professor at the college. But, from the various meetings they'd attended together, Beth knew Lucas was well respected by the team of government archeologists that had hired her to run all the underground cabling at their worksite. Like Beth, he drank from a wine glass half-filled with crimson.

"Ah! And here he is. The newest arrival to these fair shores of France, Mr. Thomas Secrist." Beth turned as a man with a slight limp twisted, sliced, and squeezed his way annoyingly through the crowded balcony as he struggled to reach their table. "I give you permission to call him Tommy because I know it pisses him off. But, be on your best behavior. Back home in Michigan where he and I live, he's a cop!" Stander handed the man one of the shots of whiskey just as he reached the table.

"Retired cop," corrected the man with a smirk as, still standing with one hand resting on the back of his chair, he downed the offered drink. Beth's eyebrows arched upwards in surprise. The man was clearly the oldest of the four men. But he didn't appear to yet be of retirement age. His salt-and-pepper colored hair had a few emerging patches of white, as did his full moustache, but she was pretty sure he wasn't ready for a rocking chair just yet. He turned towards Beth with one hand outstretched. She'd barely shook it before he snatched it back as if he'd touched a hot stove.

"Jesus! Liz?" Secrist took a backward step and nearly dropped the glass in his opposite hand. Puzzled, Beth briefly caught his eye before he turned to Stander. She saw mostly confusion within, but there was a flicker of something else not interested in any answers.

Fear.

"This is Beth, Tommy. She is the electrician I told you about. The one who, like the three of us," Stander nodded toward Lucas and Chris, "barely escaped when everything hit the fan underground."

The man seemed to collect himself as Stander spoke. Beth could practically feel his eyes scrutinizing every line on her face as he settled slowly into his chair. "Sorry about that," Secrist began. "We recently, uh... lost someone who," Beth could see him squinting slightly, "looked an awful lot like you." He seemed to grow more embarrassed the longer he spoke. "Geez," he laughed slightly as he shook his head. "Maybe I need to get my eyes checked?"

But Beth didn't believe he really thought that. She took a slow drink in the awkward silence that crowded the table. "Don't worry. I do that all the time," she said, lying. "Maybe it's my hair or something tonight. Stander did the same thing just before we came upstairs." Out of the corner of her eye, she saw surprise register on the other three men's faces. "Was this Liz someone you both knew from grade school?"

Secrist turned his questioning eye on Stander as he queried him. "Grade school?"

"I was talking about Izzy. With Beth's short hair, for just a moment downstairs, I did the same thing you did. Confused her with someone else." Stander shrugged as if it didn't matter to him. But, Beth could tell something unsaid had passed between the two men. Although Lucas seemed to be paying more attention to the band playing on stage than anything else, she could see Chris subtly eyeing her profile. Taking another sip of her wine, Beth began to regret her decision to come out tonight.

Stander, perhaps sensing her unease, started to apologize. "You must think the three of us are about as sharp as a couple of marbles." He was grinning as he laid one arm across the back of her chair. The black concert t-shirt he wore emblazoned with the face of the Frankenstein monster looking very grim under wide letters that spelled out *KrashKarma*, obviously the name of the band. Stander leaned in close and Beth felt his warmth and the slight crush of the muscles in his shoulder and chest against her bare arm. "Which is fairly accurate," his whiskey breath and cologne mixing as she breathed him in. Her anxiety, surprisingly, fading more with every intake.

"So, Beth the commercial electrician, tell us about yourself." Secrist, twirling the empty glass in his hands, asking the question in a conversational and friendly manner. But, she recognized the policeman in his tenor and demeanor. Beth had her own share of run-ins with law enforcement back in her younger days and was familiar with the tone. "You sure don't sound like you have been living in France for very long."

Lucas spoke up for the first time since Beth had joined the table. "Yes! I was wondering that as well. I can't place that accent of yours at all. You must not be native to France. Where are you from?"

Beth, nodding briefly, drained more from her glass. She collected herself with a slight smile before replying confidently. Her story, one that had been well rehearsed.

Chapter Three
Germany-16th Century

THE LIES, ONES HE no longer rehearsed since they now flowed so easily, spilled from his tongue. "I'll be certain to finish my work before then. Please don't worry or bother yourself on my behalf. I will, of course, endeavor to follow your wise counsel regarding my sustenance and sleep while you are away. In return, I only ask that you, and yes, of course the children as well, all promise that you'll enjoy my sister's hospitality. By the time you come back to our home, all of my current experiments and, as you put it, my endless questions, will have been exhausted." Herbert smiled as he lightly kissed his wife's extended hand. Then waved one final time at his young son and daughter. Neither acknowledged the farewell with much warmth or concern. Their father, a man who rarely recognized the children's presence, would not be missed by the twins.

The caroche, a luxurious carriage designed and built exclusively for Herbert and the House of Chanet, was already packed and loaded. Hans jumped down after rechecking and tightly securing the family's bundled belongings. Herbert did the opposite, scaling the front of the enclosed carriage to confer briefly with his long-tenured driver in confidence. Pressing his own personal arquebus – a handheld firearm with a custom fitted shoulder stock – into the servant's hands.

"Stick to the main road until you cross the border." He lowered his voice, "And keep clear of the moors, do you understand?" The driver, a simple fellow without the wit to disobey, nodded somberly. "Good man," Herbert said, louder.

Gregariously slapping the driver across his back before jumping down. "Off you go now."

With a jolt, the four-in-hand horsed carriage started. Herbert watched the slow descent as it rolled along the gradually sloping lane and crossed the white-capped river. His eyes never losing sight until it crested the rise before the main road. As it disappeared, he turned and pulled a sealed envelope from the breast pocket of his elegantly tailored suit. The letter, written in his own hand and in an exclusive manner, was to be delivered to his sister.

"Be certain your rider does not deliver this until after one week's time." Herbert handed the thin note to Hans.

"Yes, I understand, My Lord." Hans, aware of the planned deception, had already secured a trusted messenger in advance. He passed the flaming lantern he held over to Herbert as he tucked the ornate envelope away on his person.

"Very good. That should keep my intrusive wife and those two annoyances away far longer." Herbert spun on his heel, his step lively as he pulled a key from his front pocket. "As is often said, one can never be too careful."

"Do you fear what is to come, My Lord?" Hans walking in Herbert's shadow as they approached the manor.

"Fear?" Amused, Herbert slowed his pace, one finger tapping his chin as he grinned. "Fear must be mastered. For, if not, you become a tool that it uses to spread. Do you think me a tool?"

"No, My Lord. I beg you forgive my impertinent questions." But instead of being chastised as expected, Dr. Herbert Chanet's lolling laughter echoed in the shallow doorway they approached.

"Ah, but alas, I am. A tool, or perhaps a pliable putty in the master plan and in my master's hands." Herbert pushed the key into the lock, the heavy tumblers falling into place with the turn of his wrist. "Now, let's see if our new friend inside wants to live forever." He pushed at the thick, heavy wooden door. The metal hinges creaking and groaning as the yawning doorway opened into an inky darkness. The damp, musky, oppressive odor that immediately greeted them only hinting at the decay hidden within.

The crude stairs creaked as each man stepped onto them. Herbert scrabbled at a pile of stunted candles the open door exposed, dousing the ends of several in the smoky flare of his lantern. The tiny flames licking the misshapen wax until they tasted the charred wick and erupted in wavering light. Behind him, Hans carefully closed and barred the door. Sliding a heavy wood beam across the entryway to ensure their work would be undisturbed.

The cellar floor they stepped onto was hardpacked dirt that was free of vegetation, save a handful of colorless mushrooms sprouting in one corner. Windowless, the aged stone walls were held together by crumbling mortar and clunch – a chalky limestone material Hans had mixed and applied to patch and secure the ancient supports in various places. Massive beams lined the ceiling at their heads. Their burden, the five-stories and 31 rooms of lavish living space that made up the House of Chanet. Only a long, wide, leather curtain – hanging down from the forged fasteners Hans had pounded into place– taxing the ancient wood from below. The veil separating the hidden, underground room into two halves.

At the center of the half Herbert and Hans had entered down into, a jagged, rectangular block of solid stone dominated the clandestine space. A massive hunk of rock as wide as a person was tall and, length-wise, nearly as long as two men lying end to end. It was still partially covered by the dirt and soil that had both birthed and once entombed the oblong slab. But, where the muck and mud had fallen off or been brushed away, underneath it was black and shiny as coal.

Like the recital of a practiced dance, the two men silently finished lighting the candles and multiple lamps they'd strategically placed throughout the room. Brightly illuminating their half of the cellar, neither man pulling back or approaching the half still shielded by the heavy, leather drape. A rank ripeness, groan, and muted shuffle emanating from somewhere behind that they both pointedly ignored.

Herbert tugs off his finely tailored jacket, hanging it over the back of the chair nearest him as he begins to roll up the sleeves of his silk shirt. Behind him, Hans pulls out the freshly laundered linen he'd previously sewn and crafted into two, matching, frock coats. Holding the ends of one out for Herbert to plunge his bare arms inside before tying it at the back. Without assistance, Hans soon dons the second frock as Herbert silently eyes the long, wooden table lining one wall of the cellar. The top imbrued with rank smells and dark drippings from their past work. Much of the tabletop cluttered with an assortment of oddly shaped flasks and bottles filled with miscellaneous liquids, herbs, and milled powders of varying shades and indiscriminate textures.

The wall opposite the table was crowded with more of the same. Simple racks that held a dizzying amount of glass containers. Many were filled with fleshy things bobbing in liquids of an undeterminable nature. While others held the still husks of more easily recognized creatures. Oversized beetles, iridescent moths, and a cluster of flattened cockroaches with unmoving legs. Shrunken toads and withered bats beside colorful snakes long devoid of life. All staring blindly out of empty eye sockets.

In one corner of the cellar floor, a circular hole large enough for a man to drop down into was partially covered. Herbert couldn't be certain, but he suspected the ominous opening was likely a remnant from the original construction. Back when a towering castle stood on the same foundation. The hole likely serving as an oubliette, a dungeon in the shape of a bottle where unwanted or unruly prisoners were tossed down into and forgotten. Hans, with Herbert's blessing, now using it to dispose of their waste. Tossing the unwanted bones, scraps of flesh, and body parts they couldn't use down inside the pit. Only a few repurposed planks tossed over the opening in a haphazard manner. The worst of the stench in the cellar seeming to rise from the yawning hole of black.

"Shall we?" Herbert pointed to a wood shutter that covered a crude opening in the wall nearest Hans. "I want to remove any damaged tissue we find and extract the organs. The sooner we bath them in my elixir the sooner we can judge the results and adjust the dosage if needed." From behind the leather curtain, something unseen and wet plopped repeatedly. Periodically, the thick drape seemed to ripple and move back and forth, as if it breathed with a life of its own.

"Should I prepare a tray for the discards?" Hans made a barely perceptible motion with his eyes and head, gesturing at the swaying room divider. "It has been nearly a week, My Lord," his voice trailing off. He knew the doctor preferred to blissfully ignore the blasphemous failures of their earlier experiments. But they couldn't risk starving the undead things they'd brought back. Nor set loose something of that... that particular constitution. Hans had barely slept since the other had broken free and escaped. Though more docile, what loomed mere feet away in the hidden cellar was much larger than their second attempt. If it somehow gained the cunning intelligence of the other... Hans shuddered involuntarily.

"If you feel we must, do as you please. But first," Herbert tugged open the jagged wood shutter, "let us pull this one from the chamber." The makeshift crypt, much like the endless walls of dead entombed in the overflowing mausoleums of Paris where Hans had once lived happily, had been carved directly into the cellar wall. The brick-lined interior loaded with packeted ice of the doctor's own design to hold the rot of the corpse inside at bay.

Herbert and Hans slid the freshly unearthed body from the hole. Laying the unfortunate young man on his back across the mostly flat top of the massive stone slab. The width and height of the rectangular rock perfect for the grisly work to come. Hans stripped the corpse of its clothing. Tossing the farmer's very last belongings inside a cloth sack he'd later burn. At the wooden table beside him, Herbert unsheathed the sharp knives and glinting tools he favored.

Starting at the shoulder, Herbert expertly filleted the flesh of the dead man's hairless chest. Slicing through the epidermis and creating the shape of a cross as blade hit bone. Days beyond life, very little fluid or blood came from the cuts, but the fetid smell of death and decay filled the near airless, underground room. Rushing out of the opened corpse like one final, putrid exhale. Herbert set his knife down and began to peel back the loosened skin. Exposing the organs and baring everything inside the man from crotch to clavicle.

One by one, Herbert meticulously cut away the kidneys, the liver, the lungs, and the still, colorless heart. Only the ruptured and gored stomach was spared his butchery. The life-ending injury the peasant had sustained ruining its functions and rendering it a useless bag filled with partially digested turnips, black blood, and yellowing puss.

Save the torn abdomen, the viscera and innards were all carefully inspected by Herbert before handing them individually to Hans. One by one, each was plopped into separate vats of liquid containing a dizzying array of swirling colors. The glass containers each filled with Herbert's very own, and very special, elixir. The alchemy employed to create each batch was Herbert's most carefully guarded secret. He'd been scorned and unceremoniously derided as a charlatan and a fake by his Heidelberg University classmates and teachers when he'd first proposed and began brewing his special concoction. The narrow-minded professors eventually accusing him of heresy and booting him from the school after his earliest attempts at resurrection. Eventually, succeeding in running him out of town.

While it had taken him years of further study, secret experimentation, and countless failures before his first success, all along he'd been confident he was right. The real breakthroughs finally coming when he'd been able to work undisturbed within his own home. The hidden chamber beneath The House of Chanet allowing him to labor, at times, nearly nonstop. Refining and perfecting his alchemy until it had finally happened. Herbert restoring life to one of the stray barn cats. Though he'd been working by himself that night and ultimately celebrated the victory alone, it had been his proudest moment.

Had been. Greatness yet beckoned still more of him. Of that, he was also certain.

With the removal of the organs within the chest cavity completed, Herbert focused his attention on the exacting dissection and retrieval of the brain. Reaching for his handheld drill, a small chisel and hammer, and a second scalpel for the meticulous task. Though the unsophisticated lighting was not ideal for such delicate work, he was able to make four careful incisions along the base of the skull. With Hans cupping the head and holding it secure, he cranked the wheel of his drill until he felt the bone give-way under each bloodless slit. Then, artfully applying the chisel and hammer, he carefully opened the back of the head. Flakes of fractured bone falling away as he cracked the skull and severed the spinal cord. The ridged grey matter flopping directly into the waiting vat of his life-giving potion.

Satisfied with the success of his grisly work, the glass containers were carefully secured atop the wooden table. Each organ swimming separately in their own vat of solution. The soon-to-be repurposed tissue would remain suspended in his elixir for an entire day. Herbert believing the time soaking in the mixture helped to purify and better rejuvenate each vital component.

Finished, Herbert shed his fouled frock before sliding his jacket over both shoulders. He fished for the intricately designed porcelain pipe he'd left loaded within and, placing the stem carved from a Himalayan ram's horn between his lips, lit it. Puffing in and out until the coppery taste permeating his mouth and nasal passages finally dissipated. He leaned against the granite "table" he'd used for the autopsy and watched as Hans dismembered what was left of the peasant villager. As Herbert spoke, the repeated *clang* of the heavy cleaver striking the slab of stone chopped his sentences into bits.

"These last few days," Herbert began, speaking as much to himself as Hans, "everything has gone according to plan. The stage has now been set for what will be man's singular achievement. I must confess, I feel like a modern-day Prometheus!" Herbert laughed gaily. "This must be what it feels like to be a God!" His laughter growing shrill as Hans vanished behind the swaying curtain. The servant's dripping hands carrying a wooden tray loaded with slippery things both dense and glistening.

Herbert, pipe nestled in mouth, placed both hands over his ears as he quickly scurried up the stairs. Refusing to hear, or even acknowledge, what was taking place behind the leather veil. Closing the door and stepping into the fresh air of the outdoors. A satisfied sigh leaving his lips.

Tomorrow, the only family member he'd shared his far-reaching dreams with would arrive. The only one he truly trusted and the reason he'd toiled like a commoner these long years. Though she may not have come from the same bloodline as the rest of the distinguished family of Chanet, in many ways, Herbert was closest with her. A true kinship. The two of them, in equal measure Herbert believed, sharing intellect, impertinence, and the gall to ignore the so-called standards of upper-class German and French society. She'd encouraged and counseled him during his pursuits of life after death. Sharing ancient practices, she'd told him, from exotic, faraway lands. Entrusting him alone to decipher and apply the knowledge she imparted along with modern learnings to crack the code of life. Promising that, once he did, she had something special for them to resurrect.

The sainted bones, the entire intact skeleton, of Judas Iscariot.

CHAPTER FOUR
FRANCE-PRESENT DAY

"I'M AFRAID *MY STORY*, as you called it, doesn't start out very warm and fuzzy. I was born in the States but never knew who my mom or my dad were. I was dumped as a newborn and started life out in foster care." Around the table, Chris and Lucas acknowledged what Beth said with subtle nods of encouragement. Stander, his surprise unchecked, glanced briefly across the table at Chris before turning toward a suddenly blanching Secrist.

"Growing up, I was shuttled between a lot of different families. I had it better than most in my situation. The people I stayed with never treated me poorly or anything, but I also never really felt like I had a home." Beth smiled wanly before raising her second glass of wine and downing a mouthful. "Still don't," she mumbled under her breath.

"I kind of know that feeling." Chris spoke first, his eyes and voice soft. "I was the unwanted stepchild in my family. My mom never told me who my dad was. To be honest, I don't think she was sure herself." He shrugged indifferently, but Stander knew the hurt Chris carried deep inside from childhood. "She married a drunk, but at least the guy kept a roof over our heads." His gaze seemed to wither before turning his head and fiddling briefly with the bandage at his shoulder. Impulsively, Beth reached for his free hand and gave it a small squeeze.

"There seems to be a common theme here, huh?" began Stander. "Believe it or not, Tommy here was adopted." Around the table, Lucas, Chris, and Beth turned their astonished expressions toward Secrist.

"That sure is one amazing coincidence." Beth's tone was light, but it sounded forced.

"And I hate coincidences." Secrist stated somberly before suddenly standing. He made a show of searching for a nonexistent waitress before shuffling away with his empty glass in hand. "Be right back. I need a new drink," he said over his shoulder as he started for the nearby stairwell.

"Is that why I can't place your accent? Did you move around a lot when you were a kid?" Lucas, born in France but educated in the United States, prided himself on picking up the subtleties of language. "Parles-tu français?"

Beth smiled back at Lucas. "Oui, je parle français." Seeing that neither Chris or Stander seemed to follow, and were likely unfamiliar with French language, she translated for their benefit. "Yes, in answer to your question, I do speak French. Fairly fluently, I'm told."

"That is impressive. I still struggle with fucking English and that is all anyone ever bothered to teach me." Stander could hear the band beginning to tune their instruments and glanced down at the stage as they prepared to start once again. Their first break of the evening just ending.

"What made you decide to live here in France?" Chris asking Beth questions as Secrist rejoined the table with a full beer in his hand. "Did you move over here for work?"

"I don't really live anywhere. I'm kind of a free-lance electrician, I guess you'd say. The company I do the most work for has offices in the States, in Germany, Switzerland, and, obviously, here in France. I like the idea of seeing the world on their dime. I'll get licensed and work anywhere they send me."

"Too bad they sent you here." Lucas tipped back his glass and emptied it. "What a terrible tragedy for any of us to have to deal with. I'm sure you feel just as sick about it as we do. Except for Secrist, who flew over the week after the accident, all of us were fortunate to have escaped with our lives." Lucas looked down at his empty glass. "I lost some good friends and colleagues in the collapse," he added somberly.

The table grew silent momentarily before the band kicked off their second set of the night. The raucous beginning inciting squeals of delight from several nearby tables as the dancefloor below began filling and rolling with motion again.

"But you are still working there? At the quarry, I mean? I'm surprised the authorities are allowing that." Beth and all the rest of the university and government contracted workers had been shut down. Told the site was strictly off-limits until further notice. "How did you manage to pull that off?" She paused before adding, "Aren't you worried about safety? How stable the ground will be?"

"My work... well, our work," Lucas gestured to include the rest of the men, "has always been completely separate from the reclamation project that you were a part of in that ancient Roman quarry. Someone else owns the land we are working on. The university and government authorities have no jurisdiction despite the close proximity of the two sites. All of us, and the owner, had to sign a bunch of waivers and were advised against continuing. But, the job goes on."

Lucas glanced across the table at Stander. Though Beth didn't know it, Stander, from a recent and completely unexpected inheritance, was the landowner Lucas referred to. His own mother having vanished without explanation decades earlier somewhere within the dark, subterranean passages of the quarry. Initially, Stander had only hired Lucas to help him locate the fabled, long lost site in hopes of discovering what had happened to her. But, when a series of specialized ground penetrating radar scans had later revealed a cavernous void and a massive monolith directly adjacent to the quarry, he'd persuaded Lucas (and paid him handsomely) to begin full-time work on the enigmatic discovery. Employing him to lead a team that could unearth and potentially recover whatever was buried deep within. The cumulation of recent and barely explainable events only increasing the urgency. If answers were to be found, it would be at the bottom of their digging.

"So, sounds like you work almost anywhere in the UK, huh?" Secrist, the untouched pint of Guinness in hand, lifted the foaming beer and took a long, slow drink from his glass. His expression unreadable.

"Yes. I mean, pretty much. Like I said, I do contract work. Kind of like a freelance..."

"Do you speak German?" Secrist interrupting before Beth finished. "How about Italian or Dutch?"

"No," Beth replied with a lopsided grin. "Sorry." She looked as if she was going to say more before lifting her own glass and meekly taking a swallow.

"But you speak French fluently? How is that?" Stander, frowning slightly, turned and looked directly at Secrist, the question on his face plain. What was the retired cop driving at?

"It's... it's kind of hard to explain."

"Try us," Secrist quickly replied. Now, it was Lucas and Chris turning toward him. Like Stander, puzzlement in their expressions.

"Well," Beth began, "shortly after graduating high school I kind of got religion, I guess you'd say. Long story short, I ended up here in France for a while and never really got over the feeling of awe the entire experience left me with. Like most idealistic kids at that age, I grew out of all that other nonsense pretty fast and moved on with my life. But while I was over here, I really fell in love with the country. Since that time, this place has always felt like the closest thing to a home I've ever known. Maybe something in this land calls to me." She shrugged once before finishing her glass of wine.

Secrist, perhaps beginning to sense the awkwardness in his pressing, merely nodded amiably. "Makes sense. At that age, I think we all were super impression-able." He took another deep drink from his beer. "This is my first time in this country. Hopefully I'll find something to fall in love with over here, too."

Around the table, the discussion gradually turned to travel and some of the most memorable places each had visited. Stander bought several more rounds for the group and the Michigan bar owner, out of habit, kept clearing away the empty glasses. At any lull in the conversation, he would begin singing along with the band as it plowed through one early 2000s tune after another. When the riff started on the second Green Day song of the set, Stander finally leaned in close to Beth. "I wonder if these guys know anything else? Something current? Metal, maybe? Or some classic rock?"

"What? Dude! Why? Aren't you enjoying yourself?" Beth, the oddness of the earlier conversation all but forgotten as the alcohol had flowed, was practically dancing in her chair. "I remember every one of these old songs. For me, they *are* classics. Reminds me of going out to the bars and clubs with all my girlfriends back in our college days."

"I can tell!" Stander stood and stretched, "I'll be right back. I need to use the bathroom." Heading downstairs, he only made it down the first flight of steps before he felt a hand grabbing a handful of cloth from the back of his shirt.

"Oh my god! I am loving this band!" Beth, laughing, followed behind Stander until he hit the first level. "I need to boogie," she said giggling, as she stepped towards the musicians on stage. "Dude! Dance with me!"

Stander hollered back. "Fine! I'm not much of a dancer. But, I'm getting kind of stiff sitting up there. I'll come find you when I'm done."

"Unless I see you coming first!" Beth, laughing, turned slightly, her gorgeous green eyes narrowing. The innocuous saying – coupled with the way the flashing lights lit the expression on her face – stirred something achingly familiar inside of Stander.

Loss.

He stumbled a step after her, stammering. "Wait. What did... what did you say?" But she had vanished inside the mass of twirling bodies. Suddenly disoriented, Stander felt like he'd just been clocked a good one. The combination of booze, the loud music, and crowded revelry hitting him all at once. With his equilibrium scrambled, Stander stood dumbly and tried briefly to collect himself before an overly enthusiastic couple in matching Normandy Beach souvenir t-shirts bumped into him. The jostling seemed to clear his head slightly, and, staggering at first, he slowly weaved his way toward the men's room.

By the time he'd finished – slapping copious amounts of cold water across his features after washing – Stander began to feel better. It took him a few minutes to locate Beth among the throngs, but he soon joined her near one corner of the stage. Fighting past the surging waves of patrons to reach her as the band played. Stander moved in close to Beth, their heated bodies entwining as the dance floor churned with activity. Losing themselves in the swell - anonymous in the crowd.

Drinks in hand, neither Beth or Stander let either of their glasses remain empty for very long. Alternately draining and refilling each other's cups as they danced through the night. The later the hour, the fuller the venue became. Tourists and locals alike filling both floors of the bar with their boisterous conversations and loud laughter. Stander looked a few times for Secrist and the others but soon gave up. It was nearly hopeless in the crush of humanity. If they'd left, he'd just catch a cab or get an Uber back to the hotel anyway. Besides, his energetic and enticing dance partner was making it hard to look anywhere but right at her.

They'd allowed themselves to slowly be edged farther and farther away from the roaring stage by the tumultuous crush of the newcomers. Backed into a barely lit corner that they soon made their own. Stander was grateful for the reprieve. The combination of constant motion and the steady flow of drinks leaving his head spinning. Beth, on the other hand, continued her near nonstop movement in front of him. Bouncing playfully against his chest whenever the band played a song she really liked. At other times, her beautiful emerald eyes locking on his as if searching for something she'd once lost within.

Stander, with his back to the wall, soon found himself unwilling or perhaps unable to tear his gaze from Beth. Utterly mesmerized by the woman, he hoped the shadows hid his stare and his growing appreciation. He discreetly watched as a line of beaded sweat meandered its way down from her hairline. The trickle glistening whenever the twirling stage lights winked their way. Across one shoulder, the strap from her dress had slipped down, completely exposing the softness underneath and the gentle slope of her inviting neck. Stander could see the beginning of a faded tattoo peeking out from between the top of her shoulder blades. An inked image of a sun rising like the dawn of a new day from under the black of her dress - most of the celestial body still covered by cloth. Though hardly an unusual or unique design, something in the art and placement of the tattoo tugged at his memory like an unknown name teasing the tip of his tongue. Or, maybe an itch he couldn't quite scratch on his own. Stander fought to keep his hands to himself, longing to reveal the rest of the image. It took all his willpower to stay rooted and motionless.

In the background, the music swelled once more. *"Sex on Fire"* from the group *Kings of Leon* pulsating through the room. Beth spun with a playful smile. "Oh my God," she all but screeched in excitement. "I absolutely love this song!" And then she was on him. Leaning into and pressing against Stander before he could move from the corner she had him backed into. The band's strobe lights pulsed while most of the bar's lighting remained dimmed. Leaving Stander and Beth cloaked in utter darkness except for the flashes of near-blinding light that periodically raked their eyes. He felt Beth more than he saw her. The arms encircling his neck and two hands full of his hair, the sudden crush of her lips on his own. When his mouth opened in surprise, she leaned in and filled it with her tongue. Between his legs, he felt the top of her thigh grinding hard against the heat of his own unmistakable need.

"...I know they're watching. Yeah, they're watching..."

Breathless, moments later Stander felt Beth's embrace weaken as she stepped back, one hand left clinging to his shoulder. He could still hear the band playing and the appreciative roar of the crowd, but a dull buzz began to fill his ears with white noise. Except when momentarily bathed in the flashing strobe, the disorienting black blinded and enveloped him. Only the flickering lights of the stage illuminated Beth as her free hand slid up her thigh and vanished under the short cut of her skirt. He gawked as she deftly slipped her panties off, alternately lifting one heel behind her as she balanced herself with Stander's help. She twirled the lace once around her forefinger with a toothy smile before abruptly tucking them down the front of Stander's jeans.

He moaned at the brush of fingertips against his bare skin.

"I'll show you mine if you show me yours," Beth cooed in his ear before turning with a flip of her skirt. Teasing Stander with the briefest flash of her bare ass before strutting away. He launched himself after her just as she ducked inside a nearby door marked maintenance.

Stander, at her heels, turned and closed the door behind them. He eyed Beth in the flimsy mirror hanging from the back of the door as he slid the deadbolt in place. She stretched to yank at a fraying string dangling from the ceiling of the janitor closet. The naked bulb above her head bursting to life and swinging wildly at her hurried touch. A swaying pendulum of blueish LED light that illuminated only a portion of the tiny room at a time, leaving the other half in shadowed black with its every rise and fall. Stander stared appreciatively as Beth quickly shed the last of her clothing.

Swing.

Stander could see a white sink, bucket, and mop standing stoically in the opposite corner.

Swing.

Beth on all fours. The crumpled dress under her knees covering the grime of the cement floor.

Swing.

Stander fumbles with the belt buckle and fasteners on his jeans. Hurriedly freeing himself.

Swing.

She turns and looks up at Stander. Wait, his head spinning. Izzy?

Swing.

"*...feels like you're dying...dying...*" Stander rubs at his eyes with both fists.

Swing.

"Fuck me, Rusty." But it was Beth again. Her voice husky, low, and guttural.

Swing.

"Who... wait! What am I...? This is... in a..."

Swing.

Beth spreads herself with one hand, green eyes raging in wanton lust.

Swing.

Like the flash of a camera – an eruption of blinding blue light fills the room.

Swing.

Grunts echoing. Now Liz is underneath him. Greedily matching every frenzied thrust.

Swing.

The bucket on its side, a disturbing stirring within. The sink now splashed red with gore.

Swing.

"...consumed with what's just transpired..."

Swing.

Room spinning, spittle flew from Stander's mouth. The tattoo between his hands shiny and slick.

Swing.

A pile of splayed flesh quivered beneath him, splashing one final time upon the ground.

Swing.

Stander, confused, looks down at his gore drenched hands as the warmth cool's.

Swing.

The sink gleaming and white. The bucket, upright and empty, stood alone beside it.

Swing.

The light hurting his eyes, he screwed them tightly shut. Nothing to see here.

Swing.

Blackness.

Swing.

Stander motionless on his back.

Swing.

Alone.

Chapter Five
Germany-16th Century

With a slight grunt, Hans lifted and removed the thick beam that barred the outside world, and the rest of the House of Chanet, from Herbert's underground laboratory. Leaning the hand-hewn log in the corner nearest the cellar entrance before unlocking and opening the door. He bowed his head and lowered his eyes as the doorway filled with brightly colored fabric. The rustling of the material that made up the fine dress and gown the only greeting he received.

"Madeleine. How wonderful to see you once more." Herbert, looking up at his visitor from the bottom of the cellar stairs, also bowing slightly at her expected arrival. "I pray your travels were comfortable and uneventful."

"Thank you, dear Herbert. I was most contented despite the length of the journey. There is a chill in the air now that the sun has begun to set. But, surprisingly, I found the emerging briskness to be quite refreshing." As she spoke, Hans dared a peek at Herbert's regal but familiar visitor. Discreetly letting his gaze rise from the floor. The finely fitted clothes she wore boasted many vibrant colors, but red dominated the outfit. The well-tailored cloth both flattering and voluminous. Covering her so completely from head to toe that only her hands and face were bare and visible. At her waist, she clutched protectively at a cloth sack made of thick, luxurious velvet that bulged with the contents it held.

Though winter had only just passed, Hans recognized that Madeleine had somehow retained her bronze-colored skin throughout the long, cold months. Her exotic tone and ageless beauty, as always it seemed, once again unmarred by the passage of time. The unblemished complexion of her face and high cheek-bones perfectly balanced by the delicate bow of her lips that, when parted, revealed the straightest and whitest teeth Hans had ever seen. He impulsively leaned forward and inhaled expectantly. The sweet smell of her intoxicating perfume a welcome reprieve from the stench of death that lingered within the near-airless workspace.

Madeleine, not taking any of the steps before her, stood stiffly alongside the open doorway. Though she'd been the first one to discreetly confer with Herbert about the possibility of this once hidden chamber – pointing out the difference between the length of the basement and the first level – she'd yet to set foot inside herself. Herbert, an avid letter writer, had kept Madeleine abreast of the ensuing developments. Keeping her informed of what they'd found, his intentions for the space, and the outcomes of his work. Her written replies, always encouraging and insightful, had undoubtedly played a hand in his success. At times, her expertise or intuitions, whichever it was, leaving him certain that this monumental defeat of death was truly his destiny.

"I hope you can forgive the crudeness in which we are forced to work," Herbert crinkling his nose in exaggerated distaste as he gestured at the cellar walls and dirt floor. "But, one can never be too careful. Down here, none would dare disturb the important work we have undertaken." Herbert paused expectantly. "May I ask if you were able to successfully retrieve the... the bones?"

Madeleine, with a brief smile, merely turned toward the open doorway in which she'd entered and made a subtle gesture. Moments later, stepping aside as four men in matching outfits, obviously her coachmen and guards, descended the cellar stairs. A cumbersome and heavy stone box balanced precariously between them. Squatting, they placed it gingerly on the floor before quickly standing. Each armed man hurriedly covering their noses with gloved hands as they hastily returned outside. Hans watched as they retreated to the grand carriage that had brought them - the uniformed men taking up positions at both the front and rear. Above their heads, the sun had dipped below the trees that surrounded the House of Chanet. The ghostly white of the moon just beginning to haunt the sky. Wordlessly, Hans swung the door shut. Once again sliding the heavy wooden beam back in place and securing the entryway from the prying eyes of the outside world.

"You are wise to travel with the protection of an armed escort. There are many… dangers currently lurking in the nearby woods." Herbert's eyes narrowing as Madeleine nodded knowingly. "I hope your men remain vigilant."

"You need not worry about their fortitude. Or discretion. Like the servants you employ, they are accustomed to the unusual." Madeleine, lifting her long skirt, now strode confidently down the steps before stopping beside the stone container. "Here, it lies…" She reached down and patted the lid. "A shrine to what has passed and a carrier of the future." Joining her, Herbert stepped to the ossuary. His eyes wide and full of wonderment.

The ossuary – a stone chest meant to hold only the bones of the dead – was surprisingly bland and unremarkable. Near colorless and the size of a small child's coffin, any markings that may have once identified the interred long vanished. With a subtle nod, Herbert and Madeleine each grabbed the two corners closest to them. Their fingers finding the fitted edge of the lid before beginning to slowly lift and raise it. The subtle scrape of stone on rock the only sound as it was cracked open.

BOOM!!

A thunderous assault on the cellar door! The unexpected crash eliciting a startled scream out of Hans. He turned to the shuddering wood at his back - eyes wild with panic as something scrabbled at the door. Herbert, equally stunned, nearly dropped the carved lid he held before hastily readjusting his grip on both sides. His eyes met Madeleine's just as a shot rang out. The unmistakable clap of a fired musket followed by the thudding roar of the igniting gunpowder. Before they could properly resettle the stone cap in place, a second discharge erupted just beyond the outside doorway.

"That must be your men!" Herbert let the heavy cover slide from his grasp as he stood. He exchanged an anxious look with a fearful Hans before sprinting up the steps and racing for the door. "Pray we have not been found out," Herbert hissed as he threw open the door. Hurling himself into the emerging darkness.

One man, his long musket obscured in billowing grey, was kneeling on one knee beside the carriage. The end of his gun pointed Herbert's way. Behind him stood another, his smoking weapon leaning against a wooden wagon wheel and his drawn sword quivering in the air. As Hebert watched, the remaining two of Madeleine's coachmen or guards, whatever they were, walked briskly toward him. Even in the fading sunlight, Herbert could see the confusion plain in their expressions.

"What is the meaning of this? What has happened?" Herbert glanced up at the many windows that overlooked this side of the manor grounds. Worried and wondering if any of his servants had witnessed what occurred. Hoping the sound of the gunshots was dismissed as coming from the rim of the ancient forest that bordered the grounds. Hunters often stalked prey in the surrounding woodlands.

"Beg your forgiveness, My Lord." The man speaking was indistinguishable from the other three. Each in matching uniforms that gave away nothing concerning position or rank. "We thought we saw..." he turned momentarily, looking across at the others as if for support. "There was... uh. We saw something at your door," he finally finished.

"What? What did you see that caused you to raise weapons on my lands?" Though, based on their reaction, Herbert had little doubt what they'd seen, he enjoyed watching the commoner squirm and wither under his false outrage. "Come to it, man. I have important work to yet complete this day."

"I can't rightly say, My Lord. I've never seen such a sight... not in my whole life!"

"Ridiculous. You turned arms on my home and can give me no reason?" A practiced deceiver, Herbert knew his wealth, position, and influence allowed him to say near anything without consequence. Most witless commoners lacking the backbone to even question his ravings, yet alone his actions. "You must be fools."

"Craquehhe." The second man spoke for the first time. "Or some undead thing. It rushed from the trees and came straightaway to your door." He spoke plainly, as if commenting on a stray dog or cat merely prowling about for scraps or shelter. "Our lady had warned us such things may be near..." his voice trailing off.

"A Craquehhe?" Herbert pulled his pipe and began to repack the end. It was the most casual thing he could think of doing to show his indifference. The busyness of his hands hiding the tremble and shiver that took control of his spine. He now had no doubt what they'd witnessed. What had returned. "I'm surprised you men believe in such things. Nothing more than old wives' tales."

The Craquehhe, as told in hushed whispers for generations amongst the surrounding villages and clusters of farms, is a creature believed to have once been human. A thing existing beyond death and without a soul. It is said to be a revenant - a restless, reanimated corpse. Supposedly, as Herbert was well aware, it possessed supernatural strength and speed, despite being a rotting corpse. Often, because it is decaying, it is said the Craquehhe is a carrier of a virulent, highly contagious disease. Like a leper tainted by fate, the spreader of a plague that lives on even after the monster is destroyed.

"Pray your forgiveness, My Lord. But we worried for our lady's safety." The two men looked at each other. "We'll return to our posts unless you wish one of us to stand guard by..."

"The door!" Hans had finally dueled his fear to at least a draw. Though still clinging to the protection the doorway provided, he pointed to the claw marks that now scarred the wood on the outside. Herbert turned as he shooed away the two guardsmen. Allowing time for them to return to the carriage before looking himself. The two notches where something had crashed mightily into the wood were plain to see. Less obvious was the yellowing sliver Herbert plucked from the splintered indentations. It was viscous on one side – something foul clinging like a garden snail crushed in its shell. He brought it close to his eyes before tossing it aside with a grunt of displeasure.

"What was that?" Hans questioning Herbert as he reentered the cellar labora-tory before closing and resecuring the door behind him.

"A fingernail," he replied with a look of distaste. "I think our second Lazurus is fully aware of our intentions this evening." Herbert smiled grotesquely. "But, I'll not be deterred," he concluded defiantly. "This is my destiny."

Though shaken by the boldness of the monstrous thing that lurked nearby, Herbert descended the stairs with a purposeful gait. Rejoining Madeleine along-side the now opened ossuary, the heavy lid only covering the dirt floor where it lay. He was surprised by Madeleine's calm demeanor and indifference to the events that had just played out. Her expression seemingly one of annoyance rather than fear. "Shall we get on with it?" Her expectant gaze falling to the opened box at their feet.

Kneeling, Herbert called for Hans while he methodically collected the jumbled bones within, the men carefully accounting for and retrieving each individual piece. Starting with the skull, laying out and piecing together the complete skele-ton atop the stone slab that served as their table. Finishing, Hans retrieved the organs Herbert had harvested barely a day earlier.

"Are you quite certain this shrine," Herbert gesturing to the ossuary, "truly held the bones of Judas?" Madeleine, despite her earlier urgency, had seemed apathetic to the actual work and proceedings. Busying herself with a careful examination of the raw materials that lined the racks along the cellar laboratory walls. Barely commenting as Herbert had chattered endlessly about his process and vital components of his elixir. Extolling the virtues of his earlier failures and the often cryptic advice and instruction that Madeleine had imparted on him.

"Why do you ask?" She turned to Herbert with a look of distracted boredom. "Is something wrong?" As she strolled closer to where the work was underway, she stretched out one hand and let it brush against the room divider. The leather curtain swaying at her touch until her eyes met Hans's troubled gaze. She let her hand slowly drop with a small smile. "Or did the knock at the door dissuade your passion?"

"Nonsense. My commitment, as you well know, is the very purpose of my life." As Herbert answered, Hans handed him one glass vat after another. A harvested organ floating inside each of them. Herbert carefully retrieved the now fully saturated body parts. Positioning each within the exposed ribcage; in close proximity to where they resided among the living. "No, it is not that, my dear Madeleine. My concern is with the pelvis and jawbone. Though I doubt you would recognize the subtle differences, one educated such as I can. If I didn't know better, I would assume this fleshless outline is woman, not man."

"Ah! And would you take exception to raising another Eve instead of an Adam?" Madeleine drew alongside Herbert as he worked. Continuing to comment without waiting for a reply. "Afterall, it seems like you already raised a Cain." Madeleine's eyes drifted to the closed and barred door. "Maybe it knows you are cultivating another branch on the family tree?"

As she snickered, the stone slab upon which Herbert worked to restore life to the ancient bones pulsed once. A barely perceptible hum that seemed to add an unnatural charge to the air as if a terrible storm was brewing. "Atop a stone, no less?" The briefest flash of a blue immediately followed, dazzling Herbert's eyes as Hans gasped audibly. "The devil is truly in the details..."

The bareboned skeleton seemed to buzz and waver before their eyes. A shuddering from within as the white of the bones began to shade with color. The slop of the oozing organs Herbert had just added slipping and sliding within until they'd escaped their bone cage. Each falling harmlessly away from the shimmering, human frame. Moments later, as each bone began to grow darker and darker, blossoms of pink flesh began to sprout along the ribs, skull, and pelvis.

"No, no, no," intoned Herbert as he shoved Hans toward the glass vat of his elixir. "I've yet to add the brain." He was shaking his head in denial as, like a mushroom sprouting from the death and decay of a darkened forest floor, mottled meat began to form and ripen with blood. "The bones must be baptized in my elixir!" Herbert turned and hurried past a frozen Hans – his eyes and mouth agape in horror. Rushing, he lunged for the container with hands slippery from his earlier labors. Pulling the weighty vessel from the shelf, he watched helplessly as it fell from his grip. Shattering upon impact with the dirt floor, the pooled elixir slowly being absorbed into the soil. The next thing to fall was the sob that escaped his downturned lips. Years of work, figuratively, down the drain.

"Fret not, boy." Madeleine waved both men to her side. "Though the medicinal concoction you created is indeed both years ahead and years behind what man has learned across time, the power to create life out of death was never going to come from a bottle." She slapped the massive stone slab with one palm as the blueish hue radiating from its center grew ever brighter. The skeleton now awash in a flood of erupting gore and blood.

"But... but all my work. The successes, they... they came only after I'd perfected my elixir. This," Herbert, his eyes incredulous and wide, "this can't... I alone was destined to cheat life and defeat death."

"Oh dear," Madeleine tsked-tsked. "You truly did believe in yourself, didn't you?" She smiled wryly before adding, "Think back now, Herbert. Did your elixir ever work before you uncovered this hidden alcove down here?" She raised her hands and gestured at the surrounding cellar walls. "Had you any success working atop anything except this?" Again, Madeleine placed her palms on the radiating rock. Skin and viscera now wrapping the once bare skeleton in flesh. "At school? Or at your first lab secreted away within the tunnels below Chateau Chanet?"

After a moment of contemplation, Herbert's shoulders sagged. Slowly, he shook his head back and forth in acknowledgement of the truths she spoke. "Once or twice I thought I caught a flash of light coming from the stone slab. Maybe felt or suspected some power residing within. But, I've never witnessed such light as today. How could I have known? Why does it seem so obvious now?" He looked across the pulsing rock at Madeleine. The look of a petulant child unwilling to accept defeat clear in his body language and features.

"I may be to blame for that. This stone and I, well... we have a history." She paused then, her eyes dropping, like Hans and Herbert, as what now writhed nude upon the stone slab suddenly inhaled. Moments later, screaming as if to wake more of the dead. "Birth is always so painful," commented Madeleine as the shriek weakened to a whisper.

The stone slab still throbbed weakly as the resurrected skeleton continued to fill in. Full breasts budding from its chest while between its thighs only fair hair sprouted. "A woman!" The revelation causing Herbert to step backwards as Hans diverted his eyes, embarrassed by the beauty forming before his astonished gaze. "This cannot be Judas. You have deceived me! At every step!"

"Ridiculous," Madeliene replied sharply. She quickly untied the yellow cord that sealed the velvet bag she'd carried since arriving. Reaching inside, she dug out a human skull. "As promised, I have brought the bones of Judas to be resurrected."

"But," Herbert stammered. He was unaccustomed to not having the upper hand. "But, who is she then?"

"Does it matter? I had to be sure. Consider this," she pointed, as for the first time, the thing wrenched from death pulled itself upright and into a sitting position, "a test. You passed, Herbert. She's alive. Alive!"

Hans, his eyes never leaving the scene of the resurrection, backed slowly away. His intent to unlock the cellar door and escape the madness he was witnessing. As he staggered weak-kneed up the stairs he repeated Herbert's question. "Who is she? What is that called?" He removed the beam that blocked his way out, unlatching the lock and peering cautiously outside.

"Hmmm..." Madeleine, pondering briefly, seemed to decide right then before replying. "I think I'll name her Elizabeth. That way, with so many variations of the name, she can choose to call herself whatever she wants. And," she chuckled, "at any *time* she chooses." Madeleine started to laugh then, though neither Herbert or Hans seemed to be in on the joke.

As her rich laughter flooded the room, the undead woman's eyelids fluttered like the wings of a moth withering under flame before, abruptly, freezing still as stone. The eyes, sparkling emeralds of deep green, were open-wide and both pupils were rapidly expanding and dilating. Her head and body began to twist, spasm, and contort awkwardly before finally settling. Moments later, jerking upwards as if a marionette commanded by an apprenticing puppeteer, she lurched from the top of the stone slab. As a clear fluid ran down her chin, she appraised her audience mutely before baring wet teeth in symphony with a piercing hiss.

At inhale, she snapped her head so hard to one side that Herbert expected it to dislodge. Instead, with a snarl as inviting as broken glass, she swept up the carefully extracted and prepared organs. Biting into and chewing through the gushing exteriors before ravenously devouring each juicy bit. Bloodless gore falling from her gnashing teeth. Finishing, she shambled a few steps to the stairs before stumbling gracelessly up them. Scurrying past Hans as he fell to his knees with hands outstretched and mouth agape in fear and horror. With all the grace of a newborn baby deer – arms and legs splaying awkwardly – she dashed for the cover of the nearby forest. Disappearing into the thick timber and vanishing among the dark foliage.

CHAPTER SIX
FRANCE-MODERN DAY

STANDER, GROANING, PEERED THROUGH the cracks in his defenses. The invading light, accusatory as a preacher's stare after spending the night eye-rolling with the devil, weaseled in a fingernail at a time. Clawing at his consciousness. The fluttering of his lashes, like religion and politics, naively trying to barter a peace between the dark and the light. Sacrificing tears spilt without emotion yet full of drama.

He didn't feel the drool until his head left the concrete and it dribbled from the corner of his mouth. Stander swiped at his chin with the back of one hand as he pushed himself from the cool of the floor. He was alone in the cramped maintenance closet. No sign of Beth or any of her belongings. With a head of rolling fog thundering with confusion, he slowly dressed and tried to recall what had happened. But his thoughts were soon interrupted by the loud voices arguing just outside the door.

The tarnished and dented doorknob rattled and turned unsuccessfully several times before Stander heard the jingle of keys. Moments later, the door opening wide. The janitor closet flooding with more light as a man Stander didn't recognize filled the doorway with his bulk.

"I told you he had to be in there. I already looked everywhere else." Just behind the stranger, a scowling Secrist began to push his way past the man. "You OK? Where," Secrist was clearly surprised to find Stander alone, "did Beth go? She already leave?" He reached down and helped Stander to his feet, his eyes taking in the tiny, and not so clean, maintenance room. "Guess she wasn't too impressed by these high-class accommodations, huh?"

Stander wanted to respond but his tongue was too thick to comply. Instead, he flipped Secrist off silently as all three men exited. The key carrying man scolded and threatened Stander in French and broken English. The intent, if not every word, plain in his voice. *Get out of here and don't ever come back!* He then turned to the only other people in the place – the bar long closed and the sun now rising – the two workers inventorying the bottles behind the bar. "Abby! Becky! Où est le serpillière? As tu laissé çe idiot David travailler sans supervision? Vous deux avez porté son cul triste pendant des années..." The rest lost as Stander and Secrist hit the front door and made their way outside. The bright sun and wails of distant sirens bluntly welcoming them to the new day. Secrist pointed to the waiting Uber and they piled in. Stander, holding his head gingerly as the driver did a quick U-turn and swerved down one of the narrow streets of Caen.

Turning a corner, several screaming police cars whizzed past them. Their flashing lights nearly obscured by the brightness of the rising sun. Both men rode side by side in silence for several minutes before Secrist pointed out the filth and grime on Stander's hands. "If I was you, I'd hit the shower first thing. You look and smell like you've risen from the grave." He grabbed at one of Stander's wrists and pointed to the various stains he could see. "You cut yourself? There is blood under your fingernails."

Stander pulled both hands close to his face, scrutinizing each as an ambulance with blinking lights but no siren flew past them. "Fuck... I have no idea. You sure that is blood?" Secrist gave him a withering look that reminded Stander he'd been a homicide detective for most of his career in law enforcement. "Yeah, guess you'd know." Stander shrugged as the car pulled into a parking lot and stopped at the entrance to their hotel. "Maybe Beth was... might have been her time."

The two men entered the bustling hotel lobby. A long line of customers waiting at the front desk – either to complain, checkout, or both – forcing them to skirt around the edge of the entryway. Finding the hallway where both their rooms were, they slipped down the nearly vacant first floor corridor. "I know I just arrived and you had an... eventful night, but we need to talk." Secrist turning to look at Stander as they walked side by side. "My grandfather's diary from his time over here during the first world war was enlightening, to say the least. I already shared how his words helped me figure out the whole sword thing. But we need to scrutinize that journal together. Something else... something important might catch your eye just like the..."

"I know, I know... but fuck, Tommy." Stander peered at him from hooded eyes. "Now is not the time. I feel like I just got ran over by a truck."

"I bet." Secrist gave Stander a wry smile. "Beth looked like she was uh... energetic, to say the least. I'm just glad I found you in one piece. I mean, after everything we've experienced lately, and how closely she resembled Liz. But, seriously, in the janitor's closet of a bar?" Secrist's grin morphed into a grimace. "You get any sleep?"

"Maybe, but my body is begging for another eyeful or two..." Stander slowed as they neared their rooms. Both men staying at the end of the long hallway in suites across from each other. "I'm not really sure I'm remembering things very clearly. It was... a strange night." Stander rotated his shoulder and grimaced before tugging at the collar of his t-shirt – gingerly pulling it to the side.

"Ouch, man! Those look like some deep-ass scratches carved into your shoulder blade." Secrist, pulling back the cloth and looking at Stander's back. "Must have been a hell of an itch."

Stander snorted once as he opened the door to his hotel room. "How about you go to our dig site with Lucas and Chris this morning? Without me. They can give you the five-cent tour of our work and bring you up to speed. I'll catch up with you guys later today. We can talk more then."

Secrist stood several moments looking at the door Stander had closed. Turning to head back toward the hotel lobby when he heard the shower behind it turn on. As he walks back down the hallway, the television in the lobby catches his eye. Though muted, it wasn't hard to ascertain what the newsflash was reporting. The live-shot showing a host of emergency vehicles clustered around a building as a shrouded body was wheeled toward an ambulance. Secrist couldn't read French, but he recognized one of the words scrolling underneath. *Meurtre*. Murder in English. In the background, the bar where Stander had just spent the night.

Sitting with Lucas and Chris as they finished the last of their hotel breakfast, Secrist repeated what Stander said about the three of them not waiting for him. That he would meet with them after catching up on some sleep. Secrist grabbed a quick to-go coffee and a couple pieces of fruit before trailing after the two men. All three jumping into Lucas's car and exiting the hotel's parking lot.

With Chris riding shotgun and chattering about the weather forecast, Secrist was left alone with his thoughts as the vehicle crawled along the busy street. The buzz of the morning traffic snarled by several tourist busses as the wheeled behemoths struggled down skinny lanes that hugged the tight corners they navigated around. Just outside of the city limits of Caen, the road cleared and the car sped up. Lucas turning down a two-lane paved road with a small sign pointing them toward the village of Vieux.

Secrist, after tossing a banana peel out the backseat window, let the breeze whip his hair from side to side. The morning sun bright and comforting. As they drove along the outskirts of the farming community they approached, he looked for anything that might seem familiar. The reading of his grandfather's diary, newly discovered among his father's belongings, was still very fresh in his mind. He'd devoured the writings only weeks earlier and had spent time on his flight reviewing the scribbles again for anything that might be helpful. The pages chronicling his grandfather's time as a soldier during the first World War. Much of it when he was based somewhere along the border of France and Germany – haunting the trenches.

The French village they weaved through was quaint and unassuming. Not significantly different than the rural towns that dotted the plains of the Midwest where he'd grown up. Secrist could see a mammoth cathedral dominated the center of the clustered homes. Its silent belltower, the tallest structure for miles, topped by a single steeple. Cozying up to one side of the church was an ancient looking graveyard; the opposite end of the cemetery vanishing down a small hill that ran into a deeply timbered forest. Before he realized it, the village was behind them and the car was surrounded on both sides by meadows of wild florae.

Lucas followed a curvy lane barely big enough for two cars to pass. The road heading toward a gradually sloping valley bursting with yellow blooming flowers. The intimidating forest that had seemed to mercilessly track their journey still bordering the colorful and untamed meadows. As Lucas parked his car on a white gravel lot, Chris commented about the lack of vehicles. Explaining for his benefit, Secrist was sure, how the workers clearing away the debris from the collapsed passageways all entered in and out of the main entrance of the quarry. Their cars and trucks parked on the opposite side of the knoll from where they were. Unseen.

"We aren't as alone out here as it appears." Lucas explaining in greater detail as the three men walked up a stone pathway. "As you already know, cell phones are pretty much hit or miss around here. But we installed an old-fashioned landline that rings the supervisor's office located back at the main entrance of the quarry. Plus, it is only about a twenty minute walk back to Vieux."

"And the entrance to the quarry is over that way?" Secrist was trying to get a lay of the land and to better understand his surroundings. Part of that was, after a career in law enforcement, just professional habit. But Secrist's grandfather had marched across and into these very same honeycombed depths. The written account of his time had been almost too fantastic to believe. The things he'd encountered utterly terrifying to read about. Though he'd never admit it, deep down, Secrist wasn't keen to follow in his footsteps. Even if it was over a hundred years later. But Secrist had to touch and see with his own eyes what Lucas had discovered. The massive anomaly. There were way too many coincidences piling up to dismiss offhand.

And Secrist hated coincidences.

"Are you ready to go inside?" Lucas, keys in hand, looked over at Chris and spoke softly. "You good going down in here?" Chris nodded hesitantly, absent-mindedly fingering the collar of his shirt.

"I know Stander filled you in and shared that Chris had been attacked." Secrist nodded, Lucas looking right at him. He'd gotten the blow-by-blow via phone shortly after the collapse that had nearly claimed all of the team's lives. It had been stunning to match the events they'd experienced with the almost prophetic words his grandfather had imparted in his WW1 journal. His ancestor seemingly trodding the very same cursed land Secrist was about to let swallow him whole. He looked over at Chris as Lucas continued talking. Unsure what he sees in his eyes. Worry? Fear? Or... anticipation?

"He's only been back down here a few times since. But, don't worry. I've been working onsite nearly every day helping... helping..." Lucas looked away, his voice cracking with raw emotion. "Helping any way I can. Busying myself with all this," he gestures at the gleaming technology and bright lights, "and making sure nothing like that ever happens again." Lucas paused briefly. "Stander, he's been amazing. Generous with both his time and his money if we feel new equipment is needed. All of us still trying to process what we... we experienced down here."

Lucas turned and unlocked the reenforced steel door that led down to the monolith. Once inside the earthen cavern, the newly installed automatic lights flickered to life, briefly startling Secrist. The motion sensors reacting to the arrival of the newcomers. Lucas tossed the safety equipment each man would wear to both Chris and Secrist before beginning to don his own lighted hardhat, neon-colored vest, and safety glasses. "Yeah," he motioned at the lighting above, "we decided to upgrade all the lighting. Everything down here is both automatic and has battery backup. Plus, even though we are going up and down into the depths along a single passageway, we now each get one of these."

Lucas handed both men what looked like a walkie-talkie. "Clip these onto your belts. It is doubtful we will need them, but they are low-frequency cave-in radios that can transmit right through the rock and cave walls." He paused until both men had suited up. "OK," Lucas nodded at Secrist, "you ready to see what might turn out to be the single greatest archeological find in history?"

"I still don't understand why this find has you so excited." Secrist, his head on a swivel, followed directly behind Lucas while Chris brought up the rear. All around them, walls of colorless chipped rock sporting their wavering shadows. They passed several corridors of yawning black. Each likely a tunnel the Romans had dug as they'd raped the earth of its natural treasures. The smell of dampness in the cooling air and the sound of dripping water echoing in their ears. "Aren't they unearthing statues all over the world? Is it just the size that makes this one special?" Secrist stepped over a soggy patch of clay, his footfalls taking him ever deeper underground.

"It is the depth and the undisturbed soil above it that makes the find remarkable." Lucas turned to make his point, looking directly at Secrist. "All the dirt and earth around and below is in situ."

"I thought in situ meant the ground is still in a natural, undisturbed state." Secrist scrunched his features up in thought. "How can that be true if the monolith was buried in the past?"

"Exactly. It can't. Yet, down here, the impossible seems possible." Lucas continued walking the decline of the passageway. Secrist could see he was shaking his head in disbelief.

Chris suddenly spoke up, "Tell him about the glass you've been finding."

"Yeah, so... even stranger is the composition of the soil I've begun to collect." At their shuffling feet, the flurry of dust they'd kicked up began to settle. The ground they trod gradually dampening the deeper into the manmade chasm they walked. "It isn't really glass like Chris called it. It is what's called impactite. In the past, samples like that have only been found at known meteorite impact sites. The extreme heat literally melts the soil and rock around it as the white-hot meteor slams through the earth's crust and surfaces."

"So, what does that mean?" Secrist could feel the temperature around him dropping as the chiseled tunnel gradually arced to the left. He rubbed his bare arms to calm the rising goosebumps. "The gigantic statue came from outer space?"

Lucas laughed. "That does seem logical in a way, doesn't it? But, that wouldn't explain how the soil above, where it would have crashed through layers of earth, are still in situ." Lucas stopped walking, lost in thought. "Unless, well…never mind. That makes even less sense."

"Oh, like any of this does." Secrist pushing Lucas to finish. "What were you going to say?"

"Well, I mean, unless it happened so long ago the earth had time to form natural layers of rock above it. But, that would mean it would have had to arrive here years and years ago. Not long after the dinosaurs went extinct."

"When was that?" Chris asking a question in a hollow sounding voice. "A million years ago?"

"Over 60 million years ago." Lucas stopped walking. "Anyway, here we are."

Entering the subterranean room – the curved walls they'd hiked straightening into a cavern – Secrist was relieved to find the expanse flooded with artificial light. At the far side, adorning one wall, was a crumbled and broken doorframe. The steel door that hung from it bent and slightly ajar. Behind it, obscuring and burying what lay beyond, a curtain of rock and collapsed dirt. Stark reminders of the recent cave-in that had completely sealed off the lone corridor between this site and the adjacent Roman era quarry. Near the damaged doorway, several cluttered tables and metal racks filled mostly with equipment that Secrist could only guess were needed for archeological work.

Knowing he would want to see the sword they'd recovered – the symbolled blade likely the same one his own grandfather once held – Lucas had it laid atop one table. Secrist, immediately drawn to the aged weapon, traced the strange, inlaid script with one finger. Briefly lifting and swinging the sword several times in the air. The metal glinting under the artificial lights it was bathed in.

Back the way they'd entered, Chris stood frozen before the partially exposed, mammoth stone effigy that dominated the chiseled cavity. Secrist and Lucas soon joining him, all three men in a reverent silence as they gazed at the visage. "Pictures don't do it justice," said Secrist exhaling.

He took a step back to take in the entirety of the stoic face. The deeply carved features nearly identical in size to the famed face of the Egyptian sphynx - some twenty feet across and twice as high. The head and shoulders all that had, so far, been unearthed. The expression, though intimidating, was human and somehow genuine. Emotional. There was a tear-drop shaped mark etched deeply into the middle of the forehead. The body of the strange character filled with what looked like a series of bent crosses. The swastika-like script and ankh-shaped symbol matching an emblem recently discovered on the grounds of Stander's great aunt's old estate. "And you," he turned to Lucas, "still have no idea who carved this?"

Lucas, despite having worked for months to slowly reveal the anomaly, replied without taking his eyes off the very human-like features and expression. His amazement nearly as raw as the first day the form had been revealed. "Not yet, anyway. Often, you can see traces of other cultures in unknown art that helps you identify the artisan. The craftsman's style. Or, at least narrow the civilizations or timeline. Piece together a hypothesis. But this?" The former archeology professor stretched his arms out in the shape of a cross. "I can already find traces of nearly all the ancient cultures in this work. As if they all chipped in to bring this monstrous being to life."

Chris, his voice hushed as if interrupting a sermon, spoke as he turned towards the shelves of digging tools. "Have you told him your theory about the missing jewels?"

"Jewels?" Secrist tore his gaze from the stare of the stone. "Stander never said anything about finding jewels." He paused, turning back to the monolith to confirm the hollowed out and concave openings etched into the rock remained vacant. "Wait. Do you mean the eyes and the necklace? Or, whatever that is supposed to be around the neck of it." Lucas nodded as Chris returned holding a bucket containing various handheld digging implements, brushes, and knee pads. "Obsidian, right? That was what they said the relict found atop Mt. Arvon in Michigan was made out of." He looked over at Chris. "Same as that 'good luck charm' you and Stander found as kids."

"Right, that's what I said." Chris set the tool bucket down, the echo bounding off the walls. "Jewels. He thinks," nodding at Lucas, "ancient man somehow did this." Chris waved both hands toward the chiseled face as if frantically waving goodbye. "And then later came back and robbed it like the tomb raiders in ancient Egypt did to the Pharaohs."

Secrist cocked a disbelieving eye. "And the 1,000 year old human remains found in Skull Rock was one of thieves? I think your math is off by sixty million or so." He gave Lucas a good natured pat on the back.

"That is a mischaracterization of what..." Lucas stopped and reached down to grab a couple brushes and trowels. "I was just spouting off ideas. We only have the thing's head and shoulders exposed so far." He tossed the hand tools at Secrist. "I'll show you what you need to know so you can help figure all this out. It's a monstrous job, but we need to resurrect this. Bring everything to light if we want to find the truth and the way."

All three men bent knee to task.

CHAPTER SEVEN
GERMAN-16TH CENTURY

Herbert, sulking, leaned against the doorframe of his cellar laboratory. The ornate pipe in his hand lit but ignored. Behind him, down the stairs and behind the leather curtain, he could hear the labored moans and grunts of the first man (he supposed that was what *it* was) he'd resurrected. At the moment of its birth, he'd been enraptured by the breakthrough. Believing the thing made of bone and skin he'd parceled together and filled with the breath of life to be immaculate in its construction. But, well before the events of tonight, he'd grown to loathe the behemoth. Even as he'd made a few well, alterations he'd suppose one would call them, his disgust had not abated.

"Be still down there, goddamn you!" Herbert stuck his pipe back in his mouth before slamming the door. Crossing his arms in front of him and scowling as he watched Madeleine converse with the four men charged with her safe travels. He couldn't hear everything that was being said, but she was discouraging her coachmen from attempting to follow after the *madwoman* who had *escaped* from the *good doctor* who had been trying to help heal her *affliction* on Madeleine's behalf. Hans, for his part, had completely vanished. Hopefully, Herbert thought to himself, he'd disappeared into the house to ensure no one had witnessed what had occurred. And, if they had, be certain they were on their way to forgetting it.

Business as usual at the House of Chanet.

Of course, that was no longer true. He, Doctor Herbert Chanet, had just lost everything. Everything that really mattered to him. No one would dare say anything to his face, but it was obvious he was a total failure. All the work, successes he'd crowed about, his lifelong quest to vanquish death among man. He'd lost it all. He was a farce. A disappointment. The façade of confidence and triumph he'd so carefully crafted slowly crumbling. Down deep inside, he suddenly felt very badly broken.

Herbert watched as Madeleine separated herself from the men and began to make her way back toward the house. Each man, thus far anyway, apparently accepting the explanations of the queer events - her ruse and deceptions. Herbert began to wonder if he was equally misled.

He knew there was a part of himself that now resented Madeleine. But, conflicted, Herbert also recognized another part of him still felt indebted to her. Afterall, she'd been the first to even bring up the possibility of the additional space and hidden room within the cellar. Her keen eye picking up on the strangeness of a foundation laid centuries earlier. When later he'd written to her, confirming the discovery of a long-forgotten chamber that Hans had managed to break into, Herbert had barely made mention of the stone slab secreted within. Yet, even in her first replies, she'd encouraged him to take advantage of its placement. Reminding him of the importance of consistency in his experiments and counseling him to perform all atop the strange rock. Sharing that many ancient civilizations believed certain stones contained power beyond the scope of man.

He'd ignored the suggestion.

Instead, placing faith in the learned sciences of the day, he'd spent his time experimenting with chemical baths of varying compositions. Separating each promising concoction into its own bubbling vat. Watching what he considered life's fundamental building blocks – proteins, sugars, carbohydrates, and starches – populate and grow within. Later, introducing the simplest forms of life into his elixirs and observing the reactions. Successfully growing small cultures before finally testing his radical ideas on animals. Mice, sparrows, and frogs, among the first of his experiments. But nothing sparked with true life. Nothing returned from the infinite pool of death. No, it had only been after he'd fully embraced many of the revered Egyptian funerary practices that he'd finally succeeded.

Or so he had believed.

He'd begun removing and soaking the vital organs of his test subjects. Believing that, much like the ancient Egyptians had used individual canopic jars to secure their own life-after-death travels, each vat would be crucial to resurrection. Though, as he now sat in reflection, he realized it had actually been Madeliene who had first suggested mimicking many of Egypt's ancient practices. Supplying him with translations of their rituals that he could follow. Encouraging him to combine their sacred processes with the enlightened views of the 16th century. At first, as he recalled, it had seemed ridiculous. Herbert questioning the rationale and motives of his dark-skinned co-conspirator. But soon, he could no longer argue with the results. Her continued insistence that he add several steps for consistency had yielded the breakthrough he'd long hoped to achieve. The careful dissection, measured use of his elixir, and the consistency in the process making the difference. Each successful attempt, he now remembered, ending atop the slab of rock Madeleine had beseeched him to employ.

Never underestimate the power of quarried stone, she'd written him. *Perhaps, like the ancient Egyptians who built their monuments, or Moses with his tablets, or the ancient peoples of Stonehenge, this rock holds power beyond our understanding.* He'd initially laughed at the proposal. But, desperate for success, he had finally relented and followed all of her instructions and suggestions. Spilling the blood of each test subject atop the strange rock. The dissection always the first step in his process. While the very last step, the one Madeleine had advised he never watch, was to let his alchemy elixir do its work across the sturdy, flat surface of the strange black stone.

And it had worked! The big breakthrough coming courtesy one of the endless barn cats that prowled nearby.

It had been a stormy night full of thundering crashes and streaking flashes of lightning. Hans had already retired for the night. Leaving Herbert alone to ponder the direction his next wave of experiments should go. Acting impulsively, he'd snagged one of the slinking black cats from the grounds. Drowning it by hand at the shoreline of his lake to ensure the dying throes of the infernal beast (the damnable thing had bitten him!) would be unheard. Discreetly carrying the limp, dripping cat by its tail back to his hidden lab before sealing it in a glass container filled to the rim with his elixir. Clamping the heavy lid down tightly and placing it on top of the table-like surface of the rock. Then, lighting his pipe, he'd stepped outside to ponder his next move.

The gurgled yowling that drew him back inside the laboratory had started almost immediately. An ethereal wail that instantly quelled the chorus of nearby singing frogs. The nocturnal bustle of the surrounding countryside slowly falling eerily silent as well. As Herbert had slipped back down the cellar stairs to investigate, he'd heard the unmistakable sound of glass shattering. Reaching the stone slab, he found the reborn feline had toppled from the top of the strange rock. Regenerated, but impaled on shards of glass, it had hissed and yowled angrily at him from the ground with green eyes that poured hate and rage.

Overjoyed by the success, he'd spent the rest of the night dissecting the pitiful creature. Carefully observing and recording the cat's reactions as he'd tried to kill it for the second time. Neither poison, dismemberment, drowning, or was flame able to drive out the life he'd restored. The final solution only coming when the heel of his boot crushed the fragile skull. The endless mewling finally silenced when he'd ground its brain to paste.

He'd been ecstatic!

More experiments would soon follow. Herbert, with the help of Hans, faithfully duplicating the rebirths until he had confidence in the process. Always using his special elixir and, thought Herbert ruefully to himself, always atop the once-hidden stone slab. Later, taking a more artistic approach to his work, Herbert began to create new versions of the woodland animals that populated the surrounding forests. Generating bizarre beasts with mismatched horns, limbs, and tails – all pulled from death. Allowing those that survived the crude operations, if able, to melt back into nature. Herbert overruling the disapproving concerns and objections from Hans. Calling the abominations they churned out *his brood* as he continued with his experimentations.

On man!

Understanding he could never produce enough of his elixir to baptize a fully grown man or woman, instead, he tried pouring copious amounts of his concoction directly into the dead. Unearthing the recently deceased and, still housed in their coffins deep in the ground, loading their foul throats until they overflowed. When still they refused to rise, he'd switched to children in hopes the doses administered to the full-grown adults had merely been insufficient. But, the little brats also remained unmoving. The internalization of his elixir didn't work. Nor did the chemical baths he attempted on recently deceased foundlings he'd "adopted" from the various orphanages that appreciated his generous donations without inquiring into the nature of his business.

Frustrated by his inability to replicate the earlier successes, he'd finally written Madeleine. Her response arrived quickly; the content full of sage advice. Cautioning against the late night visits into the graveyards and reminding him of the danger if caught. Writing to him of a plan that would keep them both safe. *Should you ever succeed in raising man,* her flowing letter had intoned, *I possess the most extraordinary find. One that could dispel the self-righteous who would call your science blasphemy. For, without raising him, your work would likely get us burned at the stake as witches. That is, unless you had undeniable proof of a divine right to dawdle in the art of gods and monsters.*

Herbert remembered that he'd paused his reading then, his mind buzzing with wonderment. He certainly always felt he had the divine right. But, who could he resurrect that would be welcomed by the masses? Even Jesus himself would likely be dismissed as a madman. After all, every madhouse and fool's tower had a Jesus or two residing within. What good would one more be?

Continuing, the letter revealed she'd located the ossuary of Judas Iscariot. Without providing much in terms of details, the carefully worded reply teased the grandeur of the find. How that, if Herbert were successful in discovering the secret to resurrecting man, Madeleine would entrust him alone with the remains. *Sure as the kiss of Judas,* she'd promised him in writing. Imploring him to continue his experiments and saying that she would stand ready, so sure she was of his future success. And, true to her word, she'd made hasty preparations to visit the House of Chanet once Herbert alerted her of his triumph. Arranging her arrival to coincide with the departure of Herbert's family once he'd secured the partnership of his sister. Madeleine arriving only hours after he'd sent his family packing.

"The time is at hand." Madeleine, likely interpreting the concern corrupting Herbert's features as doubt, wrapped a comforting arm around his elbow. "Shall we descend back into the darkness that awaits?" She gestured at the closed opening that led down into his laboratory. Above her head, the moon shined brightly. Behind her, creeping out from the wall of timber at the edge of the forest, a white mist had begun to encircle her carriage. The four coachmen standing uncomfortably in the encroaching haze. Moments later, a rushed and near-breathless Hans joined Herbert and Madeleine at the doorway as the doctor withdrew his key.

With few words spared, the process Herbert and Hans had completed earlier was duplicated. Madeleine handing over her richly tailored bag as both men began taking turns fishing out the contents within. A new skeleton slowly pieced together and laid out on top of the stone slab. No longer surprised by what he was witnessing, Herbert watched closely as the strange rock hummed and the fleshless bones quivered. Once again darkening from the inside out and evolving into color.

Herbert struggled to make sense of what he witnessed one again. The coloring of the bones so vivid it seemed unreal. Bursts of cherry spreading like the sores of one doomed with the plague. Gore forming and spreading everywhere before melding into more substantial tissue. Sinewy strands slithering like the roots of a tree long starved of water until taking hold; while eruptions of muscle bound the barebones together. The body shimmering and convulsing as it teemed with layers of flesh that spread like a fire consuming everything in its path.

Beyond the outside door, desperate screams and cries began to ring out. Diverting attention from the burgeoning body atop the stone. Herbert waved an impatient hand Hans's way, silently instructing his assistant to check on the disturbance. Herbert and Madeleine, huddled side by side like expectant parents, uninterested in anything beyond the life emerging from the beyond. Both only briefly watching Hans scale the steps and crack the door before their gazes returned to the glowing stone slab.

As if in reply to the cascading sounds of desperation still reverberating in the background, the lipless mouth parted. Horrified, Herbert stared as the thing clawing itself back from death suddenly began sprouting two elongated incisors. Each canine tooth unnaturally long and sharp. He stumbled backwards as the thing wrenched out of death opened its eyes for the first time. Blazing orbs of green that Herbert refused to peer into. Turning his head, his own eyes searched Madeleine's in hopes of finding answers.

Her stare unreadable.

"My Lord! Come quickly!" Hans was hollering for Herbert from the top of the cellar stairs. The door was unlatched and hung slightly open. Someone Herbert couldn't see lay crying and sobbing just beyond. "There's been a murder!"

"Murder! Here?" Herbert roared back, the events of the evening beginning to spiral out of control. "Now?" He took several steps toward the stairs before stopping. He couldn't leave his laboratory in the middle of this resurrection. "You'll...you'll have to go see what has happened." Herbert was looking up at him as he spoke. But Hans wasn't seeing or hearing. His eyes widening in fear as he looked past Herbert before suddenly yanking the door wide. Herbert briefly saw two of his housekeepers weeping – one looked as if she'd been splashed with red paint – before Hans raced outside and slammed the door behind him. A look of pure terror stamped deeply into his features.

Herbert sensed as much as he heard the first raspy breath. He had no doubt it originated from the top of the rock. The cellar room, already dark and shadowy, seemed to somehow blacken. He heard a second expulsion of air and along with it came a rancid wave of rot. The stench causing Herbert to wince and clamp both hands over his mouth and nose. Only then did he realize he'd begun to weep – his hands warm with wet tears.

He could hear movement behind him. Something cracking like an old hand closing its fingers. Though the underground chamber was naturally cool, his body became beaded with sweat. Herbert cursed his cowardice as he tried unsuccessfully to turn. The trembling in his knees threatening to give out and drop him to the floor. Unmoving, his ears tracked the shuffling steps dragging across the soft earth of the cellar floor. Closer, and then closer still. Herbert knew something was behind him even before the hand fell heavily upon his shoulder.

Still, he screamed.

CHAPTER EIGHT
FRANCE-MODERN DAY

STANDER TIPPED THE DRIVER generously before stepping out into the bright, afternoon sunshine. With one hand shading his eyes, he watched the Uber pull out of the parking lot and speed away. Turning, his footsteps crunching in the gravel, he walked past Lucas's parked car and started up the lone path before him. He pulled his key to the outside door that led down to where Lucas, Chris, and Secrist were working and slid it in place. After entering into the chiseled corridor of stone and locking the door behind him, he paused. His eyes gradually adjusting to the artificial light as he inhaled the cloying musk of the underground passageway and chamber ahead. Frowning, he pulled up the collar on his old Judas Priest concert t-shirt. Using the black material to cover his nose and mouth as he donned the required safety equipment before heading down.

"You guys about ready to take a little break?" Stander, some fifteen minutes later, stood behind the other three. Each man bowed before the giant, stone-faced effigy. He had the enigmatic sword in hand and swung it back and forth several times, pretending to parry and block with it. The weapon perfectly balanced in his hand. "Maybe step outside for some fresh air?" Putting the sword back, he reached down and pawed at the mound of just-cleared dirt and earth, grabbing a handful. "Or, just call it a day and go get an early dinner so we can talk over a few drinks?"

Secrist groaned wearily as he pulled himself to his feet. Limping a couple steps toward Stander as Chris and Lucas stood and stretched. "What's the matter? You already getting skittish being down here?" Secrist leaned a shoulder against the rock wall and rubbed at one foot. "You just arrived."

"Nah... I mean, I don't love being down here." Stander stood and let the dirt fall through the cracks in his fingers. "But, ashes to ashes, right?" The three men congregating around him as he talked. "I'd like you," he nodded at Lucas and Chris, "to hear what Tommy found in his grandfather's diary. I haven't even heard the whole story yet, but the fact we have a written account from a hundred years ago about some of these very same lands is worthy of our attention. It strains credibility to think his grandfather," now nodding at Secrist, "only coincidently had similar experiences during World War One. But discussing things down here," Stander let his eyes wander the cave, "after everything that has happened..." He tried to shrug nonchalantly, but it seemed more like a shudder. "Anyway, I just think voices carry. Who really knows what might still be slithering in and out of all these cracks and crevices?" Stander briefly looked each man in the eye. "Plus," he pointed to the sobering monolith, "I don't trust that ugly motherfucker."

After driving back into Caen and commandeering an outdoor table at a smallish café, the four men broke bread together. With the exception of Chris, his drink of choice now carbonated water, the red wine flowed like blood. The spirit loosening the tongue as Secrist shared passages from the century old tome his grandfather had penned while they ate. Flipping pages and highlighting his time combatting the supernatural. Each man, at different times, exclaiming at the similarities to experiences they'd recently had. The ferocious creature they'd resurrected from its forgotten grave was undoubtedly the same one Secrist's grandfather thought he'd buried for all of eternity.

"I think I should share something with you guys." Lucas, who had been uncharacteristically quiet for long stretches of the conversation, shifting uncomfortably in his chair. "I'm pretty sure I know of the French chateau mentioned in the diary. In fact, as incredible as it sounds, I think it was my childhood home." Around him, the table grew silent. Briefly.

"Get the fuck out of here!" Stander looked like he wanted to stand. Or puke. Or both...

"How can... wait." Secrist thumbed the yellowed, worn pages. The binding creaking on the hard-pressed cardboard cover and spine of faded blue. "There is only the briefest mention of... not many specifics... ah! Here it is. Let's see." It had been a paragraph he'd specifically marked to discuss in detail with Stander, but hadn't yet found the opportunity. The name mentioned in the writing could just be a coincidence, but Secrist didn't really believe that. Squinting, he read the passage out loud.

"Intelligence had also uncovered the owner of the chateau to be an American woman. Some lady living in the Midwest named Madeleine something-or-other that had inherited the estate in the past from a distant French relative. None of that would have really mattered except she'd also revealed the estate included a secret underground passageway. A long subterranean corridor that had been carved out sometime in the storied past of the grand home. A hidden underground route that provided safe passage from the chateau to a nearby German village. A hidden escape route if the home was in jeopardy or came under attack. Or was bombed. The several miles long secret tunnel undercutting the border and connecting France and Germany."

Secrist let the smallish journal fall gently to the tabletop. "My grandfather mentions it a few other times but only in passing. But according to this," he tapped his finger on the cover, "the chateau was bombed by the Royal Air Force." Secrist peered across the table at Stander. "This was one of those things I wanted to talk with you about. You caught the name, right?" Stander, barely nodded, his eyes distant and unfocused.

"I was never told anything about any bombing," Lucas pulled off his glasses and began to clean the lenses on the front of his shirt. "And, to be clear, I only have the briefest memories of my time living there. I think we had moved to Caen by the time I started schooling. But, it is a very old chateau right on the border of France and Germany."

"Does that really mean anything? There must be a bunch of old houses, castles, chateaus, or whatever they are called over here along the border. The borderline itself must be hundreds of miles long, right?" Lucas acknowledged what Chris said, nodding along in agreement.

"I only know it fits the description. There is a sinkhole in the field behind the buildings. I can remember my mom telling me not play around it. She said it was dangerous because below ground there was an old tunnel that was collapsing." He looked around the table, all eyes on him. "Sure sounds similar to..."

"Does that name mean anything to you?" Stander's voice was low, "Madeleine."

Lucas was nodding subtly, lost in thought as he replied. "I was so little that I can't be sure. But, I know there was an old lady who came to visit at times. I suppose it could be my imagination, but I have it in my head she was from my dad's side of the family. I don't actually have any memories of her," he shrugged. "There are just pictures that I can recall seeing of her holding me as a baby. I'm pretty sure, when I would sometimes look at old family photo albums with my mom, that the name written on the back of those photos was Madeleine. Great Aunt Madeleine. That would have made her my Great, Great Aunt Madeleine, I guess."

"Jesus fucking Christ," Stander moaned. Chris shook his head beside him in silence. The two men had met as young boys in Illinois. At Stander's Great Aunt Madeleine's home. The grand manor known locally as Relict Mansion, or more commonly, Widow Mansion. All four of Madeleine's husbands having died on the grounds of the estate, sealing her and her home's fate as wicked and cursed. The house and land, recently inherited by Stander, had sat empty after her death until his acquisition.

"Where is this place?" Secrist ignored Stander's profane outburst, his focus on the chateau and its possible tie to his grandfather. "Do you happen to remember an address? Or at least get us close? After reading about all this," he tapped the cover of the century old journal, "I'd love to see some of the same things he did."

"I can do better than that." Lucas pulled out a set of keys and began to separate the dangling metal. "I try to keep tabs on it but I haven't been there since last year sometime." He motioned toward a muttering Stander who no longer seemed to be listening. "Ever since this guy put me to work. But you are more than welcome to explore the house and grounds." After pocketing a couple keys, Lucas slid the keyring across the table toward Secrist. "I'll text you the address so you can plug it into your phone or GPS."

"You own the chateau?" Chris, already pale, seemed to lose the little bit of blood that colored his cheeks.

"Ever since my parents died. I'm the last of my family." Lucas took a drink from his wine glass.

"Just like me," said Secrist. "The closest thing I have for family is an ex-partner's daughter that still calls me uncle." Chris nodding, his adopted family all long dead - his real heritage unknown.

"And just like me," Stander's voice barely a whisper. He turned to Secrist. "What a fucking coincidence, huh, Tommy?"

"I want to drive over there. See this place." Secrist was looking directly at Stander. "Maybe we should all go?" He cast a quick glance around the table hopefully.

"I'll pass," Lucas immediately replied. "I need to continue my work here. I'm behind where I wanted to be by now. Without the others helping, God rest their souls, I have a lot of dirt to move."

"I'll pass, too." Chris licked his lips once before looking over at Stander for his approval.

"Really?" The shock undisguised on Stander's features. "Is that a good idea? I thought you hated being underground. Especially now. I mean, after what happened to you down there. No one would blame you for tagging along with me and Tommy. And, if you come with us, at least you'll get a chance to see some of the countryside and…"

"And leave Lucas to work all alone in that hole?" Chris jabbed a thumb the archeologist's way. "What if he falls and twists an ankle or something? Besides, the physical work is helping me get my strength back. It feels good to know I'm accomplishing something meaningful. Waking up with a purpose every morning helps me focus on my recovery. Been awhile since I really felt useful."

"Well, okay I guess. I mean, it's fine if that is what you want." Stander glanced at Lucas who was shrugging his shoulders to let him know he was okay with the arrangement. "I'll book a rental car tonight for Tommy and I. We'll pack some clothes and leave in the morning, I guess."

The next day, after eating breakfast with Lucas and Chris, Stander and Secrist wedged themselves into the tiny rental car. Both annoyed the only vehicle available on such short notice had ended up being a two-door Renault Clio. It was a garish green — the color of antifreeze fluid — and had little head or leg room. Or power. Secrist, after plugging the address of the chateau into his phone, played navigator as Stander drove out of Caen. Both men had dressed casually in jeans and t-shirts for the long road trip, the bags they tossed in the trunk packed with more of the same. Once they cleared the worst of the tourist laden traffic, each settled in for the hours of driving ahead of them.

"So, after we got back to our rooms last night," Secrist pulling out the pad of paper he'd liberated from the hotel. "I spent time trying to match the area where we are headed with the writings in my grandfather's journal. I thought, since we have a destination I can drill down into, something might pop out."

"Makes sense. What did you find?" Stander glancing over at the pages filled top to bottom with Secrist's handwritten script. "Jesus! Did you write everything out? You could have just taken a few screen-shots or pictures with your phone."

"Yeah, well... old habits die hard, I guess. Things just stick with me better once I write them down." Secrist waving Stander's words away as if a pesky fly. "Anyway, unfortunately," answering his question, "I still can't be sure. He was purposefully vague about his travels and his orders." Secrist held up the tattered journal. "I think he was worried this would fall into enemy hands if he was killed or captured. He wrote a lot more about the emotions he was feeling than coordinates. His writing is almost poetic in places." Secrist flipped a few pages, lingering over several lines. "And scary as hell."

"Of that," Stander locked eyes briefly with Secrist, "I have no doubt."

"Whether the place we are heading is the same location or not, there are plenty of stories about the area online. There is a massive, mountainous forest we'll have to drive right through the middle of to get there. It kind of envelopes the cluster of villages on both the French side and the German side of the border. From what I read last night, a bunch of the ancient folklore associated with both France and Germany in general originated in the area." Secrist glanced down at his handwriting, anticipating the question to come.

"That doesn't surprise me." Stander pumped the brakes and swerved slightly. A black dog with white paws darting across the road. "I read about some of the legends when I first came over here to find out what happened to my mom." He paused. "You read about the Beast of Gévaudan? Or, however you pronounce that."

"Sure. That is the major one, isn't it? Supposedly, a huge wolf or werewolf-like creature that the king of France finally had hunted down and killed in the 18th century after the public outcry." Secrist flipped a few pages on the pad. "I wrote something... something caught my eye about that."

"Wasn't that in the southern part of France, though? I mean, where all the killing occurred." Stander kept his eyes on the road. After the dog had darted out, he realized how close the thick trees were to the edge of the road. His eyes peeled for any other animals that might dare the pavement.

"Yeah, you are remembering that part right." Secrist lifted his eyes, "I guess I didn't write it down. But, the first sightings began centuries earlier. The area we are heading for, whatever that forest is called, birthed a bunch of German folklore as well as French legends. Those ancient woodlands, if you read some of the accounts, were prowled by all sorts of creatures and monsters."

Stander, driving, kept looking straight ahead. "A few years ago I would have laughed at all this. But now, I suspect there is some truth to all those traditional stories and legends." He glanced over quickly at his passenger. "Give me the highlights. What else came out of this area we are heading into?"

"Like I said, the Beast of Gévaudan is the most famous. But, the area was supposedly overrun by witches, fairies, and goblins called Brownies, who I guess do housework." Secrist looked up and shrugged, both men sharing a chuckle.

"And ghosts, of course. La Dame Blanche is kind of like the French version of The Lady in White."

"La Dame Blanche? That sounds classy." Stander briefly cocked his head in thought. "Or, just like some goth stripper's fancy stage name," he added with a smirk. "What does she haunt?"

"I didn't write anything down. But, I mean besides being a female ghost, I think they are supposed to be harbingers of death. Or, tragedy and loss, anyway."

Stander nodded. He'd followed a disembodied apparition with flowing white hair when he'd found his mom's long-dead remains last year. It had nearly led him off a ledge before Lucas had pulled him back. Saving his life. The memory more like a dream. At the time, he'd dismissed the entire affair as a hallucination.

"Anything else besides beastly dogs, ghosts of white, and home cleaners of brown?"

Secrist was consulting his notes, the picturesque countryside outside the speeding car growing denser. "I thought the legend of the Craqueuhhe," he looked up, "probably not how you pronounce that, was interesting. It sounds like a cross between a zombie and a vampire. I was thinking about what both you and my grandfather described seeing."

"That fucking thing, what I saw anyway, had better be dead." Stander, unsmiling, looked over at Secrist. "I only survived because it let me. Toyed with me." Stander felt his ears flush. "If you hadn't sent that text when you did..." The sentence didn't need to be finished.

"Just a coincidence," Secrist sniggered once before turning back to his written notes. "There is also something named La Ankou, or just Ankou, I guess. Kind of seems similar to a Craqueuhhe so I thought it was worth mentioning. The descriptions are all over the board. But, to me, it sounds like the Grim Reaper. A skeleton with a scythe is how it's described. But, supposedly, it could also just be a servant of death, an omen or a collector of souls depending on the legend you read. In some of them, though, it is a cursed man or being that wanders the mortal plane in search of certain souls." Secrist looked across at Stander. "You said it seemed to know you."

Stander ignored the implication. "And you are saying these legends originated from where we are headed?"

"Who's to say for certain. A lot of these folk tales are all over Europe in some way, shape, or form. I imagine plenty of countries and cultures lay claim to being home to the original. I just thought some background information would be helpful. Regardless of the specific legend, beast, or monster, we'll be staying in a place steeped in folklore. I think it is worth our time to listen with an open mind when we arrive. Even a speckling of truth in a scary tale could be helpful."

Secrist tossed his pad of paper in the backseat. Outside the car windows, an endless sea of green. The timber around them growing more dominant with each passing hour. Civilization slowly falling by the wayside as they closed in on the home.

Château de Chanet.

CHAPTER NINE
GERMAN-16TH CENTURY

THE SCREAM DIED ON his lips. Waning no differently than an overlooked berry withering along a forgotten vine; a hollow husk of little substance. Herbert, immobilized by fear, rotated widening eyes and peered shakily at what clasped his shoulder. Elongated fingers – with skin stretched so tightly across the bone that it appeared transparent – twitched and spasmed. Desperately fluttering against his neck like the feckless flailing of a wind-swept bird fated to weather a terrible storm. Herbert began to quiver as he shrank from the rank breath that whispered nothing into his ear. The sound of silence ominous and filled with malice.

Trembling, Herbert watched incredulously as the ends of each spasming finger suddenly split grotesquely. Yellowing nails erupting from the torn skin and scratching at the tender flesh beneath his ear as they emerged. Dropping his eyes, he watched the process repeated as the oozing nubs of an emaciated foot sprouted gaunt toes that were slowly topped by sickly nails. Shuddering uncontrollably, Herbert squeezed his eyes tightly shut. Despite a lifetime of mocking, cheating, and chasing after death, he couldn't face the specter now that it was barely a step behind. Cowering, he waited to be claimed in exchange for his blasphemous ways.

SWOOSH!!

The ambiguous sound exploded in the still of the underground chamber. Herbert answered with a screech before desperately lunging from the wraith at his back. Each leg taking one shaky step before giving out and sending Herbert sprawling awkwardly to the ground. As he landed, Herbert spun with arms outstretched in a desperate attempt to keep his impending death at bay. "Christ," he cried from his knees. "He has risen!"

"Judas! Tama!" Madeleine, her voice firm and direct, commanded the resurrected bones. She'd swept aside the heavy leather curtain that divided clandestine cellar into two halves. Exposing what it had concealed from Herbert's denying eyes even as he cowered and sniveled along the dirt floor. Madeleine repeated herself, "Here! Tama! Tama!"

As the swaying divider slowly stilled, the light of the lanterns and candles poured into the darkened space. Dousing the hidden contents in dull, yellow light. The floor, ceiling, and walls all matched the rest of the cellar's drab interior. Except for a few discarded wooden crates and a pile of soiled hay tossed in one corner, the second half of the hidden cellar was nearly barren. A single hand-forged eyebolt, all that adorned one wall. On the opposite side, back near the corner and crowded with shadows, two thick, rose-headed spikes had been driven in the stone. The crude nails as high on the wall as a man would stand and nearly the same distance apart from each other. The misshapen tops mottled with gore as if whatever fleshy thing the iron pegs once supported had been callously ripped from the crude barbs.

Along the ground, a heavy chain decorated the otherwise nearly featureless dirt floor. Connected to the opposite end of the restraint – shackled by its gashed and torn neck – a hulking man clothed all in black stood unmoving. At his feet, a well-worn trench had been carved into the dirt by the mammoth's near endless pacing.

His face was masked by a pair of disproportionate hands. One was dark and hair covered, the other appearing almost feminine with a light complexion. Both hands badly disfigured by jagged holes in the center of them that bubbled with infection and oozed a thick, discolored puss. The top of his head, patchily covered by dark, thin hair, was severely misshapen. Squarish. Where the hairline bordered its wide forehead, as if he'd once been crowned by unforgiving thorns, discolored welts protruded and wept. Thin fluid dripping from the ragged holes.

The marred fingers of the mismatched hands cautiously splayed wide as it became more accustomed to the light. The pallid features divided by a bloodless gash that ran from the upper lip and split its broad forehead in two. Scared, but hopeful eyes peered out from behind thin digits blackened on each end by rot. Seeing Herbert first, the hands slowly dropped. A child-like grin of joy opened a mouth of grey, filled with only misshapen teeth – the tongue clipped down to uselessness. Clearly excited and happy to see Herbert, the unnatural thing made the cheerful sounds of a mute. Grunts and cries mixed with unintelligible words as if trying to mimic the sound of talking. A joy touching its colorless eyes and an openmouthed grin conveying a wonder at the sights before him.

Meak as a lamb.

"Oh dear," Madeleine began, "someone missed their daddy."

Like a wolf pouncing on a cornered sheep, the newly resurrected leapt for the simpleton. Descending on it with a swift savagery unlike anything Herbert had previously witnessed. Though the behemoth could have easily overpowered his near fleshless attacker and ripped out the thin limbs that tore into him, it lacked the sense to even understand it was in danger. Landing on its back, in moments his chest cavity was split and torn wide. Like the predators of the wild, the undead Judas feasted on the soft parts it found within. Burrowing deeper and deeper as it raked open the flesh, devouring the innards even as its victim reached for Herbert. Confusion, hurt, and tears filling the grey eyes as it was savaged to pieces. Sobbing unintelligibly before the malformed head was finally torn from the frenzied feast. Rolling across the dirt before coming to rest at Madeleine's feet.

"No!" Hans screamed from the doorway, a limp body bathed in crimson held in his arms. Tears pooled in his eyes as he looked from the carnage to Herbert and Madeleine. "You must stop this madness!" The only reply was the sound of squelching flesh as the first man Herbert had brought back to life was eviscerated before their eyes by the second. An Abel devoured by a Cain; brothers now bound by the sacrificial blood of the lamb. The exposed, white-ribbon ribcage rapidly emptied of the contents it was meant to protect. The splashes of gore painting the scene in vivid color.

"Messy afterbirth," commented Madeleine dryly. "Seems the dead develop a voracious appetite swimming in the beyond. I often wonder if it is simply nourishment they crave or if they miss the very taste of life? Regardless, what chaos they leave behind."

Finishing, Judas raised his gore-smeared chin and bellowed. An unearthly shriek that split the night and caused both Herbert and Hans to drop to their knees and cover both ears. The dripping wet corpse Hans had held rolling from his grasp. As it thumped noisily down the stairs – a red smear left behind on each step – the feasting ghoul looked up. Seeming to recognize or long for the stars and moon beyond the opened doorway, it swiftly departed. Easily scaling the steps before vaulting over the prostrate form of Hans and vanishing into the night.

Hans was shaking and sobbing as he regained his feet. He lunged for the basement door and slammed it shut before leaning heavily against the wood. Herbert remained on the dirt floor where he'd fallen. The only movement he made was the continual slow shake of his head as he tried to make sense of the night's events. Madeleine seemed unfazed by the miracles and atrocities she'd witnessed thus far. She strolled to the body Hans had unceremoniously dumped down the basement stairway. The savaged remains had come to a stop beside the stone slab, a pale hand resting against one corner of the chiseled rock.

The young woman had been dehumanized. Whatever had ended her life did so with a flair for the dramatic. Unlike the raw brutality and wild savagery of the feeding just witnessed, this was done with a certain sophistication. As if a message was intended. Madeleine stood long moments over the corpse. Not speaking or moving until Herbert finally pulled himself from the floor and joined her.

"There is no question what did this." Herbert glanced up from the body. His eyes finding Hans mutely nodding his head in agreement. Both men having seen this cruelty before. The young nanny who had taken care of Herbert's twins, and Herbert himself whenever he desired her, had been found in much the same way. Ruined. The vicious murder occurring mere days after the escape of their second resurrection. Though there was no way to identify the latest brutalized woman by her facial features – they all were missing – her nightwear and unspooled black hair left little doubt. She'd been Catherine, one of Herbert's favorites. The bed of her quaint servant's cottage often frequented by him. "Was she found by her sister?" Again, Hans merely nodded.

Her beauty had been pulverized. A sharp implement, likely a knife, had been repeatedly pounded into her face. How many times was unclear as Herbert stopped counting at six, but it had easily been twice that amount. Her nose and eyes were missing, as were many of her teeth. Flaps of loose flesh hung from her cheeks and forehead while small pools of blood and viscera filled the voided sockets. Madeleine squatted beside the unfortunate servant and reached for the soaked strings at her neck. As they came off in her hand, the drawstring sliced to ribbons, her savaged chest was exposed down to her pubis. Both breasts and most of her sex was missing. Everything that had made her a woman likely taken by her killer.

"This has happened before," Herbert, still standing, diverted his eyes from the splatter at his feet. "Shortly after we successfully resurrected a being for the second time, we had a similar... occurrence." Herbert glanced up at a still badly shaken Hans. "Bring down one of those old bedsheets so we can cover her. There is no reason to further shock or scare the rest of the staff." Hans turned gratefully toward the door. Happy to have a reason to leave the underground chamber of horrors. "And Hans," Herbert added just before the door closed, "I'd wake Jehan and have him help you move and tend to the body." Hans nodded curtly once before slipping outside.

As both Herbert and Madeleine looked on, the corpse began to gradually flush with color. Fluids suddenly pooling in the gashes and wounds her killer had left behind. Aghast at the implications, it took mere moments for Herbert to understand what was occurring. The power of the stone was slowly refilling the brutalized young woman with life. "What manner of sorcery or science is this?" His gaze hunting Madeleine's own for reason even as he swiftly separated the stirring dead from the powerful slab of granite. The figure growing limp and the pulsing fluids abating once more.

"Noviodunum Suessiones," replied Madeleine, her French enunciation perfect. The effect of the words contorting Herbert's face into a mask of disturbed confusion. She turned to him, a simple act no different than she'd done a hundred times before in previous conversations. But, in that moment, her eyes blazed with a scorching intensity.

Herbert raised his arms instinctively, and the act likely kept him from collapsing to his knees. In an instant, he understood this was the first moment Madeleine had ever actually looked at him. Truly seen Herbert. Their entire relationship, and his very existence prior to now, barely warranting a distracted glance.

So beneath her, he was.

"I understand that your father, Count Chanet, has yet to pass the full burden he bears. So disgusted by your wicked ways and excarnation of the dead that he rarely even ventures from the chateau anymore." Madeleine made a gesture behind her where, a German mile or so away, stood the Chanet's second home – a more modest chateau. Both homes strategically built to straddle the contested borders of what would later become Germany and France. "How is your father, by the way? Still deeply ashamed of the macabre work his son so gleefully pursues?"

"I prefer not to think of him." Herbert, too fearful to dare raise his eyes, took a blind step backwards. Stumbling when his heel clipped the prostrate form of the murdered girl. Barely catching himself before turning away, his mind abuzz. "Noviodunum Suessiones," his voice a hushed whisper. "I was told... My father, he said these... these are things never to be shared beyond he and I."

"Never to be spoken of. I know." Madeleine leaned casually against the strange stone. "From before your family knows why or can track, your lineage has held claim and deed to all of the surrounding lands. The aged walls of the House of Chanet, once both a fort and a keep, having withstood, witnessed, and protected, if legends are to be believed, a priceless treasure beyond the understanding of man. A sacred duty passed from a single heir down to the next heir. A supposed eternal treasure, a hidden relict with the power to end all of time itself secreted away somewhere onsite. Protected, even though none is privy to why or what."

Mutely, Herbert nodded. Madeleine's words a near match of his own father's barely two years prior. "Or, if we are protecting it from us, or us from it." He finished for Madeleine, regurgitating what his father had spewed after pouring too much wine down his throat. "And the sword?" Herbert looked up with eyes hungry for answers. Answers his own father had professed to have no knowledge of.

"Must be hidden and passed down, just as these lands."

"Why are you telling me this if we are truly not meant to know?"

"My dear Herbert, don't you see? All of this secrecy was for you. For this very moment in time. It is you that has recovered the treasure every past Chanet has doubted and feared. Here!" Again she slapped the long, squarish boulder. "You have played a most crucial role. Enabling the one you know as Judas to rise one final time."

"Treasure? That hunk of granite is..." Herbert paused, his mind spinning at the revelations. "Final time? How can I believe... was that really Judas? Where did he go? What will he do?"

"This is the fourth time the cursed being you call Judas has been restored. His original sin, his deal with the devil, if you will, sealed with a kiss back when this blue marble was first sharpened by life. He'll do what he must to survive until, much like you, Herbert, the appropriate time arrives. He has an imperfect and improbable journey over what you would call centuries before he will fully form. All to complete a purpose and destiny he has no choice but to fulfill." Madeleine, nodding towards the oblong stone, continued. "Likely, haunting this area near eternally and never straying far until that time arrives. As you have already witnessed, this and all the scattered relics it is associated with, attracts and feeds only the worst of your... er... humankind. A force far beyond the mere nature of this world. Nothing you can do will change what will happen in time." Madeleine chuckled without humor. "The one you call Judas will once again portray man and then betray man for a fourth and final time. Sure as the kiss of…"

The door suddenly burst open, and Hans held it wide for the much older man who followed closely behind. The disheveled servant, carrying a folded cloth against his chest as if for protection, grimaced before tucking both his mouth and nose under the fabric. Herbert and Madeleine stepped aside in silence as the two men descended the steps and approached the young woman's body. Hans reaching up and quickly closing the leather curtain before the man trailing a few steps back could see the partially devoured remains the divider hid.

The old servant, Jehan, flinched mightily when he first laid eyes upon the butchered remains, but otherwise worked in solemn silence. The domestic help living inside the House of Chanet unquestioning of Herbert's often strange instructions and direction. Their employer treating them no differently than furniture. Less so since only the furniture, if treated with respect, could be re-upholstered and used again. Indeed, many of the tables, chairs, and sofas that decorate the home above went back countless years and had been in the family for generations. Built and rebuilt by some of the finest craftsman on the continent. The aged wood filled by the countless number of Chanet's who had resided on these same lands and grounds as far back as anyone could recall. The family's ownership and leadership of this part of the country, as Jehan knew well, beyond reproach. So, he worked in submissive silence. Wrapping young Catherine in what would likely become her burial shroud. Anxious to depart the gloomy, dank, fetid cellar he'd never set foot in before tonight.

And hoped to never again.

"I must leave you now," Madeleine announced. "I have something I need to pick up before she starts… starts trying to scratch an itch." Grabbing the velvet bag she'd carried, its contents now loose on the world, she strode purposefully up the stairsteps. Careful to avoid stepping in the fresh blood slowly seeping into the wood and staining them darker with each passing moment.

Initially too stunned to react, Herbert didn't call out or give chase until she crested the top of the stairway. "Wait... Madeleine! You can't... I mean, I have so many questions."

Stepping into the moonlight, Madeleine tossed her reply over one shoulder. "Your father has all the answers you'll need going forward."

Herbert, exiting the doorway, noted the four horsemen had already taken up their riding positions. Two drivers up front while the other two men were perched at each of the back corners of the carriage. "Madeleine. Wait! Please..." Though she turned, Herbert understood he was again unseen. Unimportant to her. The radiant form of brilliance he briefly caught the attention of once more replaced by the distracted glance of the uninterested. "Please, can you..." Herbert sighed, "Please be careful, my dear Madeleine. I'm glad, especially this night, that you are accompanied by so many men able to protect you." He bent and lightly kissed her outstretched hand.

"Yes, I love the irony of riding with four horsemen in case something," she paused briefly, "apocalyptic rises." She turned and winked, but the gesture felt hollow. "And they'll be most excellent bait."

Unable to think of an appropriate answer, Herbert blurted out the first thought that came to his head. "Bait for what?"

"I have something I need to collect. Girls need to stick together, you know." Madeleine stepped up to her carriage and looked down the same lane she'd arrived by earlier. Back towards the nearest village and the opposite way she was now headed. "I wondered when they were going to finally show up."

Herbert turned, but he could see nothing. "Who was going to show up?"

"The angry mob with pitchforks and torches." She waved her driver on as she took her seat. "This story just wouldn't be complete without them." The carriage took off and, despite the garden of stars and full moon overhead, soon vanished within the swirling mist that encroached upon the lane.

Herbert turned and faced the mob at his doorstep.

Chapter Ten
France-Modern Day

As the music swelled, Secrist tried unsuccessfully to cover both ears. Refusing to open his eyes in hopes Stander would have mercy on him. Instead, worse, the driver began to sing along. No quarter given apparently.

"Built with stolen parts, a telephone in my heart, someone get me a priest."

"Oh! Are you awake, Tommy?" Secrist finally cracked one eye to show his annoyance. "I hope my 'singing' didn't wake you up." Stander pulled his hands from the steering wheel and made quotation marks in the air when he said singing. "Sorry, man. I just love Chris Cornell's voice..." However, the look on the driver's face showed anything but regret. The expression pure joy as he reached for the volume and turned the *Audioslave* song up louder.

"Nail in my hand, from my creator.

You gave me life, now show me how to live."

"Where are we?" Secrist, sighing, pushed himself from the passenger window. Outside, the road they traveled was dark with long shadows that stretched the entire width of the pavement. The towering trees on either side denying the valley they drove the warmth and light of the late afternoon sun. Their greedy green branches reaching for the heavens to receive the light. "What was the last city we passed?"

"Like, even if I remembered, I could pronounce it." Stander reached for the dash and turned down the volume. His phone, plugged into one of the ports, supplying the soundtrack for their drive. "But, it was a ways back," he replied with a shrug. "Not much of anything this last bit. One or two decrepit houses and a couple farms about all I've seen in the last half hour or so."

"Great. We must be in the middle of that forest I mentioned earlier." Secrist rubbed at his eyes and yawned. "I was hoping to sleep through it."

"Yeah, this area seems a little backwood-ish, if you know what I mean." Stander's eyes roamed the mountainous countryside he drove – a blur of trees, brush, and flocks of sheep. "You can doublecheck the GPS on your phone, but I think we are still about an hour or so away. I'm hoping we'll find a place to eat when we get there. I'm fucking starving."

Grunting, Secrist glanced down at his phone. Moments later, dropping it when Stander hit the brakes and swerved violently. The tiny automobile wildly swaying and rocking. "Holy shit!" Stander exclaiming loudly as he struggled to bring the vehicle to a screeching halt. The car finally coming to rest along the side of the two-lane highway. "Someone needs to pull that carcass out of the middle of the road. I almost hit it head on."

"What was it?" Secrist leaned down, his hand sweeping the car's carpeted mat in search of his phone. Finding it, he straightened just in time to hear the driver's side door close and, turning, see Stander walking along the empty pavement. In the distance, a mass of indistinguishable brown hair covered the lane they'd been driving. Secrist opened his door and followed.

"Where's the head?" Stander, a decapitated deer at his feet, looked all around the road before wandering a few steps over to a ditch that ran alongside the highway. "Nothing," he commented as Secrist joined him. "Fucking weird."

"Probably was just nosing onto the road and got clipped by a truck or something." Secrist walked over to the mound of roadkill. "Nice reflexes, by the way. If you'd hit this head-on with that tiny car, I don't think we'd be walking right now."

"Give me a hand," Stander said, grabbing one of its back legs. "We can at least get it out of the lane for the next driver." Both men work together to drag the heavy deer to the side of the road. A red smear staining the ground behind them. "Man, this really stinks of rot. I wonder how long it has sat here?"

"I told you earlier." Secrist gestured at the mountains and timber all around them, not a manmade structure in sight. "This whole area is all trees and forest. Old growth. You said you haven't seen another car for miles. This," both men dropping the deadweight, "might have sat baking all day in the sun."

Turning, Stander and Secrist walked back to their car. Just before grabbing the door handle, Stander made a dramatic, sweeping gesture toward the front of the rented vehicle. "Oh, for fucks sake," he said. The driver-side front tire was completely flat.

Secrist joined Stander as he knelt beside the wheel. With no obvious puncture or sign of an offending metal nail or screw, it appeared likely the tire had briefly slipped off the rim when Stander had swerved to avoid the dead deer. Sighing in frustration, he pulled the rental car's paperwork and dialed the number listed for emergency service. As Secrist searched fruitlessly for a jack and spare tire, none found in the trunk, Stander patiently answered the emergency service's questions. Hanging up and turning to Secrist when the call ended several minutes later.

"Well, the good news, besides the guy being able to speak English, is I paid for the integrated GPS service. They," he waved his phone to indicate the rental car company he'd just spoken with, "know right where we are. But, the bad news is, they don't have a contracted vendor anywhere near us. While I was on hold, he tried contacting the nearest towing service. But, no luck. He said it must be run by some superstitious old fool because the guy refused to come out this way after dark."

"Wonderful," Secrist was slowly shaking his head. "That sure sounds a bit ominous, don't you think? What are we supposed to do? Sleep in the car?"

"No, no, no. A tow truck is on the way, but it's coming from almost an hour away." Secrist started to nod and smile until he saw Stander raising his hand. "Unfortunately, because right now it is already out on another service call, he said it will likely be at least two hours before he finishes and can get over to us."

"Great. So, what do we do until then?" Secrist sighed as he looked at the darkening sky above with both hands thrust in his pockets. "I doubt I can take any more of your singing."

"The representative said we don't have to wait. The tow truck driver doesn't need our help or the car keys to fix the flat." Stander clicked the key fob in his hand, locking the automobile. "He also said, according to the map he pulled up on his computer while we were talking, that there is a restaurant or pub of some sort a couple kilometers or so up the road from us."

"Really?" Secrist looked both ways down the lonely stretch of blacktop. "Not a single car has passed us this entire time. Why would anyone put a business out in the middle of nowhere?"

"Maybe there is a busy crossroad. Or a nearby town." Stander shrugged as he turned and began walking. "As thick as these woods are, there could be something a few yards deep and I doubt we'd see it." Secrist snorted once as he fell in step just behind Stander. Both men walking along the side of the road as the sunlight abandoned them.

Nearly thirty minutes later, a small cluster of yellow lights beckoned the weary walkers. The modest pub had several cars parked in its gravel lot and what looked like a home on the second level. In the distance, likely several miles farther down the road, more lights twinkled in the darkness. A small village tucked among the wilds of the woods.

"Are we going to be able to order something to eat if we can't read or speak French?" Secrist pulled out his phone. "I knew I should have downloaded one of those translating apps."

Stander shrugged as he reached for the door handle. "I've only been in France a handful of times. But, in my experience, it seems like nearly everyone over here also speaks at least some English. I bet we'll be able to manage." He glanced briefly through one of the windows before opening the glass-paned entrance. "Doesn't look too busy," he said as they both stepped through the doorway.

Inside, the single-room tavern was lit by a series of small chandeliers that hung over the bar and tables. The décor of the pub's quaint seating area, painted a darkened red, reflecting the local wildlife. Stuffed and mounted heads peered at the newcomers with unblinking, glass eyes. While various fish, frozen in mid-thrash and flop, gulped wide-mouthed at their unexpected arrival. The wooden plaques holding them aloft stained a singular dark brown that matched the finish of the bar itself. The only two occupied stools had turned in tandem as the strangers had entered. But neither customer sitting in them bothered to acknowledge their arrival. Nodding amiably at the emotionless stares, Stander and Secrist sat themselves at a small corner table.

Waiting to be served, the flickering TV behind the bar drew their attention. A boxing match between two lighter weight fighters filling the screen with furious action. As a middle-aged, strawberry blonde woman emerged from a swinging door, Stander eyeballed an elderly man exiting the single bathroom in the place. Coughing behind a medical mask that hid most of his features, his liver-spotted head sported two tufts of wiry white hair that stuck up comically in the air like horns. Surprised by the two newcomers, he snorted and mumbled, "Lordy, lordy," before claiming a seat at the bar. Above his head, a ceiling fan with inches of dust atop the twirling blades, turned languidly. Only slightly more energetic, the barkeep approached their table and eyed them from behind a small pad of paper.

"Two pints of Guinness, please." Stander gave her his warmest smile, "If food is available, could we see a couple menus?" Silently, she nodded. Returning several minutes later with the beers and two menus before retreating behind the bar.

Gradually, as Stander and Secrist ordered and ate, customers began to fill the empty seats. A young family of three, a heavyset woman sporting bright green hair, and several more senior citizens wearing either cloth or oxygen masks. All were clearly regular patrons of the business establishment. Though the awkwardness of spotting the two unknown men in their local watering hole gave each pause, before long the familiar buzz of old friends sharing good stories filled the pub as more patrons arrived. When Stander told their server he'd like to buy a round for everyone, the good cheer he spread swept through the gathering. Many of the mostly male patrons raising their glasses in salute. Several making their way over and introducing themselves to show their gratitude for the gesture.

As a couple men lingered, like Stander, watching the fighters on the television, they commented on the action. Stander, though unable to speak French, could still speak their language. The one-time professional boxer gradually gaining the gathered drinkers respect with his insight into the fight game. Soon, the small table where Secrist and Stander had eaten was circled by fight fans. Their glasses of beer crowding the small table as they cheered or jeered the combatants they watched. Nearly all the men able to speak some English and conversing with the two Americans. Stander soon giving a colorful account of their near wreck and, buying a second round for the house, praising their good fortune in discovering a pub so near.

It was only as Stander and Secrist prepared to depart that the murmur dimmed. Troubled glances replacing the smiling faces as Stander ordered two more drinks and paid the bill. Secrist spoke to the man nearest him. Making a joke about fearing the long walk back to their car. Asking about the legends and what those living within the ancient forest thought about the local folklore. His questions, asked in jest and in a self-deprecating manner, soon had his companion talking. A few other men joining in as Stander returned to the table.

"These things you speak of, these tales, are as old as the hills themselves. There are places all over the world where similar stories exist. Most, if you ask me, Monsieur, are meant to keep us from danger." The bearded man who spoke, chewed the unlit end of a skinny cigar. Though his answer to Secrist's questions seemed jovial, the longtime detective sensed an avoidance in his tone. "Man is a poor match for the wilderness but he is vain. He creates stories to explain what he cannot accept as truth. Easier to make-up a fantastical beast than admit failure." Affirming nods rimmed the table.

"My grandfather was stationed not far from here during the First World War. He said there was a group of men who worshipped something that had scared him. Down in the trenches." Secrist paused, a flicker of emotion in several expressions. When no one spoke up, he continued. "These men disfigured themselves to show their faith. He referred to them as 'faceless men' or something along those lines. Does any of that sound familiar?" The crowded table grew quiet. The silence to his questions seemed response enough.

"There are things around here far older... far scarier." The man speaking was one of the two customers already drinking when they'd first arrived. He turned on his stool and spoke over the others. The seat next to him now vacant. "A madman who played at God once lived not far from here. They say it was his attempts to bring the dead back to life that inspired the Frankenstein story. The author changing the name and location to make it appear as a work of fiction." His words slurred, he stood and smiled at the attention he commanded. "Or, maybe, it was just to deny that a Frenchman could have accomplished such a feat!" Around him, enraptured by the colorful telling, his friends laughed. "The mad doctor loosed his nightmares into these very woods. These things were horrible creations from a diseased mind. Some of the abominations so wrong they died almost immediately. But some were said to be immortal. Infused with false life, they bred and spread throughout these lands. *Se reproduisent comme des lapins!* They breed like rabbits! Monstrous!"

"Roar!!"

Bursting through the swinging door, a six-foot tall rabbit hopped and yelled. The unexpected sight and sound catching Stander and Secrist completely off-guard. Stander exclaiming profanely and Secrist slopping half his beer onto the table. Both laughing uproariously as the man from the empty barstool pulled the head off the Easter Bunny costume he wore. A drunken grin stamped upon his face.

"I bought this from America! eBay!" He walked over, laughing along with them, shook both Secrist's and Stander's hands. "We don't have anything like the Easter Bunny over here. It's ridiculous, no?" He lifted the comical bunny head to his face and peered into the eyes. "What does a lapine... er... rabbit, have to do with Jesus being resurrected?" Other patrons, perhaps half of them in on the joke, slapped the costumed man across his back. A few others, also caught by surprise like the two Americans, scolded him and slapped at his face good-naturedly.

"Just keep to the main road, gentlemen. There is nothing in these standing woods worth your time investigating or worrying about." An aged and wrinkled man, likely the oldest patron in the establishment, deftly changing the subject as the laughter had died down. A maroon-colored birthmark of sorts emerging from behind the medical mask he wore, the welt-like old wound dividing his forehead in two. The men sitting in the stools nearest him murmured in agreement, most turning back to the television though the fights had ended. The spirited action replaced by a dour-faced newscaster. "It is easy to get turned around in those walls of sticks. Go the wrong way and you could walk for days without finding a soul. Unless wolves have souls."

"Are there still wolves around here? Now, I mean. I know they are native to the area. I'd read somewhere they've begun to make a comeback after being hunted to near extinction in the 20th century." Secrist downed the last of his beer as Stander spoke up, his voice doing a poor imitation of an English accent.

"Us boys should stay clear of the moors, aye?" Stander mimicked lines from the old werewolf movie he'd watched many times – *An American Werewolf in London* – using a lousy English accent. "Beware the moon," he continued before draining his glass.

Secrist stiffened, sure that the locals would be offended. But, he was wrong. Easy laughter and smiles across most of the patron's faces. A few of them lifting their chins and howling. Secrist, his concern evaporating, looked across at a now howling Stander with admiration. Wondering how the man always seemed to make friends with almost anyone. Even here, halfway around the world and an ocean away from home. Thinking to himself, the guy could get away with murder. He could probably sell gasoline to the Amish even if they were about to dare the flames of hell itself.

CHAPTER ELEVEN
GERMANY-16TH CENTURY

HERBERT COULD HEAR THE murmured buzz as the villagers descended upon him. Two baying bloodhounds, bred and trained for hunting, howled and strained against their leashes as the gap was closed. Though hardly the "mob" Madeleine described before departing, the villagers numbered nearly a dozen and many were armed with crude implements from their work in the fields. Sharpened spades and scythes, long-handled pitchforks, and flaming torches mixed with a sprinkling of unsheathed swords and a few long muskets pointing harmlessly into the air. Leading them was the local mayor, and Herbert could see many of the men with him made up the nearby town's council.

"What has happened? What is the meaning of this intrusion?" Herbert adopted his preferred air of arrogant command. Despite the titles of the elected officials, the peasants that made up the farms and surrounding community all understood the Chanet family was the real law of the land. Any important decisions or items of consequence were rendered meaningless without their authority and consent.

"Pardon the hour of our arrival, My Lord. We hoped to speak with your father, the Count." The mayor, a stocky shop owner named Karl, spoke first. "There has been another one, My Lord. We fear the worst may…"

"My father is unwell and indisposed at the moment. Your counsel will be with me." Herbert did his best to appear hurried and distracted. He needed the crowd to leave before one of the undead creatures he'd resurrected decided to make another appearance. "What has happened? Another one of what?"

"Murder!" The anguished cry emerging from the gathered crowd though none stepped forward to claim it. "A monster, it was!" Came an equally anonymous voice. The mayor, though shading slightly in embarrassment at the bold outbursts, did not correct the statements.

"It was the barmaid Rebecca, My Lord. She's been savaged beyond belief. Killed in her own bed." Karl shifted uncomfortably on his feet. "I believe you knew of her."

"Another killing?" Herbert did his best to convey a shock he didn't feel. "Where did this..." But the collective gasp of the gathered masses, along with a few sobs and sudden cries drowned out his question. Behind him, Hans and Jehan had unwittingly exited the cellar carrying the butchered remains of Catherine. Neither man aware of the gathering until it was too late. Though wrapped in material and completely covered, there was no question they lugged a body. The patches of crimson bleeding through the cloth about the head leaving the villagers no doubt something nefarious had occurred.

And no doubt that it matched the murder they'd come to avenge.

Herbert could feel the escalating tension as he watched face after commoner face turn to him. Narrowing eyes, suspicion, and fear corrupting their features with uncertainty and mistrust. Each man likely aware that Herbert, the same as other men of the nearby village, relied upon Rebecca for occasional relief. The buxom redhead, for a few coins, always willing to please.

Understanding the rule of a mob, Herbert quickly waved the two servants to him. "My home has been infiltrated by the same evil. It must be stopped!" He watched the reactions to the revelation, carefully reading the crowd before continuing. "If you have come to me for help hunting this monster, you shall have it!" Though doubt still seemed to waver across several of the more suspicious, Herbert could see the brazen deception was working. "I shall gather arms and recruit another man to join us. Surely, together this fiend will no longer be able to evade capture."

"How do we know it wasn't... that it didn't come from these lands? We trailed the murdering monster to the edge of the river." Otto, a burly blacksmith locally famous for fathering 18 children, gesturing toward the rushing waters that crossed the estate.

"That makes sense. Clever, even. The diabolical fiend must have tried to throw the dogs off its scent by wading into the rushing water. May have tried to hide or take refuge in the servant cottages tucked among the hills of the valley." Herbert, beating the man to the punch and using the blacksmith's own logic to solidify his version of events. "Poor, poor Catherine must have been in the wrong place at the wrong time. Costing her very life..." Behind him, the timing impeccable, Catherine's sister began wailing loudly. The gathered crowd and commotion having drawn several of Herbert's servants out into the courtyard. The fear and earnestness in their faces helping qualm the restlessness and heightened suspicions of the villagers.

"Hans! Bring lanterns and muskets. You and I will join our neighbors and rid ourselves of the evil that has so brazenly stepped to our door." Herbert, his mind ticking off the possibilities, understanding that tonight, along with the help of the vengeful villagers, was likely his best chance to hunt and rid himself of the second undead thing he'd raised. The one whose warning still tugged at his worst fears and whose whispered promises had rendered Han's nearly useless since escaping.

"Until we return," Herbert speaking to those he employed, "remain alert and vigilant. Help Jehan secure the body and then gather together in the main house. I pray we won't be gone long."

Herbert and Hans, each carrying a loaded musket in one hand and a lantern in the other, soon joined the gathered villagers at the edge of the ancient forest that bordered the Chanet estate. The bloodhounds pulled excitedly at their leashes; the trail outside the cottage where Catherine had been slain easily identified. Thirty paces inside the thicket the men split apart. Spreading themselves along the single line of a pitched ridge before advancing up and down several ravines. Stepping over felled logs and brushing aside barely budding branches as they moved as one deeper and deeper into the untamed wilderness. Pushing farther inside the timber until the barren trees swallowed them whole. The meager lights of their flickering lanterns, smoking torches, and the partially obscured moon above, barely lighting their way. Somewhere in the distance, wolves answered the excited yapping of their hounds. The mournful-sounding howls the only wildlife that could be heard.

With Hans walking barely three feet from Herbert's own stride, both men squatted at the edge of a small stream to hunt for tracks alongside Karl, the now red-faced and winded mayor. The blood hounds had remained excited and sure of themselves, surging forward as fast as their handler could follow. Most of the men keeping pace and now beyond earshot. A few of the older and slower men visibly straining to maintain pace. As Karl stood, no tracks of significance seen in the soft mud that bordered the trickling brook, he took a deep breath and sighed heavily.

"These woods, this part of the forest, has long been rumored to conceal the wild huntsman, Türst, and even the Devil's Stone. My own parents told me stories of gathering witches and," Karl looked down into a pool of murky, collected water, "the singing water nymphs that tempt men."

"Nonsense. As a learned scholar of science, I can assure you that no seducer of man would be content to remain submerged in such shallow waters in hopes a victim would pass by this desolate spot." Herbert and Hans stood just as Helwig, a widowed farmer who worked land owned by the Chanet family, spoke up.

"I almost wish a forest nymph or witch would come and tempt me. It's been so long since I've laid with a woman that I..."

"Don't say such things! Not here!" Hans spoke up, his head swiveling with a nervousness that was palpable. "You know not of which you speak." He seemed ready to say more until he noticed the piercing stare Herbert shot him – the message of silence clear.

"It is the bedeviled and unnatural beasts prowling this countryside that worry me. All this winter and this past fall people have spoken of the hideous creatures they've witnessed scurrying about these lands. Twisted animals of tortured physiques and dreadful mouths of barbs topped by unnatural horns. My brother told me..." Now it was Karl who killed the conversation with a look. Shushing Helwig with a glance before the rampant rumors of Herbert's supposed secret misdeeds and hidden experiments reached their town's benefactor's ears. The forest they searched may or may not be haunted by cruel and twisted creatures meaning harm to those they crossed paths with, but no one living near the House of Chanet had any doubt of the cruelty Herbert could inflict should he be crossed.

"We should catch up with the others," Karl quickly added. "Getting separated at night in these... er... any woods, is unwise." Hustling, Karl, Otto, and Helwig crossed the stream and began climbing the next gully, following, alongside Herbert and Hans, a well-worn game trail. The bobbing torch flames of the villagers still keeping pace with the excited dogs vanishing behind the crest of the next rise.

The chilling scream sliced through the still air of the night. Ending abruptly as if the source had suddenly vanished. Altering their path, the men rushed up the remainder of the hill and quickly headed for the cluster of lights visible from the peak they ascended. Soon joining the circle made by the others, the dogs hushed into disquieting whines. In the middle of the gathering, a man Herbert did not recognize lay in a pool of his own flesh and gore. He'd been torn to shreds. Lying beside him, with both hands still pressed unsuccessfully against his ravaged throat, a second man stared unseeing into the night sky above. Herbert rushed to tend the gaping wound at his neck but there was nothing to be done for the unfortunate villager. The meat of his throat missing down to the white of the bone.

"Looks as if Konrad interrupted something feeding and paid a hellish price for his insolence." Herbert stood and met the scared eyes of the remaining men. "Whatever struck him did so with claws as sharp as any razor." Herbert paused as if in thought. "May have been a bear."

"A bear! Here!" Herbert didn't turn to the voice challenging him. After all, the man was correct. This had been no bear. But there was no argument that followed. The two bloodhounds suddenly erupting in panicked whining and yelping. Straining urgently against the leather collars at their necks as their paws churned madly in the loose leaves, sticks, and soil of the forest floor. Both dogs held by a single man, he was jerked from his feet and dragged momentarily across the rutted ground before losing his grip on their leashes. The hunting dogs galloping back the way they'd come without a backwards glance. Leaving the fractured team of men to hunt the killer without the aid of their tracking skills.

"What is that?" Herbert and Hans, after helping the abandoned dog owner regain his feet, turned to where he pointed. Though cloaked in shadows with the moon at its back, the massive and fearsome outline that pawed the air with long-fingered claws and stood on two legs was still visibly disturbing. Ears, pointed sharp like triangles, sat upon its head. When it turned, the elongated snout it sported gave the walking horror the profile of a large dog. Or a wolf.

Mesmerized by the thing's eerie and unexplainable appearance, the men stood dumbly for long seconds. Rooted and silent until the howling began. The thing's eyes seemed to glint with an eerie, otherworldly light as it woofed menacingly several times before abruptly dropping to all fours. It paced back and forth along the ridge several times with a fluid, almost human grace. Though it may have been a trick of the partially obscured moonlight, its form shifted and blurred at times as if not entirely of this world. The men glanced amongst themselves, unsure if what they were witnessing was real. The doubt only erased when a large number of wild wolves rushed to join the strange beast. The snarling pack running with the hulking figure now looping down through the shadowed darkness of the hill. En masse, they descended. Straight toward the gathered men.

Though a few shaky musket shots rang out, the explosive sound and fired projectiles did nothing to deter the advancing horde. The terrified villagers were swarmed by the pack of ferocious wolves – most instantly knocked from their feet. The few who avoided the initial surge, Herbert and Hans the last among them, sprinted for a nearby ravine. The narrow gorge funneling the men down a steep-sided chasm and forcing their retreat to follow the naturally eroded pathway. Echoing all around them, the awful, agonizing throes of the less fortunate being ripped to pieces.

Tripping over gnarled roots and sliding across seasons of decaying leaves, each remaining man ran blindly. The torches and lanterns that once provided comfort and light extinguished or dropped in favor of speed. As the ravine they ran through deepened – the earthen walls at their sides gradually becoming higher and higher – Herbert became uneasy with the path they'd been forced down. The moonlight above being pinched tighter until barely a sliver of light illuminated the trail at their feet. At times, vanishing completely and plunging them in utter darkness when they passed under rotted trees that had fallen across the divide above. Much like cattle being separated and driven down chutes that would lead to their slaughter, he began to question if they'd been allowed to escape. Perhaps the hungry pack was content to consume the five or six men they'd cut down in the initial surge. But there had to have been dozens of the ferocious predators. Not to mention the hulking creature they'd first seen. Why had they yet to give chase?

In a flash, his own words, spoken to Hans just days before, came back to haunt him. Startling his tongue to speech. "What silences the brazen wolves that prowl the riverside, moors, and the bogs?" Only Hans, a step ahead of Herbert but several steps behind the other survivors, heard his gasping exclamation. It nearly stopped him in his tracks and, as he slowed, both he and Herbert tumbled to the soupy ground. The remaining men ahead unhearing and unaware they had, literally, fallen behind. Though Herbert and Hans quickly regained their feet, they found themselves alone in the darkened ravine.

Walking through a valley shadowed in death.

Chapter Twelve
France-Modern Day

Secrist dried his dripping hands across his pantlegs as he walked back to the table where Stander now served court. The paper towel dispenser in the pub's single bathroom unstocked and empty. Both men had finished the last of their drinks and were ready to head back to their, hopefully, repaired rental car. But, Stander had his phone out and was showing the gathered patrons pictures of his dog, Frazier. Silently, Secrist approached. The story Stander was telling one he'd heard many times before.

"... wandered up one evening some six years ago while I was outside cooking hotdogs on my patio. He was practically still a puppy and he didn't have any collar or tags. I felt sorry for the little guy because one of his eyes was so puffy that it was nearly swollen shut. But, despite the injury, the dog was super friendly and very chill." Stander paused and, like a proud father, flipped to another picture that he showed before continuing. "He's mostly brown but has a lot of white on his belly. You can probably tell he is a pit bull mix. Anyway, I tried to ignore him thinking someone would just come along any minute looking for him. So, I settled down to eat in one of the lounge chairs on my patio and waited. Of course, with the hotdogs and everything, he kind of sheepishly pads over and lays his head right on my chest." Stander looked up with a crooked smile. "Love at first sight."

"A beautiful animal. No one ever came to claim him?" The man closest to Secrist turning to include him in the question.

"Don't look at me. I'm just Frazier's occasional dogsitter," Secrist deferring to Stander.

"Who is watching him now? While you both are here in France?" The mostly silent barkeep asking a rare question as she cleared the empty glasses from the tabletop.

"I have a few friends I help out from time to time that don't mind watching him for me every once in a while." Stander turned to the man beside Secrist. "But, to answer your question, nope. No one ever came looking for him. I asked everyone around the neighborhood and nothing."

"Why Frazier? His name, Monsieur. Why did you name him Frazier?"

"Well, he was persistent. Following me relentlessly those first couple days and, any chance he got, laying his head across my chest. He'd look up at me with that puffy eye and it just popped in my head. He reminded me of Joe Frazier, the heavyweight boxing champion back when I was a kid in the seventies. I loved watching his fights. That guy never got discouraged, pummeling his way inside and literally putting his head on his opponent's chest and wailing away. Taking two or three punches just to be able to land one of his shots. Often, especially after those brutal fights of his with Muhamad Ali, both eyes would be all but closed. Puffy and swollen from the punches he took in his fights. As a lifelong fight fan, the name just seemed to fit..." He paused, "Man, I really miss my dog."

Stander pocketed his phone and standing, glanced across the table at Secrist. "Anyway, within a few days we kind of became inseparable. I took him over to a veterinarian office to be sure he wasn't microchipped and got him all checked out. According to the vet, Frazier is a pit bull and boxer mix. The swollen eye turned out not to be serious, having been caused by a bee sting." The men, like Stander, big fans of boxing, began to grin. "Right?" Stander nodded. "It was Ali that 'floated like a butterfly and stung like a bee', when he boxed Joe Frazier." Stander drained the last drops from his glass. "It was just too perfect. I registered him under the name Frazier and became his legal owner that very same day."

"Mon Dieu! Celine! Regarder!" The man with the skinny, unsmoked cigar exclaiming loudly and calling out to the strawberry-blonde working behind the bar. She wiped soapy hands on a soiled towel before glancing up in time to see a photo flash briefly across the television screen. "Elle pourrait être Elsie!"

In turn, the woman hollered loudly through the swinging doorway where the food she served emerged. Moments later, a bald man wearing a stained apron and woman in elbow-high rubber gloves stepped out of the kitchen area. The woman, likely related to the more mature barkeep, had her long blonde hair pulled up in a bun. She glanced shyly at the gathered customers. The majority of them with their eyes glued to the television as the volume was turned up. Scenes of police cars with flashing lights and a uniformed officer reading a statement. The newscast and his prepared speech in French.

When the profile picture was shown a second time, a phone number scrolling along the bottom, the bar's patrons gasped in unison. The rubber gloved woman stared for long moments at the image. Though not identical, the picture shown could have been her own. Or her sister - the similarity striking. She rolled her green eyes good naturedly and smiled as she turned, her co-workers and a few patrons obviously teasing her about the resemblance to the woman on the news.

Stander half sat, half collapsed back into his chair. Clearly shaken. The picture of the woman on the TV was the electrician who had worked down in the quarry with Stander and his team. The same one who had vanished after spending most of the night with Stander at the bar back in Caen.

Beth.

Even without understanding the language, it was obvious she'd been a victim of foul play. Likely murder. As the segment faded into a dog food commercial, Secrist queried the men at their table. Asking what had happened.

The tavern's regulars translated what they'd just watched as Stander stared unseeing from his seat. Explaining that police in Caen were asking for help solving a particularly brutal murder. The woman they'd shown had been attacked outside of a downtown bar a couple night's earlier. Her mutilated body found in an alley. The only way they'd been able to identify her was through fingerprints. The woman's features had been obliterated. Her killer stabbing the face over a dozen times. The viciousness of the crime, along with no one being able to identify the foreign victim for almost a full day, had made the murder national news. The reaction of the pub's customers was due to the victim's remarkable resemblance to the bar owner's sister, Elsie. The local woman who had briefly come out from the kitchen.

Thanking them for the explanation, Secrist prodded Stander to his feet. As they exited the small pub, the gathered customers clearly noticed the change in Stander. The jovial American, gregarious and generous until the news had come on, barely acknowledging their goodbyes and farewells. Walking out into the night, Secrist took the lead as they headed back toward their rental car. The full moon above so bright they both stepped onto their shadows with every footfall. When they were well out of earshot of the bar, Secrist turned to Stander.

"You know it won't take the authorities long to figure out she was with you. They'll retrace her whereabouts that evening. Police work 101." Secrist paused, but Stander said nothing. "You two weren't bashful in the bar that night. And with all those tats and your bushy white moustache, you don't exactly blend in."

"What are you trying to say?" Stander lifted his eyes from the pavement he'd been scrutinizing. Though it may have been the moonlight, the haunted pallor of his features chilled Secrist. Stander looked as if he'd just seen a ghost. "Damn, Tommy. What the fuck is going on?"

"You tell me," Secrist replied, both men hiking the deserted highway. "You were completely out of it that morning. What happened earlier in the night?"

"I can't... I truly don't remember." Stander kept robotically putting one foot in front of the other. Never meeting Secrist's eyes. "I'm not even sure who I was really with that night..."

Somewhere in the deep woods, a lone wolf howled mournfully. Secrist quickened his pace though Stander still lagged behind. "You better come up with some answers. Any detective worth a grain of salt is going pick apart every word you say. Waking up alone with blood on your hands and no idea how it got there is practically begging for further investigation." Secrist paused his gait until Stander drew even with him, peering into his blue eyes. "Did you wear a condom?"

"Uh… maybe? Not really sure." Stander dropped his gaze and kept walking. "Usually I do."

"Lord have mercy. They are going to crucify you when they catch up with us." Secrist fell in step, both men now walking side by side. "If she made those scratches on your back, your DNA will be harvested from her nails. If you didn't wear a condom, hell, sometimes even if a guy does, any semen deposited will be put forth as evidence." Secrist was shaking his head, his concern growing.

"Big deal. All I did was fuck her. Anything else I saw was just… just my…" Stander could barely meet the troubled look on his friend's face. "Oh, never mind. You know I'd never…"

"What I know is you arranged to meet her ahead of time, vanished for hours and then turned up in a janitor's closet complete with a floor drain, sink, and plenty of cleaning solvents. Couple that with your disappearance from the town of the murder that next day, and you look guilty as hell." Secrist laid a hand on Stander's shoulder. "And that isn't even taking into account any evidence of bodily fluids you two might have swapped and left on the floor of the maintenance closet. Or, what was left by you inside of her."

"Doubt my behavior that morning," Stander sighed before tossing a thumb over his shoulder, "or tonight when the news came on, will help me either, huh?"

"Only in that someone trying to get away with murder wouldn't act as dumb." Secrist tried to smile but failed miserably. "No one in that bar tonight will forget us anytime soon. What they'll say certainly isn't going to help anything."

"What do you think I should do?"

"You need to contact the police in Caen. Go in and tell them the truth." Secrist pulled his phone and looked at the time. "We could drive back tonight, but it would be so late I doubt it would make a difference. The morning should be just as good. At least we have proof of our automobile breakdown. The rental car company should have records confirming the timing and location of your call."

Stander didn't acknowledge what Secrist was saying. The two men walked in silence, their steps along the hard pavement of the deserted road the only sound.

"Did you…" Stander began, "did you see the woman from the kitchen? Elsie or whatever?"

"Sure, of course." Secrist peered over at his friend. "Why?"

"Didn't she look just like Liz?" Stander slowed his pace until both men stood still. The full moon overhead shadowing the surrounding foliage in black. "It seems like I see her everywhere. Like she's haunting me."

"To be honest, no. I didn't think she looked that much like Beth. I know some of the pub's regulars were razzing her about the resemblance, but even their response was pretty tepid." Secrist's eyes narrowed. "What is with this fixation over Liz? Ever since those couple days you spent with her back in Michigan, it's like your obsessed with her. Seeing her everywhere. Likening her to some girlfriend you had back in grade school. This isn't healthy…" His voice fading to a whisper, thoughts he didn't want to articulate percolating between his ears.

"Izzy. Izzy was my first real girlfriend." Stander turned and began walking once more. Secrist at his heels. "Never even knew what happened to her."

"Really? So, she vanished just like Liz? Like… like Beth?" Though Stander was facing forward and couldn't see, Secrist shook his head vigorously back and forth several times. The ideas populating and crowding inside nothing he wanted to consider. The two walked in silence, both lost in their own thoughts.

Cresting a rise, the rental car they'd abandoned finally came into view. The bright luminance of the moon allowing them to see nearly clear as day. Both men smiled in relief, all four tires appearing inflated and ready to continue the journey. As they closed the gap between themselves and the vehicle, new sounds began to emerge from the line of trees bordering their side of the road. Some twenty steps later, it became clear their pace was being matched by whatever walked behind the rows. Something had followed them from the bar. Though neither man verbally acknowledged the tracking, both quickened their gait.

With the rental less than a hundred yards away, a thick and heavy tree limb snapped within the dark woods, crashing to the ground. Subconsciously, the duo gravitated to the middle of the deserted road. Distancing themselves from the edge of the timber. But soon, more troubling noises reached their ears. Muted growls and the sound of tearing meat causing Stander to reach for the key fob in his pocket. Nearly to the car, his head on a swivel, he hit the button to unlock the doors. As he did, the headlights and taillights flashed in tandem with the car's audible chirp.

Startled, a shadowed figure dashed from the ditch behind the car. Something meaty and wet dripping from its jaws. Running on four legs, the creature turned once it reached the relative safety of the far side of the road. Stopping, and with a curious stare, watching as Stander and Secrist gratefully climbed into the safety of their vehicle. As Stander started the car and turned the wheel, the headlights bathed the canine in light. A grey wolf watching their retreat with a severed deer leg, likely pulled from the roadkill they'd shunted into the roadside ditch, held firmly in its snout.

Dropping the meat, the wolf lifted his snout to the air. His howl echoing through the untamed wilderness of the ancient French forest. In the distance, where the car was headed, something replied.

Chapter Thirteen
Germany-16th Century

Herbert and Hans stood unmoving at the bottom of the deep and treacherous gulley they'd been forced down into. On either side of them, sheer walls of slippery and unscalable mud rising far above their heads. Behind them, back where their panicked flight began, they could hear the agonized cries of the villagers they'd abandoned coming to an end. Their desperate screams replaced by discomforting snarls, wet growls, and the excited yipping of the hungry pack. The grey wolves of the forest feasting on those who had failed to escape into the water-carved gorge.

"We must keep moving," Herbert hissed quietly. "Catch back up with the others. Or, if we are lucky, maybe somewhere ahead we'll discover a contributing ravine that is shallower and will allow us to climb back up to the floor of these woods." Nodding in silent agreement, Hans turned and began to move forward with Herbert at his heels. Both men forced to walk single file down the V-shaped canyon of rutted earth. Slipping and sliding, their boots heavy with thick mud and sticky clay.

Herbert didn't question the sob that escaped Hans's lips. Both men seeing the corpse at the same time. It was Karl, the local mayor. He was lying in a pool of blood, the crimson it bathed in slowly seeping into the ground. But, he'd not been killed by hungry wolves, nor the monstrous beast that had seemed to command the pack. Instead, oddly, he'd somehow been decapitated. The wound at his neck as clean a cut as Herbert could ever do even with his sharpest scalpel. Puzzled, he briefly kneeled to investigate the fatal wound despite the poor lighting of the tree-filtered moon, but still came away perplexed. The single cut on both the torso and the head lying beside it was amazingly smooth.

Standing, Herbert muttered to himself in thought as the they began to move forward again. "What blade could do such a..."

"Harpsichord wire." Hans, still hurriedly walking, turned briefly and met his astonished gaze. "I was once a musician at the Palais Garnier, the Paris Opera House, My Lord."

A series of felled trees lying across the gorge above their heads completely blocked the meager moonlight from their sight. Stepping into the shadowed black, Herbert recalled the night he had successfully reanimated a human being for the second time. Though they'd already obtained and robbed multiple cadavers of the vital organs Herbert thought he needed for resurrection, he'd struggled to find a suitable and complete skeleton. For his first resurrection, the hulking dim-witted creature devoured by Judas, he had used bones from multiple bodies for the frame. Only when the experiment was completed did he realize his error. The befuddled dolt had hardly been able to stand, much less walk and talk. Herbert had finally had to nail the dullard to the wall of the cellar by its hands until it learned balance. Snipping the oaf's tongue to silence its suffering cries so he could work in peace.

As Madeleine had remarked earlier, birth is always so painful.

Hans had come to him that night with the solution. Providing him with an entire skeleton and assuring Herbert no one would recognize or question how they'd obtained it. Anxious to improve upon his first creation, he hadn't doubted Hans or asked for an explanation. Thinking little of the origins until the barebones had been laid out and Hans began carefully, almost lovingly, wrapping and covering them in a flowing white gown. Only then had Herbert interrogated Hans. But, unusually tightlipped, all he would confess is that she'd been a Parisian woman.

Stepping out from under the shadow of the fallen logs above, the moonlight streamed again. Shining down and exposing another dead body left unmoving within the ravine. Like Karl before him, his head had been detached. The manner of his execution identical. Herbert and Hans barely exchanged a glance before continuing. At another ten paces, the moon was again hidden behind more rotted trees that had fallen over the gorge. Plunging them into near total blackness.

Shadowed, Herbert recalled the awful hours of her resurrection. The crashes of lightening and booming thunder of the spring storm, the terrible shrieks as new flesh bloomed along the frame. The way she'd guzzled the squalid contents right out of the bucket of torn entrails and spoiled viscera.

Moonlit, Herbert watched as Hans stepped over yet another body. It was Helwig, the widowed farmer who'd longed for the touch of a woman. His head was still attached, the neck encircled in brass wire. The string of metal pulled so tightly it had split open the entire throat. Severed, sinewy strands dangling.

Shadowed, Herbert shuddered as the memories of her rebirth crashed into him. She'd stood in flowing white as if a virginal bride, her bright green eyes ablaze. Born with an unnatural strength that she used to pluck Hans off the ground. Dangling him by his feet down the narrow hole they'd been tossing the pieces of cadavers they couldn't use or no longer needed. Forcing him to retrieve the putrid limbs and fetid organs for her. Peeling off the rotted meat with gnashing teeth until her sickening hunger was finally satiated.

Moonlit, Herbert and Hans again sidestepped a throttled villager. Warm blood still flowing from the gashed artery at his neck. The corpse with bulging eyes and a tongue of blue that appeared almost comical in its absurdity. The death, Hebert judged, happening mere moments earlier.

Shadowed, Herbert remembered how she'd whispered in Hans's ear. How the color had drained from his face and he'd bolted from the cellar. Deserting Herbert. Leaving him alone with the horrid abomination he'd somehow managed to pull from the black abyss of death. Watching her snap a human forearm in two and gargle down the puss and marrow inside before pulling him near.

"Never again bring those who have moved on back. We belong dead." Her breath rancid and the voice breaking like shattered glass. "Heed my words, or at your final hour, I will be there with you. Ready to begin."

Moonlit, the deep trench they'd braved ended. The chasm running headlong into a channel of rushing water banked by soft gravel and wet sand. Fully illuminated, the blood soaked hands beckoned Herbert and Hans to her. The last of the men who'd fled down the earthen channel with Herbert and Hans dead at her feet. She'd evolved since the stormy night of her reawakening. Becoming bloated, folds of pale skin bunched together at one shoulder and more at the wrist of her opposite arm. A rot, judging by her deeds thought Herbert, from the inside.

Weeping and wordless, Hans went to her with head bowed. "I am the punishment you crave," her words almost tender. She wrapped caring arms around him briefly as he began to sob, a sparkling copper wire dangling from one hand. She slowly looped it once around his neck as he raised his wet eyes.

"We'll always have Paris, my bride." Hans says softly as she tightens the noose, choking the life out of him. Submissive until the end, Hans sags at her feet until his severed head dropped to the mud.

Herbert, utterly lost among the vast forest of rutted ravines, scanned the leafless, skeletal timber that rimmed the white-capped water. Unsure what, except for a miracle, he was hoping to find. His eyes, instead, landing on something far more unexpected: his wife. The mother of his two children, and the one he'd sent to his sister's home, sitting with legs crossed atop a rotted tree stump. She stood when their eyes met. Lifting her skirts and walking unworriedly toward him.

"Did you really think I wouldn't find out? About everything?" His wife strolled along the bank of the stream, closing the gap between them. "I gave our driver the day off and left the twins with their grandfather at the chateau. After all, he'll make a much better father figure than their own ever has."

"My dear!" So surprised by her unexpected appearance, Herbert's exclamations gave his fading hope a brief reprieve. "This... she isn't what she seems! Run! You don't understand! Fetch help!" But neither woman seemed to hear his words. Or care for his proclamations.

Stunned to silence, Herbert watched his bride of seven years draw even with the thing he'd brought back to life. "What are you waiting for?" she queried, clutching at the undead young woman. "He belongs dead." His wife pulling her near, and with eyes that mocked Herbert's stunned stare, covered the parting mouth with her own. The fervor of their passion leaving little doubt of the mutual attraction. When his wife pulled away from the frenzied kiss, she unsheathed a slender thrusting knife from the leather belt encircling the murderess's waist. The scabbard of the stiletto soiled and wet. "Especially since he tried to claim both our lives and bodies as something he alone commanded."

"I thought we'd do it together." The monstress turning her green eyes briefly Herbert's way as both hands explored his wife's curves. Her tongue of grey lashing at the neck and ear while his wife moaned in a way Herbert had never heard before. Breathless and somehow desperate.

"Fitting," his wife whispered hoarsely as she pulled open the top of her dress. Her bare, pale breasts bobbing in the moonlight.

Spellbound, Herbert finally broke the stunned paralysis that had kept him rooted. The sight of the bloody blade – a perfect match for the damage done to Catherine's face – startling him to action. He spun on his heel but something bit at his throat. The pain stopping him from taking even a single step. His hands flew to the wire that cut off his air, but his fingers fluttered uselessly as his eyes filled with stars and his legs gave. The weight of his body tightening the steel ensnaring him.

All went black.

Light slowly crept back and with it came voices. Flat on his back, barely conscious and muddled, at first Herbert only understood he was hearing two females speaking together. The words confusing and disjointed. "... never knew it could feel like this. Being with you these last few weeks... Long for you all the time... being with death. It... I can't explain how your touch, the coolness of your cold pale skin, the wickedness of being with you... makes me touch myself..."

With slits for eyes, Herbert tried to focus on where the conversation was coming from. If he moved his head, he lost the faint whisper of air keeping him alive and conscious. Opening his eyes wider, he recognized his wife's flushed features above his own. She was straddling him with her bare nipples, stiff and hard in the cold of the night, swaying near his face. Her conversation with someone behind him that he couldn't see, only hear.

"The throbbing stone under your home, it affects everything nearby. The sensations you felt when we were killing, the joy as we took revenge on the whores with their hooks in Herbert, was at least partially responsible for your actions." Now, as the undead bride of Hans reached across him, Herbert understood both women were in a state of undress. Her pallid lips exploring his wife's chest before encircling one engorged nipple. His wife, in turn, stretched one of her hands over Herbert to reach between the pale legs spread at his ears. Her other hand, the pointed stiletto in it, rose high. Crashing down and puncturing his chest even as the wire at his neck ended the trickle of air it had allowed. He felt the hot wetness of his blood pouring from the wounds as his wife began to rock back and forth. Moaning as she breathlessly penetrated him over and over again.

Barely aware, he felt no pain. The lasso severing his windpipe eliminating that worry. The last thing Herbert heard, the once-dead bride cooing between her moans of pleasure. "I am the vengeance he deserves. His hand was the first weapon I held."

II

THE BARREN STRETCH OF unkept ground was well-hidden from prying eyes. A windswept field of near frozen, hardpacked-earth topped by scraggly bristles defiantly erupting out of the arid soil. A near frozen desert where only the hardiest of life dared the bitter winds and retreating sunlight. Yet, this desolate tundra had seemed to call to the man who now trod unceremoniously across it. His every exhale visible in the unforgiving bite of the frigid air as he retreated into an earthen gorge. Plummeting deeper until the shadows within rose up in conspiracy to conceal his movements.

The man shuffled his thick boots as he half-slid down the side of the ravine. Wrapped in the fur of local animals, his awkward stumbling led him to a streambed crusted with the thinnest glaze of ice. Frozen dew, delicate and slim, shimmering like the tendrils of a spiderweb in the rays of the sun. An enlightened path his harried steps soon obliterated with jarring, audible crunches as he hurried. Slipping and nearly falling before grabbing hold of an aged tree for balance. As he lifted his eyes skyward, the man began to count the thick branches that earlier had caught his eye as suitable. He pulled the animal skin covering he wore to one side and laid his wind-burnt hand on the surface of the tree. His fingers absentmindedly exploring the rutted bark as both eyes scrutinized each limb. Satisfied with the choice, he began to unwind the coiled rope hidden under his furs before tossing one end up and over the branch. He let the remainder of the slack rope fall to the frozen ground as he grabbed the dangling lead. Hunched over, the seemingly earlier and earlier sunsetting already at his back, he worked the thick, rough-textured line in the bitter cold. Tying and twisting the end until he was satisfied with the result.

A noose.

When he was done, the man hurried to secure the opposite end of the rope. Winding it several times around the thickest part of the tree trunk before tying it off. He tugged and pulled hard until he was sure the knot would hold. When he was finished, he cast his eyes back in the direction he'd come. His hands began to tremble as he spied the outline of two stationary figures observing his actions from a rise in the distance. The man all but leapt for the tree beside him, quickly shinning up it until he sat on the thick branch where his rope swayed in the bitter cold. Without a second backward glance, he fitted the crafted noose over his own head.

Mumbling to himself with a wry smile, the man pulled a handful of silverish coins from his pocket. "Who wants to live forever?" said the man before softly closing his eyes as he slipped off the ice covering the branch. Plummeting headlong towards the ground below before the rope snapped tight. The force of the long drop instantly severing the head from his body. As the decapitated torso hit the hardened, frozen and dried earth under the tree, it burst asunder and all of his bowels gushed out. The gore and splatter mixing with the clinking coins.

Blood money.

The moon had risen a deep red, and the ominous sky above suddenly seemed awash in blood. A forbidding crimson hue that pricked the eyes and bruised the hearts of all those bearing witness to the executions. The three crucified men – framed against this prematurely darkening sky – each hung limply. Only one figure yet stirred, and he labored painfully through the last of his agonizing breaths. Beneath him, as he sagged one final time, the ground underfoot began to rumble and shake. The two crude and misshapen wooden beams he'd been barbarically nailed to swayed slightly in the emerging chaos but remained upright.

Below the crucifixions, staring stoically across the increasingly panicked and scattering masses, a lone woman stood apart from the commotion. Her features and expression unreadable under the thick, woolen cloth covering she wore about her face and head. Though her piercing eyes never wavered from the scene of the crucifixions, she didn't move against the warriors tasked with the grim retrieval of the bodies. The young defenders stripping the corpses and casting lots for the clothing and meager belongings of the three.

Behind her, struggling gamely to crest the icy pinnacle of what was known locally as Skull Hill, a badly hobbled girl slowly approached the woman. A tightly folded package of cloth held reverently in her hands. They both wore similar animal furs tailored exclusively for fit and though the young newcomer's speech was marred by her deformed mouth, she greeted the woman with obvious familiarity. "I've brought what you asked, Parvati. Do you want me to take it over?" The girl's claw-like fingers pointing to a small group of weeping men who stood nearby.

Pursing her lips together, the woman replied in a hushed tone. "Remember, you need to keep calling me Uma until we leave this place," she said, frowning in mild reproach. "But, no. I want to have a word with Rukah before I give him the shroud." The girl handed the woman the thick, iridescent cloth. The neatly folded material at first appearing grey, or perhaps silver, before slowly becoming more beige and brown as it was passed. The color undeterminable in the strange scarlet glow of the blood moon above.

After conversing briefly with them, the peculiar cloth was passed to the men and Parvati strode back. Muttering to herself with a wan smile, "Two down, two to go." The girl, nearly a young woman, asked shyly if everything had went as hoped and expected.

Parvati turned with a wink. "Certainly," she replied. "Sure as the kiss of Devadatta."

Chapter Fourteen
Germany-18th Century

THE FOUR WOODEN WHEELS spun at a leisurely clip as the stylish and ornamental carriage descended the dirt lane. The horse, driver, and passenger all enjoying the emerging spring day. With a hand from the warming sun above, the bursts of brightening colors and lush greens seemed poised to finally overtake the last of the withered browns and dismal greys winter had callously left behind. New growth devouring the past and turning the page on the long, cold season just ending.

As the road they traveled was gradually surrounded by dense walls of near leafless trees, the boisterous whistling and chirping of birds on the hunt for suitable mates grew monstrously loud. Only as the carriage crossed the rushing river that separated the House of Chanet from the emerging village below did the incessant songs fade. As if out of respect for the town's recently expanded cemetery they next rolled past, the avians' gay songs faded into the background.

Doctor Francois Chanet sat patiently as he rode to the office he kept in the nearby village. His medical practice as much of a hobby as anything else. Still, he did enjoy the often colorful interactions with the local townspeople. Hearing their petty gossip, tending to those truly in need, bringing the power of knowledge and learning to lands his family had called home for generations. The rural peoples scattered among the deeply forested areas long deprived of any true medical expertise. Plus, though Francois would loathe to admit it, his home these days now seemed extra cold and lonely. Unmarried and childless, the woman he'd hoped to marry had abruptly abandoned him just weeks earlier. These days of charity helping him withstand the ache of the loss.

"The usual time, My Lord?" The driver tipped his felt, tricorne hat at a passing duo of older women tiptoeing around puddles of questionable mud. "Or earlier?" Francois freed himself from the carriage interior and closed the swinging door behind him. "Rumor says they found another downstream. Some say the madman has returned." The man crossed himself though he knew his lord disapproved of such superstition.

"Same time," Francois said this casually though the news caused his heart to skip a beat. "I'll be waiting."

The doctor watched as his driver and black carriage started back down the cobbled street. All around him, the hustle and bustle of new construction as the burgeoning village continued to build and expand. Skeletal structures of measured wood scaling the sky, while behind his own office, plans for a new street were well underway. He nodded, smiled, and waved at those he recognized. Most having been friends and neighbors nearly his entire life.

Scattered among the familiar faces, desperate newcomers anxiously searched his own for charity. Some were hoping to find employment amid the ongoing village building projects. But most arrived with the change of season to work in the soon-to-be-tilled thawing fields. The surrounding farmland requiring many strong hands to clear, plant, and harvest over the coming months. The locals often willing to trade room and board in exchange for the seasonal labor. Until that time, as those hoping for work slowly migrated in, many were left scrounging and begging. Surviving any possible way until the promise of honest work arrived.

Francois turned and slid the key out from his pocket before disappearing into his physician's office. The modest space was fronted by an imposing desk that once adorned the library of his home. The rich, dark wood contrasting starkly with the drab, unpainted interior. The doctor having ordered printed sheets of papier dominoté, or domino paper, that would be adhered to the stripped interior walls once it arrived. Until then, much of the space was left bland, colorless, and with little decoration.

The one-armed widow who lived in the rooms upstairs already had the lamps lit and a warm cup of tea set out for him. The older, grey-haired woman helped him as needed with the ill while maintaining the office and building in exchange for his kindness. And a place to live. The woman's family had left her behind when they'd moved to Paris in search of a better life. The parting, though sad, was what she'd wanted. Born and raised in these mountains, she swore she'd die here as well.

"Good morning, Irene. How are we feeling this fine morning?" The doctor handing her his coat, hat, and gloves. "Did you sleep well?"

"A spot of whiskey before bed keeps me unaware of worrisome things." Irene had smartly tucked his beaver furred gloves between her breasts as she hung the coat and hat with her one hand. Putting them inside Francois's own dark tricorne hat when she was done and placing it beside the well-tailored jacket. "Especially if that fiend hiding out in the woods is back." Irene, frightfully slim and not much taller than most school-age children, nodding toward the street.

"I wouldn't believe everything you hear. As of yet, no one has contacted me about finding a body." Sitting at his desk, Francois lifted the cup of tea and blew the rising steam away. "The last was more than a year ago, wasn't it?" He eyed his elderly tenant as she pulled a short-handled broom from the corner and put it to use.

"Oui." Irene shot the doctor a look of surprise. "The deaths arrived with that first traveling fêtes foraine and menagerie. The first circus our little town ever had visit. How can you not recall? It was such an event!"

"Of course. Yes, of course." He shook his head, the black ponytail of his thinning hair wagging in the air. "That was also about the same time my fiancé first arrived. I suppose I was a little distracted back then," he added sheepishly. Though still sweeping, Irene looked across the room with some concern. The kindly doctor, though tied to a name still notorious for impropriety, was well-respected and loved not just by her, but by nearly all of the surrounding community. The recent decline of his normally sunny disposition troubling to all who knew him.

As the doctor perused several notices needing his attention, Irene began sweeping the wooden stairs that led to her living quarters on the second floor. Reaching the top step, a small gathering in the shadowed alley behind the rows of commerce drew her eye. "Bah! Une sorcière!" She spat on the floor once before using the bristles to wipe it away. "A witch!"

"Irene!" The doctor admonishing the outburst. "What have I told you of such prejudices?" Francois pushed himself from the desk and, seeing Irene's attention and slur was directed outside, soon joined her at the second floor window. "Are you cursing the migrant workers? These gypsies too dark-skinned or too light-skinned for your taste?" He followed her gaze where it fell to the ground below. "Or just dressed differently enough to make you uncomfortable? I can't keep up with all the revolving reasons for your mistrust of foreigners and strangers. I prove one ridiculous bias false and you come up with another."

Below them, likely having used the back wall of the building overnight for shelter, milled a small crowd. To the doctor's eye, nothing seemed out of the ordinary. Only when Irene pointed did Francois identify what had drawn her suspicion. Among the bobbing heads, one raven-haired woman stood apart. "Witch," Irene accused again.

"What do you... you mean her hair?" Irene's eyes narrowed knowingly as she nodded. Though neither could see anything but the very top of their heads, the one she cursed did look different. A thin line of lighter or white hair splitting her otherwise black hair down the middle. Francois dropped his gaze and scowled at the superstitious old woman beside him.

"Does the devil now anoint his disciples with shades of different hair color? Is that how you tell the wolves from the shepherd's flock of sheep?" Francois couldn't help but raise his own voice in exasperation. "Wouldn't the witches just pull all their hair up if that was the case? Or, wear a bonnet or piece of cloth atop to hide the devilish mark? What would you then find to demonize? Their language or the cut or color of their dress?"

The doctor turned and stepped toward the stairs before stopping himself. "Out of all of us, you should know the feeling of being treated differently for something you have no control over." Francois nodded at her missing limb - his voice softer. "My father took you in when no one else would. Others said you were cursed. A Loup-Garou or werewolf. Bitten by the monster we now have come to call the Beast of Gévaudan." The old woman's scowling face began to break. Her righteousness cowering from the bite of reality. "And why? How did that make you feel? Still make you feel?" The doctor made his way back down the stairs. "Aren't there scriptures about loving your neighbors instead of constantly throwing rocks at them?"

The ravenous flames began consuming her. Making it clear the mercies she'd pleaded for had been denied. Again. The burgeoning demon-fire inside erupting and purging every trace of her for the hungry palate of what so relentlessly pursued her. Using her like a well-worn possession - with familiarity and ease. The pain, searing like a red-hot ember impossibly inhaled, splitting her head. Surely, the last of her reason argued, the very fires of Dante's hell had been liquified and poured through every crack in her skull. Boring through her from the inside out. The agony of burning alive – an instant later – swapped for the unfeeling numb of worthlessness. Dead inside.

Her body, as if possessed, no longer under her control.

The young woman with the strange, thin stripe of white hair contorted awkwardly in the shadows. Her eyeballs rolling up and vanishing until the sockets were as colorless and sightless as the dead. Both hands crooked and clawed as her body shuddered violently in the dirt. Spittle and drool wet her chin as she soiled herself. Her trembling and kicking feet in the woolen skirt making the spectacle clear.

Terrified and concerned for her safety – hiding the newcomer from the judging eyes that passed near – the young woman's friends dragged her deeper into the shadows. Concealing the violence she was doing to herself. Each trying to keep her hidden while at the same time comforting and tending to her. Slowly, as her seizing body began to settle, they drifted away like leaves after their fall.

Hours later, only one caretaker remained by her side. Her head in his lap, the lashes of both eyes began to flutter. "Dieu merci, Zorrie. Thank goodness!" She didn't recognize the person looming over her. But the wide-eyes her face filled were both kind and simple. A young man with brown hair and dirt on his forehead. "Am I doing this right?"

The question, like his face, went unrecognized. Though huddled in the shadowed valley of tall buildings, even that meager light reduced her eyes to slits. With a shaky hand, she pulled at her black hair until it fell across her features. The rays of the sun all but unbearable as she struggled to sit upright. Gamely, she tried to speak but seemed unable to form any words. Or think of words to say. Unaware of where she was, who was with her, or even her own name. What had he called her?

"Zorrie?" Her jaw popped and ached as if she'd been beaten. The inside of her mouth seemed full of gravel – dry and jumbled. Sitting up on her own, slowly language returned. "Did you call me Zorrie?" The young man beside her had the unlearned gaze of a child. He guffawed loudly once before wiping at the moist slit beneath his nose.

"Zorrie! Zorrie!" He clapped his hands together in excitement. "What else would I call you?" He laughed loudly once more, the sounds much like barking, before passing a wooden cup of gritty water. As she drank voraciously, her senses began to return. She smiled at her friend.

"Thank you, Jean-Baptiste." Drinking more slowly, the veiled haze she seemed cocooned within slowly unraveled. Fragmented memories, her senses, and fondness for her simple-minded friend slowly filling the blank spots in her mind. "Thank you for watching over me." When she smiled at him, her face and neck ached.

"Zorrie! Zorrie! White stripe of glory. Zorrie! Zorrie! White stripe of glory. Zorrie! Zorrie!" She reached up and caught his attention. Stopping his excited clapping and chanting.

"Jean-Baptiste," she started, knowing she could only briefly hold his gaze and limited attention. "How long was I out? Where was the sun when I started…" Not needing the rest of the prompt – the question always among her first upon waking – the man-child pointed to the sky opposite of the sun directly above their heads. "Most of the morning, I guess, huh?" *No wonder I'm so weak and shaky,* she thought to herself. *My spells don't usually last that long.*

Her *spells,* as a kindly priest had once explained, were natural and not to be feared. The learned man-of-God likening them to the dramatic swings of the sea. Counseling her to track how she felt and what was happening inside herself just before the spells arrived. Comparing the affliction to the shifting tides of the ocean. Eventually, he explained, man learned how to avoid being overtaken and dragged away by the undertow. Telling her to do the same. To watch for and learn the subtle signs within herself so she could prepare. Have enough time to find a safe place to hunker down and ride the tempest about to blow through her mind. Reminding her that when the spell eventually recedes, just like water after flooding, what gets left behind is often distorted and strange.

As she would sort through her scattered thoughts, much like walking among the tidal pools, she often discovered things she didn't recognize. Some so bizarre they frightened her. This usually happened right after she would reawaken. Fleeting glimpses of things that made little sense to her without the context. Often, returning memories explaining away the mysterious. Other times, what passed before her were more like dreamy premonitions. Fantastic images that compelled her though she had no reason or understanding why.

She shuddered. This had been one of those times. A badly misshapen and ruined body was all she could recall. Horrible. Flesh spilling and hanging loosely. A thing hardly resembling humanity laid out as if for inspection. A monster.

Zorrie felt the familiar pang of loss as more of her memories returned. Pushing aside the unknown vision of horror she'd had. Replacing it with people she'd once loved, and things she'd once held sacred, until she'd lost her grip. Self-consciously, she tugged her sleeves down to cover the zigzagging scars that ran unchecked up and down both arms.

"Zorrie, is it?" With the help of Jean-Baptiste, she gained her feet. "Right, right," her memory still filling back in. "Someone said I looked like a zorilla the other day," she gestured to her striped hair. "Told me I looked like a polecat because of this."

"Zorrie! Zorrie! White stripe of glory! Zorrie! Zorrie!" Jean was grinning, but, with the gash above his lip and oddly jutting teeth, few would recognize it as such. He wiped at the perpetual drool that dribbled from the wound he'd been born with. Most villagers teasing him as a *harelip*. The local folklore and superstitions associating the hare with the devil and lust. Though Jean, like Zorrie, without a mother or father, his very birth likely resulted in his mother being labeled a heretic. Or worse. The affliction often considered proof of rendezvousing with the devil.

"Let's go find the others. We need to see if anyone has found food or work yet. If not, we need to help." Zorrie pulled her hair forward so it hung down and covered much of her features. Her long sleeves and wool skirt covering nearly everything else as they made their way out of the shadowy alley. Her memory still badly scrambled from the episode, she had the vaguest sense she should stay hidden, her eyes darting about. Did something stalk her, or was she in hiding? Rubbing her temples, she willed the answer to come but came up empty. Unsure, she reached out and grabbed Jean's hand so they wouldn't get separated. "Stay close to me," she whispered to her smiling friend.

Though it pained her to admit it, keeping Jean close had another benefit. Strangers often more sympathetic and generous when they were seen as a pair. The man-child unaware of how others viewed him, he sometimes drew them near with his kind eyes and joyful disposition. Letting the light in his eyes blind him to much of the teasing and taunting. While she, guarded and ashamed of her scars, stayed dressed in greys that smothered her personality. To say she fared better beside Jean was an understatement. Without him, she was unsure she'd last a week.

Hours later, having found their friends but no work, those without homes huddled near a sagging barn on the outskirts of town. Sharing the limited bounty of food they'd managed to scrape together with the others, Zorrie and Jean ate. Passing their wooden cup and dipping it in the collected water of a barrel. Listening to the others discuss the rumored new murder and debate their next move. None wanting to be without shelter when the sky turns black this night. The dense woods that encircled the burgeoning village was scary enough. The notorious forest surely harboring fearsome creatures some say are immortal, others say diabolical. The dark expanse of ancient timber beyond the House of Chanet, a place long cursed and feared. Some believing it to be the birthplace of the Beast of Gévaudan terrorizing, it seemed, the entire countryside of France.

But now, even the village itself seemed tainted. The rumor of a most terrible murder haunting the townspeople. The features of the victim, they say, gone.

Faceless.

Chapter Fifteen
France-Modern Day

"Wheel seem fine? No wobbling or anything?" Secrist, lost in thought since returning to the repaired rental car, finally breaking the silence. Stander, his mind occupied as well, flinched before shaking his head back and forth in the greenish glow of the automobile's dashboard.

"Nope, no shaking and," Stander lifted both hands from the steering wheel, "there doesn't seem to be a pull to either side. I think we should be fine driving this the rest of the way."

"That's a relief." Secrist turned and looked out the passenger window. "I can't see even a single light. It feels like we are driving through the middle of nowhere."

"No kidding." Stander let his eyes roam over the moonlit hills, bridged valleys, and dense timber that lined both sides of the two-lane road he drove. "But, once we finally get out of this forest, we should start seeing signs of civilization again. What does the GPS say? How much longer until we reach the chateau?"

Secrist glanced briefly at his phone before replying. "Less than an hour now. It looks like we should be exiting these mountains soon."

Stander nodded with a grunt, his eyes never leaving the road. Up ahead, just beyond the reach of the small car's headlights, a dark mass flowed across the pavement. "What the fuck?"

"You see that eyeshine?" Secrist leaned forward in his seat. "What the hell is that? A bear?" Wordlessly, Stander took his foot from the accelerator. The vehicle slowing as its headlights brightened the painted highway stripes that vanished under the bulk of the thing's hairy hide. Unhurried, the thick figure seemed to grow larger even as Stander began to pump the brakes. The car coming to a halt on the traffic-free road as the beast slowly turned toward the approaching vehicle.

The thing's pelt was dark grey. What appeared to be the tail of a horse swishing casually behind it. The rotund, dense body balanced on four muscular legs with comically mismatched black hooves. Defiantly, the bizarre creature seemed to purposefully block the bulk of the road where it stood. A cunning intelligence gleaming behind its baleful stare. The shape of the profile, muzzle, ears, and eyes that of a wolf. Gradually, it raised its long, black snout and began sniffing the air.

"What the hell is that thing?" Secrist spoke in a hushed tone as he melted back into his seat. "It's like the devil tried to one-up the platypus." Beside him, Stander merely nodded mutely.

Moments later, a torrent of tawny-furred wolves poured from the dark foliage and tall trees that crowded the lane. The pack yipping excitedly as they pranced across the road. The canines crowding the massive, malformed beast as it moved to peer directly into the stopped car. Briefly locking eyes with Stander, the gigantic beast's black lips pulled slowly back from its snarling jaw of rowed teeth. The twin incisors, as long as fingers, flashing with menace.

"Fuck this, man…" Stander cranked the steering wheel hard to one side before slamming his foot down on the gas. The car shot forward and whizzed past the furry behemoth. In the rearview mirror, Stander watched as the smaller wolves all darted into the lush greenery at the side of the road. The entire pack instantly vanishing into the woods. Bathed in the dwindling red of the rental's taillights, the last to turn was the cobbled-together creature with the wolf head. Sauntering almost casually from the pavement as if wanting to be certain the vehicle wasn't going to turn back around.

"Step on it!" Secrist craned his neck to view the speedometer. "Can't this little French car go any faster?" He spun on his seat to see if anything was giving chase.

"Quit pissing your pants, Tommy. That scary-ass, wolfy-looking thing isn't following us." Stander's eyes bounced from the windshield, to the rearview mirror and the side mirrors before refocusing on the road ahead. "Haven't you heard? Big bad wolves with such sharp teeth prefer little girls in red hoods and grandmas in soft beds over pigs." Stander turned with a smirk, huffing and puffing dramatically. "Unless it can get three at a time." Secrist, a lifelong cop, didn't even look Stander's way as he flipped him off. "Besides, until we get past all these hills and curves, I'm more worried about the road ahead of us. That's twice now we almost ran into something trying to cross."

Nearly thirty minutes later, Secrist, glancing periodically at his phone, began warning Stander of the upcoming lanes they'd be turning down. As the mountain range faded behind them, the roads became both straighter and less hilly. Periodic lights began to wink at them from the occasional farmsteads they drove past and for the first time in hours, oncoming traffic welcomed them back to civilization.

After stopping briefly to refuel and check on their repaired tire, Stander finally pulled onto the deserted lane that climbed the rise Chateau Chanet sat atop. The car cautiously navigating the shadowed switchbacks until abruptly cresting the hill and entering a circular, dirt drive. Stander pulled the vehicle around what was likely once a courtyard. Killing the engine just outside a set of double doors before, along with Secrist, stepping out into the night. "Finally," the only thing his passenger said as he hobbled out. Both men stretching as they took in their surroundings.

The full moon in the cloudless sky above was no longer impeded by the mountainous forest they'd driven through to reach the chateau. The bright luminescence allowing both men the opportunity to appraise the stone and brick structures. The dirt drive where they stood, partially overgrown by encroaching grass, was like a roundabout but with only a single entry and exit. The courtyard completely enclosed by the patchwork of two-story buildings that circled it. The building styles and materials used – likely spread across centuries – made for a complex of mismatched structures. All assembled from the graveyard of past architecture.

Frankensteined, if it was a real word, would be the word that comes to mind.

The grandest structure, both in size and intricacy, was likely the original home and, at one time, a standalone castle. At its back two corners, crumbling and unstable looking ramparts reached for the sky. The tops of both, shaped and jagged like rooks on a chessboard, looking out across the sweeping valley below. The rolling hills mostly farmland and pastures of green. On the opposite side, crowding the chateau, an aged wall of timber. The trees hugging the grounds marking the end of the woodlands and thicket they'd just driven through.

Flanking the elaborate stone centerpiece, stood the reminders of how grand the entire site had once been. Along one side, the most dilapidated of the buildings. Nearly half of its reddish, slate roof had collapsed inward, and many of the second story windows were glassless openings. The simple structure had the look of the chateau's servant's home or quarters. Next to it, sharing a wall but separate, stood the stables and barn. The nearly empty buildings were silent and dark. The wooden doors still attached occasionally creaking in the breeze, nothing of note behind them. On the opposite side, the buildings were less recognizable. Nearly windowless, the stone-colored walls of dull grey had been patched haphazardly in various ways across the centuries it stood. Much of the outside covered in ivy, both green with life and brown with death. The competing vines cannibalizing each other across several of the facades.

A smallish maze of shoulder high hedges crowded the grounds between the buildings. Sprinkled among the dead ends were mostly crumbling figures of stone. Vaguely divine in appearance, yet unlike any saints or deities either Stander or Secrist recognized. Most missing limbs and weathered to near featureless. Faceless, even.

"You got the key Lucas gave you?" Secrist pulled the bags they'd brought from the car's backseat. "Did he tell you what door it fits?"

"You mean keys. As in plural." Stander pulled a jangling keyring from the front pocket of his jeans. "He said this big one," Stander held it by one end, "would fit the lock on the metal, double doors." He nodded at the doorway he'd parked in front of; the entrance into the original castle. "Lucas said even he wasn't entirely sure what all the other keys unlocked. But, that we were welcome to use them to explore the grounds."

Secrist handed one bag over to Stander as they approached the locked doorway. As Stander slid the cartoonish-sized key into the rusted lock, Secrist appraised the unlit windows above. Wooden shudders bracketed each glass-filled window. The unique styling and aged wood matching the décor of the other building's windows and doorways. Glancing around him, the effect of the ancient architecture and the barely touched upkeep of the grounds was stunning. Enclosed by the building's aged walls, the edifices seemed to transport them back in time. Everything looked, felt, and even smelled like history. Secrist felt a grin forming under his moustache. He was about to stay in a bonified and authentic French chateau!

"Motherfucker!" Stander, the keyring back in his pocket, twisted, pushed and pulled on the circular door ring to no avail. Leaning his shoulder against the tall steel door, he shoved mightily until it finally began to move. A deafening screech echoing about the otherwise deserted courtyard. Pulling away from the opening, flakes of rust fluttered to the ground while Stander wiped at the reddish stain the corroding metal left on his shirt. "Great," he muttered to himself, "this was one of my favorite *Volbeat* shirts."

Secrist turned on his phone's light before stepping past his grumbling friend. Finding a modern light switch just inside the doorway, he flipped up the three toggles. The entryway and several rooms beyond inviting them in with a soft, yellow glow. Each space illuminated by brass-colored chandeliers last in style back in the '90s. The cheap fixtures in stark contrast to the rich splendor of the aged furniture inside.

"Lucas said we could have our pick of the rooms, but suggested we stay on the first floor." Stander dropped his bag before closing and locking the door behind him. "He said there are a couple bedrooms to the right that should be made up and share the only working bathroom."

"I wish we hadn't arrived so late," Secrist was turning in a circle as he spoke. "Just look at this! I'm dying to check this place out." He couldn't wait to explore the grounds and compare what he found with the notes in his grandfather's diary. According to what he'd written, there should be an underground tunnel connecting the chateau to the actual location his ancestor watched over during the First World War. If any of it was still standing.

Stander nodded and grabbed his bag from the floor. "Now, let's go check out the rooms and get settled in." Like Secrist, he was anxious to see if he could find any trace of his Great Aunt Madeleine. Specifically, if some of the puzzling symbols he'd found in her home back on the border of Iowa and Illinois were duplicated here.

The home on the border of France and Germany.

Chapter Sixteen
Germany-18th Century

The sparkling, silvery dew hadn't frozen overnight. Though neither Zorrie nor Jean-Baptiste had been roused by the cold as they had previous mornings, the clingy dampness in the cool grey air was still uncomfortable. Zorrie had woken with a start; her heart thundering inside her chest. But, hearing the calm, blissful drone of her companion's untroubled sleep, she lie unmoving beside him. Pondering the ghastly image that had propelled her out of the lake of calm she'd swam in most of the night.

It had been the same abomination that had frightened away her spell the day before. Only this time, the monster had seemed to reach for her. A fleshy thing with stubby fingers and eyes of anger. The features of the fearsome nightmare distorted and squished together. The skin straining and bursting from some sort of internal pressure. As if something deep inside was trying desperately to reach the surface.

Or reach her.

Zorrie squeezed her eyes tightly shut. Forcing herself to revisit the dream, memory, vision... or whatever she'd experienced. Exploring the nightmare in hopes she might spy a clue as to the origins of the troubling visage. But, soon the frayed edges of the picture in her mind unraveled. Leaving her pulling at the strands until even they flittered away. The only realization being the hideous creature had been prostrate. Lying on one side as it gazed upon her. She puzzled over this new bit of information until, shuddering, she abruptly sat up. Her eyes troubled and wide as the thought bloomed.

Had it been watching her as she'd slept?

Later that morning, after scrounging bits of stale bread and finishing off some partially eaten vegetables left lying in the street, Zorrie and Jean made their rounds. Lingering near the market stands in docile hope that others might take mercy on their plight. Cruising the alleys behind businesses with sharpened eyes sweeping the ground for anything of value they could potentially barter or trade. Hoping to find something that might help them endure until the next day when the cycle would be repeated. The daily grind of survival; safety, something to eat, a place to sleep.

But, now around every corner, Zorrie felt as if she was being constantly observed. Tracked like an animal being hunted by an unseen predator. Each passersby's stare giving her pause; each avoidance of her eyes questioned. If the fiendish murderer had indeed returned, was she to be the next victim?

"Zorrie, Zorrie, why the worry?" Jean cocked his head so far to one side he nearly fell over. Smiling, he reached over and swept away the hair she used as a mask. Briefly, exposing the scars circling her neck before she pulled the black locks back down. "Zorrie, Zorrie," he started again before she stopped him. Covering his drooling mouth with one hand while turning to those resting beside them.

"Is it really true," she began, "about the murder."

"Yes, Mademoiselle. I heard they found a body tangled among the branches of a tree that had fallen across in the river. Murdered dead." The man speaking was seated nearby and rocked an infant in his arms. Zorrie couldn't remember his name, but his nursing wife, snoring contently beside him, had been kind to Jean. The tiny family never separating from each other.

"Barking mad, he is." The man standing was Jacques, his bulbous nose perpetually red and dripping. "Eats his victim's faces right off, he does." Finishing, he dragged a crusty sleeve across his weathered face.

"How do you know this?" Zorrie slid one arm around Jean's shoulders. He'd sat up straight and moved closer to her. "Did you see them bring the body to the doctor?"

"No need. We all know it is the same madman as before. Killed plenty, he did. Lives in the woods with the beast." Jacques leaned over as if to hide a conspiracy. "I heard tell they are one and the same. Man and beast. You won't catch me waltzing through that place." He gestured past the outskirts of the town. An inferno of green stretching beyond the village's oldest, and by far grandest, home. The House of Chanet. The home of the local Noblesse - neither crown, clergy, nor commoner.

"What happened before?" Zorrie shushing Jean at her side as a few more of the gathered listened in.

"This was nearly a year ago, before you arrived." Others nodding in agreement as Jacques began to tell the story. "At first, they blamed it on the circus. Saying a caged beast had escaped. But the victims... well, no animal kills that way."

"What way? Eating faces?" Zorrie didn't understand. "Don't the scavengers of the woods often start with the eyes and tongue."

"Full of holes, they were. Their faces! Like a giant bird had pecked them to death." Jacques turned to the others for confirmation, nodding along with them. "The circus had cages of animals most of us had never seen before. The first murder happened the same night the menagerie's wagons arrived."

"And they never caught the killer?" Part of Zorrie wished she would stop asking questions. The answers not likely to bring her comfort. But, if she was being stalked as feared, she must learn all she can. "Where was the body found?"

"Bodies, dearie. Bodies." The voice, feminine, rising from the gathered though Zorrie couldn't tell who had answered her.

"How many?" Her voice sounded timid in her own ear. Hollow.

"I do not know for certain." Jacques cast a glance among the others in hopes another might have the answer. When no one spoke up, he shrugged and continued. "I know after the first one they tried to pin the devillish work on one of the poor freaks in their sideshow. Hauling one of the human curiosities up to the Seigneur, the Lord of Chanet manor." Again, he gestured at the home that overlooked the village and valley it was nestled inside of. "Never to be seen again."

"What happened next? Didn't the murders stop?" Zorrie could see uncomfortable shuffling among those standing while others dropped their gaze.

"Hard to say, Mademoiselle. These lands, these woods, well... death is never far from this wretched place, eh? Some have always vanished from these parts. Still disappear," several listeners crossed themselves. "Some say the Chanets are the reason these lands are cursed with terrible beasts and horrors not meant for this world. But that was long ago. Our Dr. Chanet is full of only kindness. Whatever his family may have done in the past, he would have had no part in. Most you ask are saddened he lives alone with his servants. Wishing he'd be blessed with love and family. Whatever haunts, or has returned to haunt these cobblestones, is not of his doing."

"What happened to the freak." Zorrie hated the word. In her mouth, it tasted like blasphemy. "The one accused at the beginning? The human curiosity."

"I heard it was carted north to the Confédération Suisse. The good doctor taking pity on the unfortunate soul and finding a clinic able to care for ones with similar afflictions." Murmured agreement among the gathered. "Paid for out of his own pocket, he did."

"But we don't know if the murdering fiend remains? Perhaps spending the winter months in hiding? Waiting for spring." Zorrie said out loud what she was thinking. "Or being hidden by one of the villagers?"

"Waiting for the migrants." Zorrie let the confusion and question show on her face. *Why would that matter?* "Waiting for victims no one would miss. Waiting for others who might be accused and then hauled away. Getting away with murder one planting and one harvesting season at a time." The father with the baby in his arms speaking up. He'd obviously wondered the same things before. His eyes betraying the helplessness of his situation. The local fields his best chance at finding work and bettering his family. Risking his life to support his children and wife.

Zorrie leaned against Jean. Were they just as trapped? Just as helpless?

Dr. Francois Chanet watched the dust glide across the sunbeams. He turned his face to the warmth as the villagers outside went about their daily business. The busy street beyond his office window crowded with their clamor. As his thoughts drifted, the day's work behind him, he recalled the night he'd heard of the first of several murders that had plagued his hometown one year prior. How the local mayor and village officials had barged into his office making wild accusations.

He remembered the cart pulling up and stopping in the street. How with only a glance, he'd known what to expect. Sighing, and looking out this very same window, he'd turned from the all too familiar scene. The elders likely burdening him, he suspected, with another drunk or some poor gypsy scapegoat. His medical office expected – out of civic duty – to take care of the town's troubles. His family the closest thing to law and justice in this part of the country.

First, they'd carried in the victim's body and laid it across one of his examining tables. Covered in cloth, only the head showed signs of trauma. The linen so wet with blood it had hooded the deceased in crimson gore. Pulling back the dripping wraps, he'd nearly exclaimed out loud in fright. The savagery both so calculating and brutal that it had left him weak-kneed. The dead faceless and pocked with so many holes that they were uncountable.

Next, they hauled in the accused. The village elders explaining the murder had occurred the same day the first wagons of the circus caravan arrived. The much anticipated spring festival set to begin in mere days. Each of the men imploring Francois to act quickly and decisively. The only way to ensure the inaugural fair's success was to quickly take care of this problem. Unexplained disappearances and deaths were not uncommon among the community – the woods full of fearsome creatures. But this was different. It had been no beast.

Though, what they hauled in, was no man.

Hidden under woolen blankets teeming with lice and parasites, the prisoner was walked in. Soiled straw sticking to the excrement stamped on the heel on one filthy, bare foot. The accompanying smells forcing each to cover their nose and mouth. Hump backed and bent forward as it shuffled, its gait was unsteady and slow. The wheezing accompanying each step sounding like it may be the last breath it would draw. As it struggled to sit, nearly losing balance until settled, the raspy wet cough it struggled through left yellow and green phlegm splattered across one arm of the chair.

Francois remembered he had looked from victim to the accused. The murdered was unnamed and faceless, but had been a young and healthy man. Likely, a son to one of the farmers based on his emerging tan and rippling muscles. The suspect on the other hand, struggled to even walk and sit. Turning to the local posse, Francois began to ask questions. "How did this happen?" Pausing, he'd rephrased the question. "How *could* this happen?" The look on his face explanation enough.

"I don't rightly know, My Lord." The mayor, hat in hand, couldn't bring himself to meet Francois's gaze. "Poor Jules," he gestured to the body, "was found just as you see him, sir. Not far from where the wagons for the circus are being unloaded."

"Why is this the suspect? Did someone see what happened?" Around him, shaking heads of denial. Not surprisingly, it soon came out, no one had actually seen what happened to Jules. Looking for a scapegoat, the men had scooped up the most recent arrival. Admitting the timing and close proximity had prompted their actions. Francois gave each man an opportunity to speak, admonishing their silence with his glare.

"Am I to believe this poor soul, who can barely walk, overpowered and killed this young, healthy man? What would be the reason for the attack? Why would anyone murder a local so shortly after arriving?" Francois did his best to remain measured with his comments and questions, but felt his anger begin to rise.

"A mad beast this one is." The mayor's son stepping forward and yanking the frayed and thin blanket off of the accused. "Do you think this monster reasons like a man?"

The gasps that followed the reveal first drew the doctor's attention. A small crowd of the curious gathering outside his opened office door. Though it contained women and children, the more fragile turned from the atrocity sitting in his office. Even the men still staring seemed to no longer want to see. The sight one not easily forgotten.

Whipped raw in places, the lashes were old enough to have scarred over most of its back. But a few raw and weeping wounds meant the beatings hadn't ended. The tortured flesh a testament to years of abuse. Badly misshapen, awkward lumps rolled under the pale skin. Some may have been bruises or contusions from blows, though it didn't seem likely. The uneven patchwork extending the length of its back and reaching around both shoulders. The head, warped as any gourd or squash, was wrapped in contusions. The little hair on the crown so light and wispy it was barely visible.

Unmoving, clearly ashamed of its appearance, tears dropped from the closed eyelids. The streaming carving lines into the filth caked around the face and neck. A trail of mucus coating the raw and chapped lips. As startling and troubling as it looked, only after circling back around to where it faced did the doctor become truly ashamed of his fellow townspeople. The pitiful creature was obviously unable to commit the murder of which it was accused. Francois sought out the poor thing's frightened gaze. Smiling, he gently patted one of the malformed arms. The doctor understanding the being before him was simply a mistreated freak from the circus sideshow. Monstrous and frightening on the outside, the villagers assumed the same lurked inside. Had he not been here to provide counsel, it would have likely already been swinging from a tree.

Taking full responsibility, Dr. Francois Chanet shooed the curious onlookers from his office. Pulling the mayor aside, he did his best to explain the types of diseases and potential causes for the severe physical deformities. Assuring the official they had the wrong person. That if they truly feared a murderer had come to the village, the real monster still lurked nearby. Loudly letting him know that he was so certain of innocence that he would take the pitiful soul home with him. Provide care that had clearly been long deprived in hopes something could be done to soothe the pain and suffering. As the men piled back into the wagon that had brought them, Francois told them he would speak directly with the owner of the circus in the morning.

Soon, with the help of his driver, Francois loaded the pitiful creature into his carriage. Taking the accused murderer up to his home. The House of Chanet.

Chapter Seventeen
France-Modern Day

The following morning, Secrist woke, cleaned himself up, and dressed before exiting the bedroom where he'd slept. Surprisingly, he felt fairly well-rested despite having arrived so late to their destination the night before. The enormous, four-poster bed he'd slept in as soft as it was grandiose. The bedchamber, though lacking most modern amenities, was dark, cozy, and quiet. Had he not been so excited to start exploring the grounds of the ancient chateau, he would have lingered longer in the silken sheets. The aged look of the room unique and charming.

Stepping out into the main hallway, he backtracked toward the foyer until he found Stander's bedroom. The echoing of his footsteps on the marble floor loud in the quiet and stillness of the empty chateau. The door to his room was open and after briefly knocking on the thick, baroquely carved wood and calling out without reply, Secrist began to search the massive home. Glancing into shadowed halls and wandering through assorted rooms of all sizes. Many of them plastered with ornate wallpaper from centuries past that demanded your attention. The wooden trim and floorboards that framed the gawdy patterns all stained a deep, rich brown. The curved banisters of several stairways leading to the second floor tempted his eye and step, but he continued searching the ground floor. Strolling into a weapons hall devoid of its namesake near the rear of the chateau. A few sober-looking busts on chest-high pillars eyeing his search and a vaguely familiar coat-of-arms hanging on one wall.

Giving up finding him inside, Secrist made his way outdoors and was relieved to see the rental car still sitting where Stander had parked it the night before. He hollered several more times but only succeeded in scaring a murder of crows to panicked flight. Their accusatory cackles drawing his eye as he watched their hurried retreat into a blackened opening near the top of one tower. Frustrated, he finally pulled out his phone but was dismayed to discover he had no bars and no service. With growing concern, he started walking the lane they'd driven up to the Chateau Chanet. Remembering that he had a signal when they'd arrived last night and trying to recapture his lost cell service. With his phone held high above his head, he squinted in the morning sun as he walked the graveled road.

"That isn't going to work." Startled, Secrist nearly dropped his phone as Stander suddenly crested the top of the hill and headed toward him. "I just walked halfway down to the main road and still couldn't pick up a signal. I wanted to let Lucas know we arrived but no dice." Stander flashed his phone at Secrist. Neither of the devices able to communicate. "Maybe there is a local tower down or something? I figured I'd try him again later."

"And call the police back in Caen." Secrist put his phone away.

"Huh?" Stander shielded his eyes from the morning sun with one hand. "Oh, well, yeah. Of course. I was going to try them once I spoke with Lucas. I was just hoping he'd tell me they caught whoever did that to Beth and save me the dime." He chuckled, but it seemed forced. Slowly, the two men began to walk back toward the chateau.

"Where do we want to start looking?" Secrist scanned the buildings that made up the estate. "I'm most interested in trying to find the underground passageway my grandfather mentioned in his diary. The tunnel that connects this chateau with the tenant housing or apartment building he watched over. He described it, granted this was over a hundred years ago, as being the tallest building in the village. Said the chateau was supposed to be roughly a mile or so away from it." Secrist stopped walking and turned. From their vantage point atop the hill, they could see two small towns in what would be the correct direction. The one farthest to the west appeared to hug the border of France. All but straddling both countries. Both close enough to be candidates. "It has to be one of those. But, assuming it is still standing after two world wars, even if we drive over and find what we think is the right building, I doubt they'll let us two just waltz right in and..."

The sound of an approaching small engine cut Secrist off. Moments later, an all-terrain vehicle crested the hill of the long driveway. A single man drove the ATV and as he pulled alongside, he gave them a guarded smile and nod as he killed the engine. Bearded and deeply tanned, he smelled of the outdoors and of farming. The sides of his four-wheeler splashed with what looked like a mixture of mud and feces. Roughly their same age, he pulled off his cap and ran weathered fingers through his thick hair. "Puis-je vous aider, messieurs?"

Stander and Secrist exchanged a confused look. "Sorry. We only speak English. Come again?"

Unsmiling, the man repeated himself in English. "No problem. Can I help you, gentlemen?" The translation didn't immediately cure the confused looks, so the farmer continued. "This is all private land and property around here. If you are tourists looking for castles to explore, there are some nearby I can help you find. Otherwise, I must ask you to leave. I live not far from here so the family who owns this home asks me to watch over the place. In exchange, they allow my herds of sheep to graze on the property."

"Whoa, whoa, whoa." Stander smiled and dug the keychain Lucas had given them out of his pocket. "We have permission from the owner to be here. He even gave us the key to the front door."

The Frenchman didn't move from his seat, but he clearly recognized the oversized metal key Stander held. "May I ask the name of the person who gave you that?" The tone wasn't unpleasant, but direct. From atop the ATV, his eyes scrutinized both men and the parked rental car.

"Lucas. Lucas Chanet. He works for me." Stander paused, unsure how much he should say. "We are visiting from America and my friend Tommy here, well, he has an interest in this part of the country. He recently found out his grandfather fought near here during the First World War. I guess he was stationed close by and described some of the places and things he saw. We, well, mostly Tommy, we wanted to check his story out. See what might still exist that he had written about." Stander shrugged in hopes it conveyed a sense of nonchalance.

"Ah, Lucas. Of course! I haven't seen him around lately. I hope he is doing well." Again, the man spoke in friendly tones but made no move to leave. After an awkward moment of silence, he faced Secrist and continued. "I'm afraid that while France has many monuments and memorials to World War One, there are none nearby. What is it you hoped to find? Perhaps I can point you in the right direction."

"What I'm looking for is supposed to be under the ground." Secrist, eager to learn more, stepped close to the ATV. "My grandfather wrote of a tunnel that connects this chateau to one of the neighboring towns. Have you heard of such a thing?"

The neighboring farmer frowned slightly as he nodded. "These lands are riddled and pocked by old tunnels, mines, and quarries. Even now, it is not uncommon for portions of fields to collapse from time to time, and for livestock to be lost in sinkholes. I know nothing of any specific passageway that may have existed back then. But, I can show you a cave-in just over yonder. It is definitely part of a tunnel system, but whether it is what you seek or just another collapsed mine is anybody's guess. It is not far. Follow me, messieurs." Restarting the motor, the man drove slowly toward the back of the property. Passing several dilapidated buildings and a collapsed shed. Five minutes later, all three men peered down into an earthen opening of foreboding black. Several thick, broken timbers crisscrossing what looked like the opening to a small den.

"Don't let that tight gap fool you. It may be an uncomfortable squeeze getting in. But, once you get past this rubble you see, it opens up. You can standup and walk once you get a little ways in."

"So you've been inside?" Stander asking the question while Secrist dropped to his knees and poked his head in the hole of black. "I'm surprised someone hasn't filled this all in. Don't you have a bunch of kids going in and out of here all the time?"

Solemnly, the farmer shook his head no. "You won't catch anyone, adult or child, willing to go inside. I only went in far enough to see which way the underground passage went. I keep my animals far away from any part of the land that seems unstable. With the recent resurgence of the wolves, enough livestock disappears as it is. I can't afford to lose any more than I already do."

"Are you kidding? If I was a kid there'd be no way in hell anyone could have stopped me from exploring this." Secrist pulled his head back out. A boyish grin on his face and loose dirt speckling the top of his head.

The neighbor frowned once more. He seemed ready to drive away but sat stoically in the ATV's seat. "May I ask how much you know of the Chanet family? Of their ties to these lands?"

"Lucas has worked for me for the better part of the year. I feel like I know him pretty well." Stander pulled the keyring he'd shown the farmer earlier. "He must think we are trustworthy as well. Otherwise, I doubt he would have handed over all these keys."

"Of that, I have no doubt." The farmer smiled briefly before stretching out one arm, gesturing across the nearby meadows and rolling hills of green. "The Chanets were Lords of these lands as far as the eye can see or a horse can ride in a day. For generations and generations they ruled. The family was rumored to have ties to Egyptian royalty, the Templar Knights, the Catholic church, Freemasonry, the Illuminati, you name it. But, according to my great-grandfather, much of that was always just jealous rumors and gossip."

"Why is that?" Secrist, done brushing the dirt out of his hair stepped to Stander's side. "What did your great-grandfather think they really were in alliance with?"

The Frenchman shrugged with a slightly bemused smile. "Before their ruin, he said they likely would have founded most of those sects I mentioned, not just belonged as members. The family in league with something far older."

"Before their ruin?" Stander turned and looked at the chateau. "Seems like Lucas is still doing alright for himself."

"All of the family's original property, except the little bit you of land you see here and the forest just beyond, was all sold off long ago. Whatever treasure the Chanets supposedly held apparently exhausted centuries earlier." The neighbor, seemingly embarrassed he'd gotten so wrapped up in his tale, smiled timidly. "Please forgive me if I am speaking out of turn, messieurs. Lucas is the last in what was once a storied legacy. I'm sure if he could, he'd sell off what he owns around here and wash his hands of this whole place. And his ancestry."

"Maybe he is holding onto it for sentimental reasons?" Stander shrugged while Secrist nodded agreeably. "Or, he just hasn't found the right buyer yet."

The man revved his ATV as he shook his head back and forth slowly. "This crumbling chateau and the forest of black that butts up against it will likely never be sold. No one wants these cursed lands. Even if it was given to them. Nobody wants to be responsible for what makes those dark woods home." The farmer made a show out of checking his watch. "If you do decide to explore that tunnel, and I can't condone it much myself, keep your eyes peeled. I'm certain plenty of... of creatures use the various collapses as dens and burrows. It would be easy to surprise something." Nodding once, the local man waved as he rode away.

"Or be surprised." After watching the farmer vanish over a slight knoll, Stander turned to Secrist. "I don't suppose anything he said has changed your mind about trying to see if that is the right tunnel?" Secrist shaking his head as both men began walking back to the chateau. "Yeah, that's what I figured."

"I'm not saying we do anything crazy. Let's just climb down in there and see if it looks promising. If it does, the tunnel is only supposed to be a little more than a mile long. Shouldn't even take us an hour to walk there and back." Secrist smiled reassuringly at his friend. "Now, let's go grab those flashlights we brought with us."

Passing the ramshackle shed and remains of the other collapsed structures, Stander slowed. Seconds later, stopping completely, he looked back toward the thick foliage that rimmed the grounds. He raised his arm and blocked the glare from the sun above with one hand – staring into the nearest thicket of trees. Had he seen a figure observing them from the woods?

"What? Do you see something?" Secrist looked across the windswept weeds, tall grass, and the yellow wild flowers that waved their way. He could see nothing out of the ordinary. "What are you looking for?"

Stander shrugged. "It's likely nothing. I'm probably just being paranoid with everything that has been happening. For a moment I thought I saw someone standing over there. Kind of felt to me like we were being watched while we were talking with our new friend, the ATV rider." Stander shrugged, his steps slowly resuming. Both men retrieving their flashlights from inside the chateau and returning to the collapsed ground.

Stander waved Secrist in first. "After you, you curious motherfucker."

Chapter Eighteen
Germany-18th Century

Francois's favorite steed was already saddled and waiting for him. The dark brown horse nuzzling and leaning into him with pricked ears as he spoke in soft, soothing tones to the animal. The stallion clearly anxious to begin their ride in the crisp morning air. After mounting and adjusting his épée de cour (the gentlemen's sword he wore on social occasions), the doctor was handed his personal flintlock pistol. Both weapons, brought along as much for show as a precaution, safely tucked away before the journey began. Dr. Francois Chanet dedicating his morning to inquiring after the owner of the newly arrived traveling circus. The poles and tents of the upcoming spectacle already being raised at the opposite end of the village.

Starting off at a trot, Francois turned his face to enjoy the warmth of the early spring sunshine. Above him, hardly a cloud in sight. Both rider and horse crossed the rushing river at the end of the House of Chanet's lane before turning toward town. Briefly traveling the main road until Francois suddenly veered off. Cutting across a weedy meadow at a gallop before slowing and guiding his horse into the woods at the opposite end of the field. Following a well-worn game trail into the darkened timber that he knew would cut his ride in almost half. Ducking under branches as the shadowed forest took them in.

It was the day after he'd rescued and taken in the accused human curiosity. The pitiful creature had been blamed for the gruesome death of a villager the day before, but Francois had found the reasoning unsound. Opening up his own home to the alleged murderer in hopes he could rescue the pitiful thing from its tortured existence as a sideshow attraction. The fresh wounds and jagged scars it bore reflecting a lifetime of pain. The pouch of jangling silver coins tied with leather strings at his waist, he hoped, would be enough to buy its freedom. A noble notion some might say. But deep down, Francois knew his actions were not entirely a selfless act.

In exchange for the freedom, he hoped to examine and eventually diagnose what had caused such extreme deformities. His personal interest in medicine demanding he try to understand the affliction. The curiosity driving him with the same ambition that originally spurred him to open his office in town. The emerging science of surgery something he'd become completely enamored with. Though infrequent, the ill and lame of the town gave him opportunities to explore this interest. Learning what hid under the skin, draining abscesses and swellings, extracting tumors and, occasionally, performing various amputations.

Experiment, if you will.

An interest in healing, Francois had been told as a young man, was in his blood. The Chanet family – nobles and owners of these lands going back generations upon generations – had a long history of medicinal studies. Many of his ancestors doubling as not only the law of the land, but also as the only healer of the land. *Unless you count the uneducated barber surgeons and their crude skills,* one of his favorite relatives had once shared with him, *which often leaves the ill even worse off,* she'd finished with a laugh. The bronze-skinned woman, a benefactor of the Chanet family with royal ties supposedly going all the way back to Egypt, had been the real force behind his decision to attend university. Pointing him in the direction of the burgeoning skill of surgery which was only now beginning to gain acceptance in polite French and German society. Prophesying to him about the benefits that would come from the science and encouraging his studies.

For Francois, this favorite relative of his had always been both dark and mysterious. A stunner from a distant branch of the family that lived in far-off, exotic lands. Her infrequent visits to the home as he'd grown some of his favorite memories as a child. Both her accent and dialect strange and unplaceable; her entertaining tales even more obscure. As he got older, though Francois was unsure exactly when or why it had happened, he and the rest of the Chanets began to affectionately refer to her as their aunt.

Aunt Madeleine.

When Francois had once pressed his father about the binds holding her and the Chanets together, he'd confessed to having had some of the same questions growing up. "When I was young like you, I think it must have been either her mother, or maybe her grandmother, that would occasionally travel here and visit. At least they looked the same..." His father had seemed to reflect briefly then, his eyes drifting up in tandem with the downturn of his mouth before continuing.

"Anyway, just like now, the visits were so rare it is hard for me to recall. But, I'll tell you as my father told me. Never doubt she is truly one of us. There is a distant branch of our family tree named Scotia that originally settled these lands. Long, long ago our ancestors came here from what is now Ireland and Scotland by way of Egyptian royalty. Queen Scotia, our family's matriarch, was born to a powerful pharaoh, but she fell in love with an outsider. This forbidden and taboo love angered her father and he banished her from his kingdom. Exiling his daughter and her lover, they fled across the seas. Baring children together and claiming lands in what is now Spain, Scotland, and Ireland. Eventually, the branches of the family tree reached these lands. Where she came from is responsible for all of this." His father had swept an arm before him, gesturing at the castle and countryside around them. "In exchange, we watch over these lands. Protecting an ancient treasure that one day will change the world."

Francois had not seen his Aunt Madeleine for many, many years now. He'd expected she would accept the invitation to his wedding and they would recultivate the relationship between the branches of their family tree. But, with his engagement now called off, he wasn't sure when or if she'd visit again anytime soon.

Though he loathed to admit it, he had hoped the proposed wedding and expected tributes from the joyous occasion would refill his coffers. The Chanet family no longer as prosperous as they'd once been. The downturn in fortunes robbing Francois of the untroubled future his ancestors had all enjoyed. The family, in recent times, forced to sell much of the land they'd owned just to keep up appearances. Both he, and his father before him, offering parcels and plots to those wanting to grow their own businesses and the nearby village. The town elders grateful for what they assumed was generosity. Many were shocked Francois was allowing the town to encroach so close to the House of Chanet. None aware how near financially ruinous he'd become. A family scandal involving a long-dead ancestor nearly destroying their good name and, for a time, turning many in the area against them. Several families that had diligently worked their lands for generations abandoning the farmsteads and turning once profitable fields into unwanted meadows of weeds. The wooded timber eventually overtaking and claiming the loss as its own.

Francois, frowning, tugged on the leather reins he held. Something was rotting nearby. The horse, likely spooked by the smell of death in the air, neighed loudly once before stopping. Tracking the rancid odor, Francois guided the horse off the mud-packed trail and led him down into a gulley. A trickling stream of crystal-clear water meandering between banks of wet sand and gravel. Dismounting, Francois secured his horse to a nearby tree and pulled his loaded musket. Carrying the firearm loosely at his side, he jumped to the opposite bank by navigating across several large stones clustered close together in the water. Looking down at the trail that caught his eye, he froze before dropping to one knee.

The path had been easy enough to spot from the other side of the river. A series of tracks that came out of the woods and stopped at the water's edge. A little farther down the bank they seemed to resume as if whatever made them had briefly waded into the stream. There was nothing unusual about the trail, only the tracks. The pawprints were undoubtably wolf: four symmetrical clawed toes with a single lobe on the back of the pad. Francois had hunted enough over the years to easily identify the print. But these tracks were far, far larger than any he'd previously seen. Regaining his feet, he cast a nervous glance down each side of the untroubled water. The awful smell that first drew him wafting somewhere nearby. Looking back at the ground, Francois pressed his own boot into the soft mud beside the wolf track. His footprint dwarfed by the massive pawprint.

Intrigued, Francois followed the tracks that emerged out of the water a little farther downstream. Wondering if he might be able to catch a glimpse of whatever had made them. But, as the sandy mud gave way to higher and firmer ground, the prints faded to nothing. Looking farther up the bank, where the tracks had seemed to be heading, Francois found a toppled tree of enormous size. A busy mass of tangled roots overhanging the crater-like cavity its fall had left behind. Drawing his sword, his flintlock pistol already pointing ahead of him, Francois boldly advanced upon the sheltered depression. With every footfall, the deepening stench of death tried unsuccessfully to hold him at bay.

Peeking over the rim and looking down into the earthen hole, the vile odor wafting up caused his eyes to burn and water. He'd found a killing pit. A bone pile so varied that Francois could only guess what the unfortunate quarry within had once been. Feeling fortunate that whatever used this hidden spot to ambush and consume its prey was gone, Francois turned and beat a hasty retreat. Recrossing the stream and unhitching his horse before reclaiming their spot along the game trail. Continuing through the woods toward the newly arrived circus.

Zorrie felt the familiar, dull throb beginning to build at her temples. Her spells often preceded by a seemingly ordinary headache. She'd been separated from Jean-Baptiste for much of the afternoon. Her simple-minded friend accompanying some of the others crowding the market square. With the day nearing its end, occasionally the street peddlers would leave behind scraps of near-spoiled food they knew could no longer be sold. For those still in search of work, the unwanted bits could be collected and cobbled together into a stew of sorts. The weak broth it produced shared among those unable to find food of their own.

Alone, Zorrie tried to think of a safe place she could shelter and hide. If this truly was the beginning of one of her spells, wherever she ended up would likely double as her bed for the night. With the skies above beginning to darken with ominous clouds, it seemed certain rain would soon present another obstacle to deal with. Hoping to reach her new friends before either storm arrived, the one in her mind or from the troubled skies above, Zorrie began to make her way toward the center of town. Ducking down shadowed alleys and hurrying along cobblestoned streets. But before Zorrie made it even halfway to her destination, the sky above opened up. A jagged streak of lightning crackling in the air just before a thundering boom announced the downpour. Startled by the sudden deluge, she quickly ducked inside an arched doorway.

Hoping the burst of rain would be short-lived, Zorrie leaned against the wood at her back. The doorway just big enough to keep her sheltered and dry. She waited until the streets emptied before beginning to dry herself. Bunching her sleeves and skirt together in places so she could squeeze out the excess water. The few villagers still hurrying from the spring shower not noticing the long lines of scars that ran up and down her arms and legs as she briefly bared them. Finishing, Zorrie looked to the sky above in hopes she'd find the clouds thinning. Instead, her eye catches movement across the street. A shadowed figure in a second floor window facing her. The glint of metal flashing in one hand.

Zorrie pretended not to notice. Keeping her face neutral as she scrutinized the sky above without actually seeing a thing. Her mind parceling out the options. If she continued on her way, the town square was only a couple streets away. Jean-Baptiste and the safe refuge of the others, if they hadn't already run for cover themselves, could be that close. But, noting the town square was likely visible from the window with the watcher, if she found herself alone, there would be no place for her to go. Or hide if, as suspected, she became incapacitated by another spell.

Zorrie shuddered. The thought of being paralyzed and at the killer's mercy terrified her. Without her friend's vigilant protection, what chance would she have? She stole a quick peak up at the window across from her. Was the figure looking down at her? Moments later, the window brightened from the inside. Her watcher vanishing.

Zorrie gasped! Now would be the best chance to escape unseen!

Bypassing a reunion with Jean-Baptiste and their friends, Zorrie bolted the opposite way. A desperate gamble she hoped would buy her enough time to find someplace new to hide. If the watcher from the window had been following her as suspected, she had to find a safe place no one would expect.

Zorrie splashed across mudpuddles full of tiny rings, the rain still coming down but slowing to a sprinkle. She chanced a glance behind her, but the curvature of the lane she ran limited her view. As she crossed several streets and alleys, her head spun in every direction. Pounding footsteps seemed to echo down each. Her desperation now pairing with panic as she hurried to find a safe place to hide. The last of the village's streets merging into the single road that snaked its way outside of town.

Inside her head, the all-consuming heat was building. Zorrie could feel her ability to reason slowly dissipating like steam escaping the kettle. The spell brewing within raging like hellfire and slowly overwhelming her. The curse or disease, whatever one had faith in, pushing Zorrie aside to take possession. Slipping inside her like a well-worn shoe. Trampling her will under an onslaught of fiery pain. Above her head, lightning streaked across the sky. The emerging wind pushing her faltering step as she stumbled beyond the outskirts of the village. Disoriented, she was past the cemetery before realizing the road she walked would lead her nowhere safe. Just ahead, a bridge spanning a swelling river. Beyond that, only deep forest and the House of Chanet.

With a screaming head of fire, Zorrie lunged toward the wooden overpass. Though her mind was scrambled, she still recognized how exposed she was on the open road if her stalker came this way. Understanding that if she was able to make it under the bridge unseen, she could safely hide there and wait out the spell ravaging and pulling apart her mind.

Nearly blind from the pain, her only rational thought, though already no longer sure why, was to hide. An instinctual feeling of danger propelling her forward as she staggered to the river's edge. Sliding on her backside down the muddy bank, unaware of the ball of mating snakes writhing below until her feet touched the sloping ground. Zorrie choking back a scream as she watched the squirming mass of desperate males between her shoes overwhelm the female buried within. The serpents untroubled by her arrival, each driven to ensure the survival of their own.

Scrambling for the protection offered by the bridge, she dove headfirst into the shadowed black. Crawling blindly over slimy sticks and slippery stones. The rank odor of rotting marine life all but overpowering as she pulled herself along the soggy ground. Her unexpected intrusion startling long-dormant insects and resurrecting hidden spiders as their webs were ripped asunder by the clumsy passing. Zorrie flattening herself and squeezing deeper and deeper under the wooden bridge until finding a slightly elevated dry spot. Collapsing as her eyes rolled up in her head and her body began to seize.

Somewhere nearby – as the agony splitting her head finally dissolved into nothing – a desperate shriek was drowned in rolling thunder. But Zorrie was already lost in her affliction and unable to feel, hear, or see. Her body twisting, contorting, and shaking under the bridge. When the second scream came moments later, the one choked off immediately, she never heard it.

The spell leaving Zorrie dead to the world around her.

Chapter Nineteen
France-Modern Day

"Here goes nothing." Secrist, flashlight in hand, crawled through the split in the earth. Vanishing into the black chasm the local farmer had shown them earlier that morning. Scuttling down the dirt collapse that had buried the opposite end of the tunnel in tons of debris. The cave-in cutting off the clandestine passageway before it reached the Chateau Chanet. "That was actually easier than I thought it would be." His voice echoing and reassuring.

Stander didn't immediately respond. His attention drawn to a spooked fawn hurtling through the nearby weeds. Behind it, back where the deer had erupted out of the timber, several thin branches slowly stilled. Stander strained to see into the dark woods as he replied. "How tight of a fit is it in there?" Leery, but spying nothing of note, he soon squatted beside the earthen gash and played his light around the rim of the opening. "If we have to crawl, you can count me the fuck out."

"Relax," came the excited answer from below. "Once you slide down, the whole thing opens right up. The tunnel ahead looks completely free and clear. Come on." Sighing, Stander forced his way inside. Contorting his wide shoulders to make the fit and joining Secrist inside the underground passage.

Stander spoke in a hushed tone as he surveyed the manmade channel. The collapsed rubble at their backs as their flashlights lit the underground tunnel stretching out before them. "I don't know if I can do this, Tommy." Their lights fading at the first curve of the blackened passageway. Nothing visible beyond the first twenty feet or so. "Fuck me…"

"Oh, come on, Russ. I don't think we have anything to worry about. This all looks really solid to me. And from what that farmer told us, no one around here explores these old shafts and underground passageways anymore. They are all abandoned and forgotten. Besides, nothing bigger than that crack we just came down can get in here anyway." Secrist played his light around them. Reaching out and touching the chipped walls of the tunnel.

"We got in here," Stander mumbled. His light pointed straight ahead of them. The uniformity of the carved passage numbing. A dank, wet smell permeating the entire underground channel. Stander felt the rise and march of goosepimples conquering the bare skin of both arms. It took all of his willpower to remain rooted. "I don't know if I can do this," he repeated.

"You can go back up to the surface if you want. I understand." Secrist knew Stander, as well as Chris and Lucas, had all nearly lost their lives in the recent quarry cave-in. Portions of the unstable ground near where the monolith was discovered collapsing and killing several workers. That accident, coupled with similar experiences in Stander's past, undoubtedly messing with his head. "But, I told you we would climb back out at the first sign of danger. So far, this underground passage looks solid as a rock." Secrist rubbed his hand along the tunnel's walls. "Hell, this is rock I'm pretty sure… Anyway, I'm not dumb enough to try and walk this alone. If you say no, we can forget this side and try to find the other end of it in one of those towns. Maybe we'll get lucky."

Stander sighed. "Well, I guess we are down here now." He stepped to Secrist's side, "Lead the way, Tommy. I'll do my best to keep from shitting my pants." He gave Secrist a wry smile as he gestured for him to go first. Both men walking single file down the arch-shaped cavern.

The ground was solid under their feet. A gentle breeze whistling from an unseen opening somewhere ahead of them helping to keep the air fresh. The ceiling, mere inches above their heads, and the walls at their shoulders, were all uniformly shaped. The dimples from thousands of chisel and hammer falls scarring them both. Clusters of free-falling rocks that had dropped to the floor causing the men to weave and hurdle the obstacles periodically. Their footfalls in the soft gravel and dirt the only audible sound. The constant bend of the channel keeping their sight limited to less than thirty yards ahead of them. A halo of light around the duo, behind them, the constant advance of the darkness their flashlights left behind.

"Wait a minute," Stander, breaking the silence of the somber walk. "We are right on the border of France and Germany, right?" Ahead of him, Secrist glanced back long enough to shake his head yes. "Didn't your grandfather write that this tunnel connected France and Germany? That the chateau where we just spent the night was on the French side, and that this tenant housing or apartment building you're hoping to find was on the German side, right?"

"Yeah, that's true." Secrist answered without turning, his eyes trained on the path ahead of him. "But the border of Germany and France has fluctuated big-time in this area over the years. Except for the Rhine River, which serves as kind of a natural border, much of this land was pretty much always under contention. Loads of treaties across centuries kept things in flux. In fact, unless I'm mistaken, the current border wasn't officially established until well after the Second World War ended. So, don't sweat it, Russ," Secrist turned slightly and gestured around him to include the entirety of the underground passage. "This would all be closed off if the tunnel actually undercut the current border. I bet we'll come out the other side like five feet from the actual German border." He looked back and gave Stander a quick smile. "Or something equally ridiculous and..."

"What was that?" Stander stopped and turned completely around. The flickering of his flashlight illuminating the path they'd just walked. "Did you just hear something?" Both men stood still and silent for a long minute. When whatever Stander heard wasn't repeated, they began to move forward once again. Walking in silence until they both started to relax once more – conversation resuming.

"I know you have hiked similar underground passageways in the past," began Secrist. His voice sharp in the oppressive silence they waded through. "But I am amazed at how straight and perfect this tunnel is. How long ago do you think this was done? Is this the same style of construction you've seen around the quarry and the monolith Lucas is uncovering?"

"Lucas could tell you for certain, but it sure looks the same to me. And Lucas says the catacombs surrounding both of those has to be more than 10,000 years old. All of this," Stander waved his arms to include the entirety of the passage, "would have been done with pickaxes."

"That job must have sucked. Can you imagine the amount of..." Secrist stopped talking and walking briefly before continuing. "Is that a skeleton up ahead?"

Both men circled the fleshless bones. Whatever died had remained untouched. Each bone laid out the same way they would have been in life. The small mammal, likely a coyote, wolf, or dog, had seemed to collapse and expire in that very spot.

"Looks like it. The poor thing must have gotten trapped down here." Stander looked across at Secrist. "Great," he added sarcastically. "Maybe we should take the hint."

"I don't know. I kind of think this is a good sign." In response, Stander simply frowned and shook his head. "Seriously," Secrist continued. "Think about it. No signs of predation. I bet it wandered all alone down here in the dark. Pacing these tunnels until it finally keeled over and died. Probably of starvation."

"Aw, geez. What a terrifying way to go. Thanks for that image, Tommy." Stander shuddered as he nudged the tip of the articulated tail with one foot. "But, I suppose you are right. If something wandered this way it would at least have upset these bones. Maybe we really are the first to walk these tunnels in a really long time." After a few moments, both men continued moving forward. Their lights bobbing with each step, the cool air comfortable as the floor of the tunnel began a gradual decline. The sound of unseen dripping water keeping time with their footfalls.

The men walked in silence for several more minutes. More piles of fallen dirt and loose stones that they easily navigated past. The tunnel itself remarkably stable and remaining largely intact the farther down the passage they crept. A blueish grey clay appearing in places along the walls and ceiling as if later applied to stop cracking and water leaks. Secrist, still in the lead, held up a hand and stopped. Silently directing Stander with the point of his finger. Some ten yards ahead of them, a shadowed opening. The tunnel, perhaps, splitting into two.

"What do you think?" Stander shrugged at the question and waved Secrist forward. Both soon peering into the void. "Empty," commented Secrist as he pulled his light from the shallow opening. The hole simply a smallish room with nothing inside. Stander sighed with relief until he saw similar gaps in the tunnel walls just ahead of them. The rock hallway they walked down suddenly forcing them to pass multiple yawning openings of pitch black. Creeping forward, they peered inside each as they passed.

"What the fuck?" Stander could think of nothing else to say as their lights illuminated the toys spread across the ground. The dirt floor of the third room littered with the broken pieces of two rotting dolls. One looked as if it had been disemboweled, the straw stuffing spilling out of its chest. The other doll stared at them from one painted eye. The porcelain atop the mostly cloth effigy broken into shards. Both of the toys were incalculably old and clearly handmade. Shaking their heads in silence, Stander and Secrist turned from the room. Continuing past more doorways of black with interiors so small they were no bigger than closets or a cubby. Neither of them able to walk by without glancing inside each one.

Most were empty. The ones that weren't, both men wished they were.

The random carcasses they came across weren't yet completely fleshless, but the dried husks were more bones than meat. Many appeared to be twisted versions of recognizable animals. Yet neither man could clearly identify the creatures they found. Badly misshapen heads connected to contorted spines. Wingless bats mixed with legless sheep. Goats with horns protruding from all sides, and un-shelled turtles with stilt-like legs. Speechless, each hollow compartment a horror show onto itself, Stander and Secrist stoically peered in each of the first several chambers they came to. Stopping only when they began to discover the unsuccessful births. Hollows of tortured mothers split wide by the unsuccessful delivery of their offspring. Many, many left bloated by their breeched babies. Still birthed litters of unrecognizable masses of tiny claws and barbed canines.

"Are those clothes?" Secrist paused before taking two steps back and reshining his light inside one of the chambers they passed. A frayed cord dividing the room, pieces of cloth hanging down. Reaching out to touch them, the cord suddenly gave and they fell to the dirt floor. Two pairs of what looked like homemade pants landing in the dust. "What the hell?"

"Tommy. Come here." Stander waved Secrist over to the next room. A battered suitcase of stained and cracking leather rotting atop a squarish boulder. "I know that is really, really old. But I'm not liking us finding manmade stuff down in these 'long-forgotten' underground passageways." Stander made quotation marks in the air when he'd said *long-forgotten*. "What do you say we turn around?" Secrist looked as if he was about to object when they both detected a strange noise.

Click-clack.

Behind them, back down the long passage they had just walked, something stirred and scraped. The sound like rock skidding across stone. With troubled eyes on each other, both men strained to hear more. Moments later, the noise was duplicated.

Click-clack.

Stepping back into the tunnel, Secrist shining his light back the way they'd come. Shadows jumping at the hurried wave of the flashlight. Once more, the sound came.

Click-clack.

"For fucks sake, Tommy. This whole underground wonderland is starting to freak me out! I vote we forget about this tunnel and head back up. We can go into those towns and see if we can't find the building you're hunting. I'm feeling a little bit claustrophobic and caged down here." Stander cast a glance ahead of them. The tunnel continuing beyond the reach of his light. Behind them, where Secrist still shined his flashlight and keenly peered, more shadows flowed along the walls.

"No argument here. But," Secrist turned and locked eyes with Stander, "which way? You really want to backtrack and find out what's making those noises?"

"Fuck no! And I also don't want to walk past all those creepy fucking animal corpses ever again either." Stander turned and began walking the same way they had been. His stride longer and his pace quickened. "You can follow me this time, Tommy. I'm hauling ass out of this fucking hellhole." On his heels, Secrist trailed close behind. Periodically turning to ensure the passage behind them remained empty. The small cavities they'd encountered earlier tapering off and ending. The chiseled walls on both sides continuing uninterrupted.

Ten uneventful minutes later, Stander abruptly switched his flashlight off. Behind him, Secrist hissed out his concern. "What are you doing?" Swinging his light forward, he peered over Stander's shoulder. "Is someone up there?"

"No. But I see light up ahead." Stander turned with a grin as he reengaged his battery powered torch. Unmistakable relief radiating from his eyes. "I hope that means we are almost out of here!" Both men hurrying towards the glimmer.

"No way! You gotta be fucking kidding me!" Secrist started to question Stander's outburst, but saw he had no need. Ahead of them a barricade of barred metal. A thick padlock shining under the beam of Stander's flashlight. "I can't believe it," he muttered.

The door of bars was made of thick, heavy, aged iron. As both men reached the barrier, they pulled, pushed, and shook the barely rattling door. The keyed lock, though discolored by the passage of time, held firm. Looking beyond the obstruction, more of the light they'd seen streamed across the floor and walls of the passageway. Sunlight and fresh air just beyond their reach.

"I guess we should have figured this end might be locked. If this is the same subterranean channel my grandfather described seeing, we should be directly below the town." Secrist pointed to where the light originated. "That might lead right up to the building I'm hunting."

"Wonderful. But, without a key, we won't be able to..." Stander suddenly grew silent. He reached into the pocket of his jeans and pulled out the keyring Lucas had given him. Holding it up, he said, "You don't suppose one of these might work, do you?"

"Worth a shot. Unless you're eager to find out what followed us down here?" Secrist tossed a thumb over one shoulder. "Better make it quick, Russ."

The handful of keys on the ring were thumbed one by one. Most were clearly much newer and smaller, but there were several candidates. One by one, Stander fit them into the padlock. Though the first one failed to engage, the next one turned easily. The massive lock popping free as if oiled just the day before. Both men clamoring to open and close the barred iron gate behind them. Snapping the metal padlock back in place and turning, Stander and Secrist walked toward the light.

Chapter Twenty
Germany-18th Century

Zorrie woke with a mouthful of coppery gore. Though she couldn't see it, a crimson tide had overrun her chin before pooling and congealing at her neck. Sightless and cold, the smell of wet earth filling each nostril, she was certain death had finally caught back up with her. The entirety of her body blanketed in an exhausting discomfort, Zorrie's first thoughts were of eternity. Had she been buried? Was the mud she lay in the grave of her eternal sleep?

Slowly, her senses began to awaken. The most acute was a throbbing pulse that ran along one side of her jaw. Wave after wave of unrelenting pain. She fought back nausea as she shifted her head to the right. Spitting out the thick blood gathered before probing the inside of her mouth with a tentative tongue. Gently caressing the splintered edge of one tooth before it ignited a fiery pain that caused her to freeze in agony. She'd shattered a tooth during the spell.

Bone in the blood.

Dully, Zorrie wondered if the excruciating pain in her mouth had been what woke her. All of her reasoning still dimmed by this latest episode, she tried to recall what had happened. She remembered the beginnings of the headache, how she'd ran and searched for a safe place to hide until it passed. Jean had been off with the others when the spell had come; her friend nowhere to be found and unable to watch over her. Something chasing her as she'd fled. How she'd ran until seeing the bridge. Pulling herself underneath it and hiding among the waterlogged branches and river debris.

She'd heard a scream, hadn't she?

Zorrie struggled to make sense of the distorted images and scrambled memories left in the wake of her latest episode. She also felt certain something had been watching her again as she'd slept. A thing with piercing green eyes and a mouth of barbed red scrabbling up the riverbank on its belly. Creeping closer until... until... Zorrie cursed the fuzzy image in her mind. Had it even been real, or just her imagination? A trick played by her tortured mind? Merely a dream?

Slowly, as Zorrie began to claw her way back into consciousness, she became aware the day had dissolved into nighttime. Her unfocused gaze falling upon the water serenely running past the shoreline closest to her. The beams of the full moon above reflecting off the shimmering waves. The sound of the tumbling water calm and relaxing as a chorus of nearby frogs serenaded her awakening. All around her, the luminescence above created long shadows that hid much of the surrounding forest in black.

As Zorrie began to push herself from the ground, she heard something *plop* into the river. The sound eventually drawing her eye to an ever-expanding ring of water. A fish jumping for a meal? A turtle abandoning a log? She gave it little thought until the *plop* came a second time. Curiosity sharpening her focus, her eyes quickly sought out the disturbed water. The undulating rings lapping against something pale bobbing near the surface of the river.

Zorrie strained to see the shapeless mass as it tumbled closer to her hiding place under the bridge. Though floating leisurely down the waterway, it was big enough that it seemed to catch the bottom of the river at times. Rolling and sinking briefly before suddenly breaching the surface again as it neared. Spinning as it popped up, the brief flash of a deathly white human face framed by long hair left Zorrie gasping. Though it quickly resubmerged, she recognized the victim from the village. It was the breastfeeding mother. The nursing wife of the migrant worker who'd shared what he knew of the recent murders with her and Jean just days before.

She stifled the moan that partially escaped her quivering lips. Afraid to let it go completely lest the screams bubbling up inside her might all spill out. Another murder! There could no longer be any question death was truly haunting the community. Had she not run, the body floating down river could have been her own! Instantly worried for the others, especially Jean, she began to make her way out from under the bridge that hid her. Determined to report what she'd seen in hopes the village's nightmare could be ended.

Thud!

Zorrie froze. Something, most likely a rock, had hit the floating corpse. The blow slightly altering the trajectory of the body at the water's surface. The sudden change exposing the hidden ruin at the neck, everything below her chin savaged and ripped open. The sightless eyes accusatory as they stared at the shoreline under the bridge.

Zorrie crammed both hands in her mouth to silence her scream – eyes wide in fright. Directly above her head, a whispered chuckle followed by heavy steps that echoed across the water. The footfalls slowly crossing the bridge. Zorrie heard a brief grunt before something once again splashed in the water beside the floating dead. Moments later, the methodical footsteps continued. Though she could see nothing from her hiding spot under the wooden bridge, her eyes followed each creak of wood. The hollow-sounding and unhurried footfalls fading as they crossed over to the opposite side of the bridge. Ending as whomever made them stepped from the wood of the river-spanning arch back down to the dirt. The road it walked continuing on through the forest. Just ahead, a lane splitting off that led up to the House of Chanet.

For long moments, Zorrie didn't move. Barely breathing for fear she'd be heard. But, as the river rolled past and the frogs began singing once more, she began to curse her cowardice. Why hadn't she tried to sneak a peek? Clearly, whomever so casually strode across the bridge and tossed rocks at the latest murder victim was the same fiend who had killed the young mother. The same murderer that stalked the village. Stalked her!

Her head clearing, the recent effects of her latest spell fading, Zorrie wiggled free from her hiding place. Discreetly peering over the edge of the bridge and carefully scrutinizing the road ahead. Empty. Behind her, the few feeble lights of the village helped embolden her. If she could just catch a glimpse of the killer, that was all it would take. The murderer couldn't be very far ahead of her. She could follow behind and then run all the way back to town and report everything she'd seen.

Ducking into the thick foliage that grew along both sides, Zorrie began to follow the road. Careful to stay hidden, she trailed after the killer as silently as possible. An owl helping cover her stumbles with repeated hoots and calls. Almost instantly, her long skirt and shoes were soaked by the swaying grass she trod upon. The earlier shower leaving the weeds at her thighs and the branches at her head dripping with rainwater. The combination of the two, though chilly in the dead of night, helping to cleanse the worst of foul-smelling river muck she'd slept in.

The light of the partially clouded moon revealed the fresh tracks she followed. The footprints in the mud of the road easy to spot from her hidden pathway. What made them remaining somewhere ahead of her and out of sight. Peering through the trees, Zorrie froze when several twinkling lights suddenly appeared. Quickly ducking down, she trembled silently in the tall grass for what felt like an eternity until realizing the lights were unmoving. Creeping closer yet, she exhaled loudly as the outline of the House of Chanet came into her view. Windows uncluttered by curtains letting the lamps within be seen. Obviously, the lights she'd seen from afar.

As Zorrie admired the tall and ornate structure, by far the grandest home in the village, a lone figure appeared near the lane leading up to the house. Unwittingly, she caught and held the breath she drew in.

Her quarry!

Thin and gangly, what she'd followed was dressed all in black. The shine off its hairless head a twin to the obscured moon above. The murderer seeming to effortlessly glide up the lane until abruptly changing course. Veering from the path, it cut unhurried across both lawn and garden. Trekking to one side of the huge manor, away from any entrances. Though in the darkness and from that far away it was likely an illusion, whom she watched seemed to vanish.

The silhouetted figure dissolving into darkness. No opened door nor lit window appearing. Almost as if sinking into the earth itself.

Sure she'd tracked the murderer, Zorrie turned back. Fearfully picking her way along the hidden trail until reaching the bridge once more. Crossing back over the running water and making her way stealthily back into the village to look for her friends. Moving among the places she knew them to haunt.

Francois guided his horse off the winding game trail. Emerging from the woods just beyond the village and following an overgrown path choked with wispy weeds. The rutted wagon tracks at either side of the lane the only evidence of its recent use.

As he spurred the horse up a grassy knoll, the tops of several sagging tents came into view. A steady and rhythmic clanking filling his ear as the spikes that held them aloft were driven into the ground. Cresting the rise, the breeze greeting both rider and horse turned foul. Below them, a line of wagons bearing cages filled with filthy creatures panting listlessly in the sun. Bored monkeys crowding into a sliver of shade, two pacing ostriches with endlessly bobbing heads, and several big cats unmoving on the floor of their enclosures. Just behind the cages, teams of horses, donkeys, and camels with their backsides caked in excrement were tethered to nearby trees. As Francois drew closer, a single elephant with haunted eyes tracked his approach. Black clouds of flies hovering above all the animal's heads as the nearby workers prepared for the upcoming spectacle. Men sweating under the bright sky as they positioned and gave rise to the coming attractions.

After dismounting and hitching his horse, Francois strode into the middle of the bustling workers. Thanking the men who pointed out the owner of the traveling circus and gradually making his way over to him. Natural curiosity slowing his feet as he passed several weathered and moth-eaten shelters. Discreetly peering inside the frayed flaps but finding all but one still unoccupied. The very last shelter housing an ancient looking woman clothed in dark green and crowned by a long scarf of red that covered her hair and ears. A wooden sign – lying in the grass and waiting to be hung – proudly proclaiming the occupant to be the fortune teller Madame de Warens.

Stoic and unmoving, only her eyes followed his path. The aged lines that crisscrossed her face untroubled by his return stare. She called out to him in a raspy voice, beckoning him inside and promising to reveal all for a few coins. Unsure what tempted him, Francois smiled politely as he stepped through the opening. Inside the tent, the small table she sat at was hidden under brightly colored cloth covered in, he assumed, supposed magical symbols. Beside her, across from the empty chair he faced, stood a wheeled cart with a number of small compartments. Each opening closed and hiding whatever was held within.

"Do you wish a reading?" The wizened eyes seemed to twinkle as Francois cast a dubious glance at the stack of cards she hovered over.

"I'm afraid I don't really have much faith in fortune tellers, Madame de Warens." The inside of the enclosure was unadorned, the only furniture the table, chairs, and wheeled cabinet beside her. "And I've never had much luck at card games."

"I do not read cards. These," she tapped the top of the deck, "are merely a cure for my boredom. A game I can play alone to entertain myself."

Nodding agreeably, Francois sat in the chair opposite the fortune teller. The fee he paid quickly squirreled away by the old woman as she began to pepper him with a series of seemingly ordinary and benign questions. His age, if he was married, the year he was born, the age of his mother when she'd had him, if he had children, and so forth. With each answer, the strange seer pulled pinches of sage, dried tobacco, and various herbs from out of the strange cabinet beside her. Carefully selecting, based on his replies, each ingredient. When her inquiries were completed, the nips of the various dried plants she'd collected were spread upon hemp paper and expertly rolled together. Finishing, she lit one end of the short and stubby handmade cigar. Taking several generous puffs for herself before handing it over to Francois. Gesturing he should continue to smoke, she placed a small ceramic plate in front of him.

"Think only of what troubles you as the smoke fills you. The questions you wish answered." The fortune teller pointed to the plate. "I will read the ashes that fall."

Francois nodded. Though he thought the concept utterly ridiculous, he did his best to follow her instruction. The smoking pleasant and surprisingly tasty. In short order he finished the fortune teller's cigar, a few small piles of grey ash scattered across the dish. He looked expectantly at the strange old woman as she spread the soot several ways with one finger for long moments before abruptly stopping and licking it clean.

"See anything in my future? I mean, besides a cough and sore throat." Francois grinned from the chair he sat in. "Maybe a new woman on the horizon?"

"I see only reflections in your smoke." She looked up at him, her expression more confusion than answer. "Smoke and... smoke and mirrors in your life." The inflection in her raspy voice making the statement sound like a question. "Apologies, sir. It is not often I find one with their fate so obscured. There seems to be a dark shroud I am unable to see past." She pulled back out the coins Francois had paid her with, laying them flat upon the table.

Francois thanked Madame de Warens, waving away the coins she'd offered to return before exiting her tent. Whatever his destiny was to be, still unknown. As his eyes slowly adjusted to the bright sun, he searched once more for the man he'd originally traveled to see. Spying the circus owner directing a team of bleary-eyed men sporting shadows of day-old growth. Several still smeared in fading masks of smiling greasepaint. The hopeful facades of forced grins running down their faces in streaks as they labored to hoist a net of rope under the swaying swings of a highwire trapeze act.

After introducing himself, Francois was invited to sit at an outdoor table shaded by a towering tree. His host, the owner of the traveling circus he'd come to see, pulling out two glasses and pouring drinks from a bottle filled with a murky liquid. The man, his white shirt damp and yellowing at each armpit, gulped down half his drink in one swallow. After loudly belching, he dragged a browning sleeve across his mouth. A wide smile that didn't touch his eyes emerging from under the cloth.

"So Monsieur," he began, "what pleasures you? I have many attractions, as you can see." Proudly, the unshaven man who smelled of old sweat and stale urine gestured at the cluster of half-raised tents and sagging wood wagons. Most with once-hopeful signs of faded colors and dubious promises. "But, I also have many other attractive rides for men who clamor for more, shall we say, clandestine encounters. Do you wish to see the women that can either be ridden or ride you for a small fee?" The man drained the remainder of his glass.

"No, no, nothing of the sort. But, thank you. I have come to inquire after another. The one taken from here yesterday. After the...uh... incident." Francois reached for his drink, forcing down a small swallow before turning to cough. His throat burning from the fermented apple cider.

"Oh, Monsieur! A terrible thing!" The circus owner shook his head back and forth slowly. "It is not uncommon for excited boys and young men to take an interest in our travels. Some out of curiosity while others press for work. How can we be blamed for this?"

Francois's eyes narrowed. "The young man's body was brought to me. Curiosity didn't plant all those holes in his head. He was most viciously murdered! My family keeps the peace and protects these lands. One of your own was implicated but I am not easily swayed without justification. If you wish for the return of your... your charge, you must show me where this happened. Explain to me how this..."

"Please, Monsieur!" The owner stood with arms raised in the air. "We have been invited to your town and came when asked. Yet, it is the guests your village wishes to blame?" Indignant, he turned and waved Francois after him. "Gypsies, tramps, and thieves. We hear it from the people of every town. Share..." Francois trailed behind the grumbling man, his words becoming unintelligible. Moments later, stopping suddenly beside a cage built upon a wagon. The line of carts it sat among set aside from the other tents and a mere twenty paces from the edge of the forest.

"See?" Reaching up, he shook the locked door of the wagon cage. "Locked as always."

"Why are you showing me this? What animal do you keep here?" Francois, confused, pointed to the straw laden enclosure. One corner of the filthy cage was hidden from view. A cheap dressing screen providing the barest of privacy. Two overturned wooden buckets lying on the deeply stained floorboards. Walking to the front, Francois read the sign attached at the top. The first line written in large, bright lettering easily read from a distance. The second line, directly beneath in much, much smaller script, obviously meant to demean the interred:

Eve – The first woman ever

that no man would touch!

"This is Eve's. Where she stayed until the men of your village took her." Not waiting for a response, he spun on his heel and pushed his way into the nearby woods. Dumbly, Francois followed. His head buzzing with the revelations. His anger building at the cruel treatment. Ten steps inside the foliage, the ground sloped down into a shallow gully. In the middle of the depression, leaves shiny with dried blood. "Here is where I found the body." He turned a solemn eye toward Francois. "I stepped in here to relieve myself."

"Why did... who...?" Anticipating the question, the carnival owner retraced their steps until they both stood before the locked cage once more.

"The closest witness to what happened to that young man was Eve. Even though she was locked inside, the men we notified from town took her away. Brought her to you, it seems."

"Eve? You keep calling her Eve. Is that her... I was unaware she, that it was a she?" Francois was infuriated. Had this man kept a woman as an animal? Had his fellow villagers done so little simply because of how she looked? Had the world gone mad?

"I can assure you, though no man would ever guess, what I say is true." The owner pulled out a bottle of brownish liquid from one pocket of his pants and took a swig. "Hardly even human, if you ask me."

"I cannot allow her to be returned." Francois yanked the leather pouch tied at his waist, tossing the bag of silver coins and watching, with some satisfaction, the disgusting man drop to his knees as they spilled along the ground. "Take this for any inconvenience and loss of revenue this may cause your... business. Do not call after or try to claim her ever again as yours. Is that understood?" Without waiting for a reply, Francois left the owner digging in the dirt for the silver coins.

Blood money.

Chapter Twenty-One
France-Modern Day

AFTER UNLOCKING AND PASSING through the barred gate, Stander and Secrist had to turn sideways to squeeze through the last bit of the underground tunnel. Their backs scraping against the chipped stone walls as they navigated the remainder of the tight and twisty carved crevasse. Both men chasing after the light ahead.

When they were finally free of the constrictive channel, the two men found themselves in a tightly quartered cavity of natural rock. All around them, a mishmash of discarded tools and construction signage of varying sizes. Red-bordered triangles with shoveling stick figures and stacks of barricade beacons with unlit yellow lights atop each. Alongside the weathered signs, five or six empty and unused trash barrels. Just beyond the piles of maintenance equipment, a single staircase atop a cracked and discolored concrete slab. At the top of the steps, a series of metal rungs bolted into the wall like a ladder found in a chlorinated pool. Above them, the light of the outside sun streamed through an unsettled manhole cover. The sunshine beckoning them both back to the surface.

"That's our exit," said a relieved Stander as he made a beeline straight for the staircase. "God knows I could use some fresh fucking air, right about now."

"Wait a minute," Secrist was studying some of the signs as they walked past them. "These are all..." But Stander was already balancing himself on the rungs and muscling the heavy lid. Pushing aside the metal far enough to pull himself through the opening. Turning, he hollered for Secrist and helped him through the hole. Partially sliding the manhole cover back in place without letting it close completely once they were both on the surface.

Standing, he turned to speak with Secrist but found him turned the opposite way. His eyes looking up and his jaw hanging down. A tall apartment building capturing all of his attention. "I kind of don't believe it," all he said.

"Is that what you were hoping to find? Some shitty apartments?" Stander asked the questions as he gradually took in their surroundings. They had surfaced in an alley of what appeared to be a recently revitalized downtown area of a small village. Many of the buildings sporting hopeful signs of commerce. To their right, a small café awash in greenery and bright, cheery flowers. The criss-crossing vines budding with multiple colors. The shop next door to the quaint eatery, a bookstore with overspilling carts looking as if they'd been hurriedly filled and pushed outside for quick liquidation. On the corner, a duo with matching acoustic guitars busking and singing their hearts out in a language he couldn't follow. Across the street from the musicians, a tiny jewelry shop. Far beyond that, he could see a portion of a river that rolled unhurriedly toward the outskirts of the downtown area. The town square itself bustling with foot traffic and peddled bikes that whizzed past them without slowing.

"God... God almighty." The bright shine of discovery ran away from Secrist's face. The excited and attentive stare sagging bit by bit as if tumbling down uneven steps. His eyes dropping to the ground as he took a backward step. "Then... then it was all true. The rest... all of it!" Secrist looked across the bustling streets before his gaze returned to the building he'd sought. His expression growing haunted and dim despite the brilliant sunshine and cheerful pedestrians strolling past. "All those horrible things I read really happened."

For the first time, Stander turned his full attention to the apartments Secrist was babbling about. Five stories high, the tenant complex was grey and unre-markable. Though clearly aged, the construction and style was not what he'd expected. The façade appearing more modern, and likely only a few decades old. *Perhaps,* Stander reasoned, *it had been rebuilt after it was bombed in World War*

One? Or, for that matter, maybe again after World War Two. That, he supposed, would account for the differences described in the old war journal.

"How can you be sure this is the right place?" Stander gestured at the building Secrist continued to gawk at. "If I had to guess, I'd say these apartments were built sometime in the 1960s, not in..."

"It's the right place." Secrist pointed as he spoke, his face ashen. "The tunnel and the opening exactly where my grandfather described it. The buildings, of course, are more modern looking. But check out the foundations. Crazy old! No one builds with stone like that any..." Secrist's eyes suddenly grew wide as saucers, all but bulging from his head as he turned to Stander. "That corner!" His head on a swivel, Secrist looked at something behind them and then down at the manhole where they'd emerged. His gaze quickly returning to the apartment building. He repeated the process a second time, his head shaking back and forth as if in disbelief by what he saw.

"Lord have mercy, that corner facing us, maybe one of those very windows, has to be where the vampire crawled from. My grandfather watched him do it multiple times. Somewhere underneath that building is its lair. Or was, anyway." Secrist turned and looked at Stander. "Where it slept and kept watch over that big hunk of glowing stone that I told you he described in his journal."

"That radiant rock is why I'm so interested in your grandfather's diary. There has to be a connection." Stander suddenly pulled Secrist toward him, his voice dropping to murmur. "Fuck. Don't look now, but I think we are drawing some attention. Those two over there are pointing our way. Maybe someone spotted us coming out of that manhole? Probably looks suspicious. Afterall, we aren't exactly dressed like sewage workers from, uh..." Stander looked at some of the spraypainted graffiti on the walls nearest them. "I don't know much when it comes to written languages. But, isn't that German?" He pointed to the scrawling letters of slanted white.

For the first time, Secrist took in the rest of their surroundings. As Stander had just pointed out, the signage all around them was German. "Oh, oh, oh... this isn't good." Trying to appear casual, he glanced at the two citizens Stander had pointed out. The pair suddenly joined by someone in a uniform, all three now looking their way as they talked. "I think we need to reverse our path, Russ. Play it cool. But, when those three aren't looking, we better climb back down and get the hell out of here. I can't understand how, but I think maybe we did actually cross the border into Germany."

"Get the fuck out of here," Stander matched the urgent whispering of his friend. "Neither of us brought our passports. I thought you said there was no way that could happen."

"It shouldn't," he hissed back. "But, here we are. Just be ready to open that up if they start our way. In the meantime, let's keep talking. Maybe we are just being paranoid."

"Do you know any German?"

"Just, *Sprichst du Deutsch* which means, 'do you speak German?' I think." Secrist shrugged.

"Great. I think we know the answer to that question." Stander sighed.

"I just thought of something," Secrist squinting in thought as they both anxiously watched the trio across the street from them. "Remember when we were at your Great Aunt Madeleine's house on the border of Illinois and Iowa? The place all the locals affectionately called 'Relict Mansion.'" Stander nodded, the trip mere months ago. "Remember how we discovered that hidden, underground passageway that we followed away from her home for about a mile?"

"Sure. We ended up coming out down by the lake. Where Izzy and I used to meet when we were kids." Despite the uncomfortable circumstance they currently found themselves in, Stander couldn't help but grin at the memory. Izzy had been the first girl he'd been sweet on. "Why?"

"Doesn't it seem like we kind of just did that same walk, but in reverse? I mean, we just hiked toward what was centuries ago likely once an impressive manor instead of away from one. But, both of the tunnels' construction techniques, and the distance they run, are virtually identical. And when we discovered that secret passage at your great aunt's old place, it was in a hidden subterranean room with what amounted to a freaking zombie inside. Almost like it was left there to guard something. We pulled that weird cloth or shroud off it and unwittingly let the monster loose."

"I mean, maybe. Yeah. So?" Stander's confusion was reflected in his expression. Secrist, the longtime police detective, putting pieces together he would have thought were part of a totally different puzzle.

"Well, we just walked about a mile and, though we were stopped maybe fifty yards or so from its basement or cellar, I bet this tunnel also originally began in a subterranean chamber. Just like at your Great Aunt Madeleine's, in a room hidden somewhere beneath this old manor. Of course, that would have been long before it was converted into this tenant housing we see today." Secrist turned and looked across the street that divided where they stood from the apartment building. "Doesn't that make you wonder what kind of monster might have been hibernating here? Or guarding something? Maybe it was that same bloodsucker you tangled with in the quarry? Or, maybe there is something else slumbering in the darkness under that street. The more I think about it, I find it hard to imagine the secret passage didn't originally begin, or end, there." Secrist pointed to the building with rooms for rent.

"There were two doors leading out of Relict Mansion. Maybe what we walked to get here was, like at my Great Aunt Madeleine's, just the first door." Stander tossed a casual glance over his shoulder. The nosy trio taking a step toward them.

"Exactly. What do you think might be behind door number two over here?" Secrist saw where Stander was looking, the three now crossing the street and heading toward them. "Shit." He moved to block their view, turning his back on the trio's advance. "Time to go! Move that manhole cover and jump down. I'll be right behind you."

Squatting, Stander slid the cumbersome lid aside and scrambled down the ladder. As soon as Secrist joined him below, he reached back up and tugged at the hatch until the access point was mostly covered. Both men racing back the way they'd come as he pulled the keyring out of his pocket. Slipping down the tight fissure, unlocking the iron gate, and slamming it shut behind them. As Stander reset the padlock, urgent voices rang out. Someone was following them! Secrist and Stander ignored the exclamations as they ran back down the tunnel. Both of their flashlights swinging wildly, shadows growing and shrinking on the rock walls beside them. Jogging together back the way they'd come until certain no one was following. Soon, slowing their pace to a cautious walk. Both men leery of what they'd heard trailing them earlier.

Ahead of them, the passage of ominous darkness that led back to the Chateau Chanet. Whatever may have followed them earlier down into the black abyss unseen. Creeping forward, both men strained to see what might lurk ahead of their step. The exit they sought, and now their only way back to the surface, was the mile of black ahead of them.

Chapter Twenty-Two
Germany-18th Century

Francois barely recalled the return ride after his contentious visit to the traveling sideshow. What he'd seen and learned from the owner of the gloomy and depressing carnival giving him plenty to consider. He'd been appalled at the mistreatment and squalid living conditions he'd found. The pitiful creature he'd taken in obviously cared for no differently than the menagerie of beasts they kept.

Anxious to return home, Francois was excited he would be able share such good news with her. That when the tired, old circus finally packed up and moved on from their village, it would be without Eve. He'd secured her freedom. The doctor shook his head as the horse trudged on. Incredulous that the misshapen thing he'd invited into his home had turned out to be a woman and not a man as he'd assumed. The insufferable treatment she'd endured at the hands of her previous *owner* infuriating him the more he thought about it.

As the House of Chanet came slowly into view, Francois wondered how the morning had went for his new guest. Last night, understanding the malformed circus attraction to be a man, he'd tasked Frederic, one of his three remaining butlers, with the poor thing's care. Suggesting that upon awakening, he help bathe and find suitable clothing. Chuckling as he dismounted and handed the reins of his horse over to the stableboy, he wondered if Frederic had been as stunned to learn the truth as he'd been.

Finding Frederic alone with Eve in Francois's private bathroom a short time later, there was no question the butler had been completely surprised. The servant's face a twin to the young man found murdered the previous day. A feature-less mass of pulverized gore full of holes.

"For the love of God!" Francois, unaccompanied, quickly closed and locked the door behind him. Frederic had bled out on the decorative mosaic that lined the bathroom floor. His ashen body awash in blood and lying in a pool of shimmering red. Behind his cold corpse, overturned pails and Francois's copper bathtub. Inside the dirty, darkened water, his guest. The misshapen head facing his way as if floating atop.

"You... you did this?" Francois gesturing at the pale body. "Why?"

"Hurt." The single word, barely a whisper. The puffy lips speaking, struggling to form the right sounds. Raising a dripping, lumpy arm, she seemed to point at a mark near her forehead. Her eyes glazed and unsteady. "Hurt," the word repeated.

"Frederic tried to hurt you?" Francois scoffed at the notion. Frederic, unmar-ried and childless, had been working for the Chanet family for years without incident. The idea he'd purposefully disobey Francois or suddenly somehow turn violent seemed absurd. "I find that hard to believe."

Francois grabbed towels from a nearby stack of linens and covered as much of Frederic's remains as he could. Pulling another towel, he stepped over the corpse and neared the bathtub. Out of respect for her privacy, he diverted his eyes as he approached. Holding the towel out in front of him as he spoke. "I want you out of the water so we can have a proper conversation. I can't understand how this could have happened."

Francois busied himself with soaking up the pooled blood on the floor. Ignor-ing the struggles of Eve as she pulled herself from the soiled bath water, attempted to dry herself, and donned the robe Frederic had previously laid out. By the time she'd finished, Francois had begun to ring the bloody towels out over the tub. Rinsing out the thickening gore and letting it mix with the dark water inside. The filth and scum floating along the top helping mask the contents. The doctor only stopping when he felt a tug at his sleeve.

"River." Looking up, Francois turned to see where Eve gestured. A crooked finger pointing at the body of Frederic. It took several moments for her to speak again. Her thick tongue crowded and constricted by the swelling and contusions along her jaw and mouth. "River," she repeated, her breathing like gasps.

Francois sighed. He'd clearly made a terrible mistake bringing this woman into his home. Though he couldn't work out how she'd done it, with two nearly identical deaths happening in her presence, Eve was clearly disturbed. Her barely intelligible speech, rambling about rivers of all things, forcing him to consider if she was able to reason at all. He stepped to her, for the first time seeking out her eyes. Surprisingly, they were green and dazzling. Two perfect emeralds surrounded by the chaos and ruin of her body. Tears streamed down her cheeks as she struggled to form another word. "River," she repeated for a third time. Her eyes beseeching his own. A desperation and loneliness within.

Like the eventual recognition of far off thunder, Francois slowly grasped the message she was trying to communicate. Eve wanted him to dispose of Frederic's body by tossing it in the river. Surprising himself, he reached forward and brushed the strands of wispy hair away from her face. Peering deeply into the eyes of pure green – intending to explain why he couldn't do that – his own tongue grew awkward in his mouth. The words dying in his throat.

Her eyes were intelligent. Beautiful even. Pure, but full of fear. In them, he recognized the agony her lifetime had been filled with. Francois found himself longing to help her. His own eyes slowly boiling and burning with anger as he recalled the sign above her cage.

Eve – The first woman ever that no man would touch!

Perhaps, Francois reasoned, it was no wonder she acted as she did. An existence and life filled with only taunts and teasing. Made to parade herself as a mockery. Likely beaten if she ever refused. Barely able to speak, she could hardly advocate for herself. Perhaps she had somehow killed the young man. It seemed hard to argue when compared to what she'd done to Frederic. The murders identical. But, could he really fault her? Francois began to wonder if he might be able to give her a new life. What if he could somehow heal her? Cut away the growths and resurrect the life she'd lost.

Heal her as Jesus had the lepers.

As if she'd heard his thoughts or somehow felt his heart resoften, her scared eyes grew hopeful. The spark in them emboldening Francois to action. Using the buckets to drain the rancid bathwater and, careful not to be seen, dumping the foul water outside. Concealing Frederic's body within his locked bathroom until late into the night. Loading it onto a horse drawn cart and, as Eve suggested, dumping it into the river. The swift current quickly pulling it into deeper water and sending it downstream. The faceless corpse stripped of any identifying factors.

Francois understood that Frederic's abrupt vanishing would cause alarm among the household staff. However, he also knew that the people of the village and surrounding area would hardly question his disappearance. The notorious and seemingly cursed forest that surrounded the village always considered responsible for the unexplained. The fearsome and terrible creatures residing within blamed anytime something tragic occurred. Frederic had been a well-known and avid mushroom hunter and gatherer. Often hiking alone for hours within the nearby timber. Though he abhorred lying and deception in general, it would take only a small bit of prompting by Francois to ensure the narrative he crafted would be believed.

And since it had now been over a year since it happened, the story had went unchallenged and unquestioned. Frederic, by all appearances, had simply been another victim of the feared woodlands.

***

"No one will believe you, Zorrie. Even if they did, what do you expect will happen? You can't accuse the most powerful family in the land of harboring a murderer." Jacques pulled a handkerchief and blew his nose. "Besides," he added while tucking the soiled linen back in one pocket, "you aren't even sure what you saw. What proof would you offer?"

Zorrie searched for courage in the eyes of the others. Most of her and Jean-Baptiste's friends turning from her stare. None, it seemed, willing to join her accusations. The husband and infant child of the woman Zorrie had seen drifting dead in the river nowhere to be found. The family of three vanishing sometime during the previous night. Like so many others gone missing, the dangers in the surrounding woods were blamed for the disappearances. The entire town, it seemed, numb to the fate of others.

"I know what I saw. I'm certain what truly curses and haunts the people of this village can be found in the House of Chanet. I don't know why, but the murderer I followed takes refuge there. If you don't believe me, that's fine. I'll return and discover the truth for myself. Someone has to help these poor people." Zorrie stood and began walking away without waiting for a response. "Come on, Jean," she hollered over her shoulder. Uncertainty stamped upon his face, the man-child joined her. The pair turning down a side street before making their way outside of town.

As the evening sky turned black, both Zorrie and Jean huddled close together behind a stand of trees. After a day of scrounging for scraps, her broken tooth making the simple act of eating and drinking torture, Zorrie had retraced her path from the previous night. Finding a hidden location within the timber surrounding the House of Chanet that gave them a clear view of the home. Her focus on the side of the manor where the killer she'd followed had seemed to gain entry. Though no doors were visible on that side of the house, she noted a portion of the wall stood out as different. What may have once been an opening – judging by the size, it had been a doorway – had been bricked up with stone sometime in the past. Though she couldn't be certain, the mismatched stonework seemed to be about where the one she'd followed the night before had disappeared.

Together, Zorrie and Jean watched for anything out of the ordinary. By the time the moon had risen, Jean was snoring contently beside her. Though noisy in the calm of the woods, the peaceful droning was an improvement over his constant questioning. The simpleton often babbling when he was scared. Zorrie, though grateful for the company, gladly letting him sleep as she kept watch.

The House of Chanet was the biggest home she could recall ever seeing. Sitting atop a slight rise and looking out over the encroaching village below, the burgeoning construction gradually closing the gap between the village and the home of the noble family that governed it. Standing five stories tall, Zorrie could barely count the many windows that looked across the land. Though several were lit with a warm light, most remained dark. The massive home, it seemed, was largely unused.

She'd heard the current noble was neither married nor had children, and she couldn't help but wonder what could possibly fill such an enormous building if not family and loved ones. Struggling to keep her eyes open, she tried to imagine all the wonderful things each room held. Visualizing sitting rooms and bedrooms glittering with shiny things, each with a warm fireplace. Private bathrooms, kitchens full of wonderful aromas, and dining rooms with twinkling chandeliers and clinking cutlery. The fantastic images swirling together and evolving into dreams as her head drooped lower and lower. Her deep breathing matching Jean's own as the slumbering soon shuttled Zorrie into a deep sleep.

Beautiful and unmarred, she looked down at her glowing and unblemished skin. Rubbing one hand across a bare arm just to feel the supple softness. The dress she wore was finely fitted, a flowing gown of satins and lace, jewels at her neck and ears. Looking up, she was briefly blinded by a series of lights that seemed to radiate in front of her. The lumination dazzling and brightly lighting everything around her. Though normally shamed by her appearance, she bathed in the attentive glow. Twirling once and feeling the gorgeous dress she wore flapping about her ankles and feet.

Gradually, she became aware of the music. It was coming from behind the row of lights, and when she shaded her eyes with one hand, she could see the glint of the shiny instruments and hurried sawing of a multitude of bows across tightened strings. An orchestra. The booming music somehow familiar. Only then, as she bowed, did the shortness of her breath surprise her. Her throat slightly sore with exertion.

She'd been singing!

An adoring crowd rose before her. Thunderous applause nearly overpowering the instruments still playing at her feet. Her heart pounded as the realization crashed into her. They were cheering for her! She looked expectantly for someone offstage to her left. The handsome man she yearned to see standing there was clapping along with the rest. Inside, her heart fluttered. She knew she loved her husband. But it was the shadowed figure beyond, standing high above on some wooden scaffolding that caused the fluttering between her thighs. The broad silhouette, she knew, equal parts terrifying and exciting. The things they did together, nothing a fine cultured woman would ever admit. But she knew she couldn't help herself when he called for her. Couldn't keep away though she knew she should. He was a breath of fresh air, an intoxication she drowned in, a ride she wished never ended.

An itch she needed scratched.

As she bowed a second time, several long-stemmed flowers were tossed at her feet. Not from the figures at the side of the stage, but from the paying customers in the seats. Overjoyed, she bent to retrieve them. She must have pricked a finger on one and she quickly held it to her mouth. The taste of blood sullying the moment. Pulling the blossom to her nose and inhaling deeply, she quickly turned from the offensive odor. The stench suddenly overwhelming her. Gagging, she soon began coughing. As if death itself stood breathing beside her. The rancid smell all around her and unescapable.

Coughing so hard, Zorrie woke herself up. Beside her, Jean was also just waking. The look on his face a mirror of her own. Both woken by an awful stench. Though neither could see nor find where the putrid smell had originated, it eventually dissipated in the nighttime breeze. Zorrie tried to ignore the flattened weeds next to them. Not entirely certain whether the emerging spring foliage had already been pressed to the ground or not. Hoping that whatever had laid down there had done so well before they'd arrived. If not, what had bedded down beside them as they'd slept?

Chapter Twenty-Three
France-Modern Day

Stander, leading the way back down the underground tunnel and several steps ahead of Secrist, saw the flickering first. An erratic light ahead of them winking in the darkness as if it's on/off switch was being repeatedly flipped by an unruly toddler. Slowing their hurried steps, both men palmed the lenses of their own flashlights. Covering the glare to hide their approach as they crept forward. Neither able to identify the intermittent glow haunting the pathway ahead.

Hidden in total black, the slow blink of the light seemed to gain strength and brighten the longer they watched. Vanishing completely for long seconds before once again brilliantly illuminating the passage ahead. The contrast nearly blinding in the utter darkness that surrounded them. The surging pulse dizzying like the repeated flash of a camera or the swing of a pendulum slicing through the black.

Initially mesmerized, Stander soon had to turn from the confusing strobe. He reached for Secrist's shoulder with a groan, the piercing light digging into his skull. The bright flashes, much like the swaying of the corded bulb when he'd been with Beth, disorienting. Stander suddenly felt very queasy and certain he was about to puke. Spying one of the chambers cut into the wall of the tunnel, he lunged for the void. With eyes closed, he stumbled blindly into the small chasm, running and hiding from the light. Immediately dropping to all fours and burying his face in his arms in a desperate attempt to stop the nauseating spinning. But, as the rotations in his mind and the gurgling of his stomach gradually relented, his memory of that night at the bar with Beth returned with shattering clarity.

Rising with a chafing, bruising intensity. The eerily similar pulse, like a beacon guiding his fractured memory home, dragging the previously obscured past out into the light.

Beth had been on top of him when he'd first noticed something strange. Straddling his hips and leaning back, she'd begun to ride him. Urgently. Both of them nude, Stander had slid one arm behind his head like a pillow to admire the rise and fall of her perky chest. Every fourth or fifth stroke dramatically rotating his hips and bucking hard against her deepest grind. His other hand, firm and decisive, was fastened at her neck to keep her saddled in place. The vice-like grip at her throat pacing her greed; his squeezing fingers right where she wanted them.

Though they'd barely met and never been together in the biblical sense, both seemed to anticipate the other's wants and desires. Their rhythm, like musicians lost in the flow of creation, somehow easy and familiar. The guttural sounds out of his parted lips and the delighted wince on Beth's face, a match in lust and desire. Drawing close to completion, Stander moved both hands to her hips. Pushing down hard to bury every bit of himself inside her with every thrust. Teeth bared, Beth seemed to relish the rough treatment. Her pace quickening to match his own intensity.

Yet, abruptly, she'd soon slowed and then stopped completely. There was no physical change he could see, but Beth's expression seemed to grow soft. Though her green eyes remained unchanged, the look behind them did not. As their heated frenzy stilled, she let herself fall forward and into Stander's arms. Burying herself in his chest for long moments before raising her chin. When she did, though the body remained the same, someone else stirred within. It was undeniable in every breath she took and recognizable in every line on her face. Only one name fell from Stander's shocked lips.

"Liz!"

"You have to leave." Though nearly breathless, she gasped out the words in a rush. "I can't hold her back. Or help you this time. Something is..." Her head abruptly snapping violently backwards. When she next looked down at Stander, Liz's expression sagged as if bits of it were being torn off and wiggling down.

Replaced. The love and concern in her emerald orbs vanishing. Both eyes briefly rolling up until only the white showed. When they rotated back, the green eyes were the same. But the message in them had returned to the heated need of the other. Beth once more in control, lust streaming out of each orb.

"Fuck me harder," she grunted with a tortured exhale. The desperate slap of her thighs against his hips resuming. The tiny janitor closet echoing as a startled Stander suddenly flipped her onto her back. Pulling himself out, he felt her legs desperately trying to corral him. Both hands digging painfully into his back as she clutched at his shoulders. "No! Dude, I'm so close... close... close to..."

Glancing at the back of the door, the cheap mirror hanging there reflected the deception. The glint of a sharpened blade being pulled from the tiny bag Beth had carried. Stunned at the betrayal, Stander scrambled farther backwards until he'd completely separated himself from her. His shoulders slamming against the back of the janitor's closet door.

Rising in front of him and covering Stander with her swaying shadow, Beth hissed as she lunged for him.

Throwing his hands up and darting to one side, Stander waited for the bite of the blade. Instead, silence filled the room. Peering through outstretched arms, he found Liz had somehow reclaimed control. The blond figure in front of him wavering, transfixed as she stared into the flimsy mirror reflecting her attempted violence. "You hold the body but not the mind," she said to the image. Before turning slightly and focusing once more on the cowering figure at her feet.

"Your little watcher sure has a powerful will. I've never known such fervor and affection as what I feel through her." Absurdly, a teardrop fell to one cheek. Then another. Both eyes suddenly welling with emotion and tears. She wiped at them with a frown and a balled up fist. "Sorry. Her love for you is hitting me in the vacuum where I once had a heart." She gave him a weak smile. "I can't even love myself as much as she adores and longs for you."

Stander slowly pulled himself from the floor of the maintenance closet. He was confused and still feeling off-kilter from all the alcohol he'd consumed earlier in the night. Exposed and vulnerable, he'd couldn't recall ever longing for a pair of pants more than in that moment. Cupping as much of himself as he could with both hands as he staggered to his feet. "I don't understand what's happening right now. Or who you think..."

"She uses those she can control to stay near. The look-alikes that came down through her bloodline. Most of them never even realize she's been there. Watching over you like some sort of guardian angel. I guess this body is a close enough match to her own that it can be used as a conduit. Allowing her to take possession and control my actions." She paused then as if in reflection. "Daring to defy even my master?" The tone of the statement coming out more question than reveal.

"Guardian angel?"

"Angels, celestials, spirits, demons, immortals... whatever name you want to use." She remained unmoving as she spoke. Perhaps unable. Her eyes never leaving her own reflection in the mirror. "But, though I was born of her same tribe, if you will, I will not go quietly. Resurrected from death and forced back into this body against my will, I am not a tool to be used. By anyone! I'm tired of losing... losing myself."

As Stander listened and tried to make sense of the ramblings, he could see the internal struggle manifesting itself before him. Subtle changes in expression, posture, and demeanor reflecting the battle within. The revolving evolution profoundly disturbing. Liz seeming to pull herself through on occasion and rise to the surface. Each time, infuriated, Beth seemed to drive her away. Though, as he watched, the will in her fight seemed to falter.

"I'm exhausted, beaten down by all the lies and deception." Stander could practically feel her surrender. In the mirror, her eyes sought out his own. "I've been a puppet for so long that all I truly feel is the rutting of Mithras's hand inside me. I'm tired of an eternity spent always pleasing others before myself. I've been a faithful wife, a freak, and doting mother. Murdered and a murderer. I've walked this earth and buried beneath it. I've hunted those who deserve death and been hunted by those seeking righteous vengeance. Given up my body, lost my mind at times, and sold my soul to the closest thing to a devil I could have ever imagined. I may have failed the will of Mithras, but there are others still coming for you."

Though he was certain it was Beth speaking and not Liz, Stander felt a pang of real emotion. Was she warning him against what was still ahead?

"Mirrors are a far darker magic that runs way deeper than most people ever understand." Beth was once more turning to face herself in the mirror. "They tell the truth." Seeming to surrender, Stander could all but see Liz emerging. His heart swelling as she gained leverage and control over the relinquished body. A moment later, her expression splintering.

"See this truth!" The stiletto swiftly rising and puncturing the face. "You can't use me!" Blood now pouring from a second wound. Screaming at herself, "I won't let you whore me out!" Beth driving her stiletto a third time, and then a fourth, into her own face. "I'm done being," another savage stab that split her nose, "powerless! No control..." now she split her own eyeball, "over my..." the next piercing sending several teeth flying, "own body!" Mercilessly, she brutalized herself. Shredding her own face. The blows reducing her beauty to ribbons of red. "I belong dead..." Blood cascading down until, weakened, she finally collapsed. The final strikes taking out her second eye and slicing one ear in half. The last blow severing an artery just below her chin that streamed crimson as she convulsed on the floor. Her features and head reduced to a pulpy mess.

Faceless - masked in gore.

Stander groaned as he lifted his eyes. Secrist looking down at him with concern. Behind him, at the opening of the chamber they'd ducked into, eerie howls had begun to echo through the subterranean tunnel. Stander, confused and terrified. Secrist, worried and scared. The periodic flashes of brightness continuing like a lightning storm without thunder. Reaching up, Stander let Secrist help pull him to his feet. "You alright? What the hell happened? Did you just get sick?"

Stander waved the questions off as his equilibrium slowly settled. Taking in several shuddering breaths before relaying the memory. Both men watching the doorway as he explained what had happened. "OK, but where did the body go? How did it get out of there and who cleaned the room all up?" Secrist peppering him with questions.

Stander gave him a shrug and a confused shake of his head. "I don't know. Maybe I did?" But Stander didn't really believe that. "We can figure that out later. At least now I know what happened and what to tell the police. But right now, we need focus on getting out of here or none of that matters much." Both men grew silent as they watched the flashes of light and listened to the howling.

"I really think that is a man's voice, not an animal." Secrist poking his head back into the earthen hallway. "It also seems like that light is sort of blueish like a halogen lamp." He turned back and looked at Stander. "I think we need to get closer. I mean, if you are feeling up to it. I suppose we could stay here until that shit goes away." Secrist gesturing into the tunnel.

"We can't wait if we are being followed by the fucking border police." Stander stood and shook his head. "Let's do it," he said, gesturing towards the opening. "I don't imagine you have your gun on you by chance, do you?"

"You know I didn't bring that. Too much paperwork." With their flashlights off, both men crowded together. Only moving forward when the unknown light ahead illuminated their path. Creeping silently forward down the rounded channel. Both the light and strange howls becoming more pronounced with each shuffling step.

Chapter Twenty-Four
Germany-18th Century

Jean-Baptiste couldn't keep still. He seemed compelled to speak every fifteen to twenty paces as they'd crept forward in the darkness. "Where is everyone else at? Why is the stripe in your hair wider now? Aren't you scared out here? I'm scared…" Zorrie shushing him several times as they began to make their way across the meadow. Just ahead, The House of Chanet. The lights within finally growing dark.

"Zorrie, Zorrie, I don't like all this worry," he chattered once again. "The smell out here is stinky and bad. Can we go back to sleep. I'm tired, Zorrie." Exhausted herself, the bit of dream-filled sleep she'd snagged earlier had been far from restful, she finally snapped. Cupping one hand over the weeping gash that split his face to stop him from both talking and walking.

"How about this," she began. "Why don't you go back to where we were?" Zorrie pointed to the stand of trees they'd hidden most of the night behind. "I'll watch until you get there and lie down. You can go back to sleep while I have a little look around." She gestured to the side of the manor they'd been approaching.

"I don't like it here. It smells funny. Why do you want to look in there?" Before Zorrie could reply, Jean asked another question. "Can we go fishing tomorrow?"

"Jean-Baptiste," she hissed, "we'll talk later. Right now, I need you to go back where we were and wait for me there. Just close your eyes and go back to sleep." The man-child's simple gaze wavered with uncertainty. "Go on now. I'll be able to see you the whole time," she added, lying. Walking a few steps back with him until he kept moving on his own. "That's it. Go lie down and I'll be back before you know it." She gave him an encouraging smile when he turned doubtfully one last time. Eventually, he made it the rest of the way before sinking down into the weeds that circled the cluster of trees. Hidden from view.

Zorrie turned back toward the house. Carefully watching each darkened window as she methodically advanced on the home. Creeping ever closer to the spot where the night before she'd watched the murderer somehow disappear. Certain she would find something that would prove what she'd seen. Find a way to put an end to the gruesome deaths haunting the nearby village.

As she separated herself from the shadows that had hid her advance, a moment of panic nearly stole all of her resolve. In the distance, the mournful howl of a wolf reminded her of both the ordinary dangers lurking nearby and the disquieting rumors of the Beast of Gévaudan. The monster said to frequent the mountainous forests nearby. Undeterred, she crept closer. Who could say if the whispered rumors of fantastic beasts were true or not?

Reaching the side of the grand home, Zorrie pressed her back to the cold stones. Flattening herself while her eyes darted all around. In her chest her heart pounded until, long calming moments later, it seemed certain she'd made it unseen. The racing of her pulse slowing as a multitude of crickets did their best to cover her clumsy fumbling with their chirping. Adding their voice to the darkness, the frogs that called the nearby river their home responded with their own chorus. The competing songs drowning out Zorrie's footfalls as she crept along the outside wall of the opulent manor.

Nothing appeared unusual as she explored the shadowed side of the house. The discolored bricks she'd spotted from afar had clearly been added well after the home's construction. Why the doorway had been permanently closed piqued Zorrie's interest. Had something been purposefully hidden? Or perhaps locked within? Sliding farther along the wall, her shoulder clipped the edge of a sealed window. Turning, she was surprised to find the opening tightly shuttered. The secured window, like the resealed doorway, no longer in use. She ran one finger along the edge until she found a gap. Kneeling, Zorrie pulled until the shudder opened slightly. Pressing one eye to the crack, she looked inside.

The room had likely once been a sitting or reading room of some sort. The moonlight streaming in from a glass paned window on the opposite wall that lit up the unoccupied chamber. To the right, a cold fireplace with a blackened hearth dominated one entire side. The wall opposite cluttered with furniture, crates, and a wide free-standing mirror that seemed to have been hurriedly shoved aside.

In the middle of the room stood a strange looking wooden, rectangular, table. The top of one side raised as if one was meant to sit atop it like a chair. A series of notched grooves in the wood coupled with lipped edges allowing it to be braced at different heights. Similarly, at the opposite end it was split in two. Each separate section able to swing independently of the other. If both sides and the far end was laid flat, the odd-looking piece of furniture could almost pass for an ordinary dining table. Zorrie, though she knew not how, recognized the odd piece of furniture. It was an operating table. The split ends for raising and lowering a person's legs one at a time. The opposite side where the patient's head would lay. That end also able to be raised and lowered depending on the procedure or surgery.

Near the operating table, gleaming implements designed for cutting flesh flashed from where they were laid out. A series of glass vats and oddly shaped containers set in a line just beyond. Underneath, a stack of linens. The smaller table crowded with things Zorrie hardly recognized. The glinting tools somehow menacing; the soiled and stained wood underneath hinting at their painful use. Directly above the instruments of hurt, a wavering curtain made from velvet hung from the ceiling. Though the sides were currently pulled wide-open and secured with cordage, the fabric divider, when loosed, would likely split the room nearly in half. As she eyeballed the finely tailored drape, something about it troubled her. Why was the room divided in two?

To find out, Zorrie attempted to pry the secured shutter open wider and squeeze herself inside. Only somewhat successful, the expanded opening at least allowed her to see more of the room even though she couldn't gain entry. Zorrie strained to peer into the corners nearest her. Several abandoned metal cages with their doors swinging freely lined the wall closest to her. The enclosures empty save for the opened shackles and thick chains hanging down from the tops. Subconsciously, Zorrie began to rub at the scars along her wrists.

She'd seen this room before.

Tears sprang from her eyes. Fear and pain accompanying a dizzying array of scattered images that Zorrie struggled to grasp hold of and make sense. The table, the cages, the curtain, and constraints tugging at her jumbled and fractured memories. Zorrie knew this room. Knew it well...

Like an unexpected fall into a lake of freezing water, the next shock took Zorrie's breath away. She'd seen the monster terrorizing the village. Seen it in this very room!

As if tumbling from a great height, Zorrie braced herself as more resurrected memories came rushing her way. The descent into her unknown past breathtaking. She'd been imprisoned in this very room. Forced to witness atrocities none should ever see. A tortured monster laid out across the operating table, a masked man carving up the horrid creature. His gore drenched hands pulling syrupy and viscous masses out of the abomination. Hacking away even as the tortured soul cried out in pain. Shrill screams ignored by the mad butcher.

No bottom, it seemed, to his pit of cruelty.

Zorrie had stared directly into the emerald eyes of the anguished soul he sliced apart. Unable to turn away from the scene, she'd cried along with the monstrous thing. Crimson pouring from the fresh wounds. Lines of red crisscrossing the body beaded with sweat. Fear and pain stamped across its features. Restrained and hardly able to move herself, Zorrie could only watch. The agony palpable in the air of the room. A hell of weeping and gnashing of teeth.

Arriving much earlier than usual, Francois heard his one-armed helper before he saw her. The older housekeeper entertaining one of her many boyfriends in the rooms she kept upstairs. After she'd walked the sheepish-looking lover out the backdoor, Irene went about her usual chores. Brewing tea for the doctor and starting a fire to chase the lingering cold from the room. As she set the steaming ceramic cup down in front of him, Francois couldn't help himself.

"I didn't recognize your new boyfriend, Irene. When did you stop seeing... uh... oh, what's his name? You know, the guy I've caught you with in here a time or two before."

"Charles came over early last night. He says when he gets to drinking, he needs a good milking." Francois couldn't stop the arch of one eyebrow as he tried to contain a chuckle. "Philippe is more of the morning glory sort, I guess you'd say. Not much I need to do this early for him but open the door and he's ready to..."

"Hold on, Irene." Francois set his tea down. "Aren't you the one accusing others of cavorting with the devil? Wouldn't Jesus question the frolicking of an unmarried woman such as yourself? Taking two lovers in such short order?" Francois tried to keep a straight face. Personally, he couldn't care less what others did behind closed doors. He'd always been baffled by how the most pious and self-righteous members of their community obsessed over where one wanted to stick their private parts. But teasing the seemingly insatiable old woman he employed was a game they both enjoyed. "The other day you accused another of being a witch just because she had a stripe in her hair."

"Nothing witchy about needing someone to get your insides all twitchy." Irene finished lighting the last of the lamps, her own eyes twinkling with mischievous delight. The doctor's office open and the front door unlocked. "What can I say? I have a hot little cauldron that needs a good stirring from time to time."

"Guess that explains the duo, *'Double, double toil and trouble; Fire burn, and cauldron bubble'* and all that?" Francois quoting one of his favorite plays. The conversation ending as the mayor abruptly stepped inside the office.

Behind him, two somber men carried a body. Laying it across the nearby examination table before swiftly departing. The rumored dead man who'd been endlessly gossiped about for the last several days finally delivered by his kin. Solemnly, the mayor reported the corpse had been pulled from the river. The man's family keeping the body within their home for a full day and night of mourning. Unable to swim, they suspected, according to the mayor, that he'd fallen in the river and drowned.

Francois began his examination almost immediately after the office had cleared. Though the body was not badly decomposed, it had begun to bloat and blacken in places. Something had gotten at the face of the unfortunate man. The eyes and tongue missing completely. Much of the flesh around the man's features eaten away. The grisly wounds reflecting the diligent work of marine scavengers and opportunistic foragers like rats, badgers, and foxes. Though horrible to consider and even worse to see, none of the wounds seemed unnatural.

Faceless or not.

Working in the solitude of the office's backroom, Francois next checked for what had slowly become a familiar mark at the neck. The doctor only recently beginning to suspect some of the seemingly unrelated, but increasingly consistent deaths, as having a common denominator. Almost like a plague. Especially among the younger and seemingly healthy villagers that suddenly turned up lifeless. And bloodless. Those that did, often with a bite-like gash at the neck. Or with throats so brutally savaged there was no way to know if the mark he'd begun to track had originally been present or not. Francois had never believed in vampires himself and wasn't about to start now. Still, the wounds and bloodless bodies consistently appeared in the area. He knew it was up to him to uncover the cause.

As Francois scrutinized the dead before him, the doctor was reminded it had been one year earlier that the mayor had his servant Frederic's body delivered to his office in much the same way. Like the man atop his table, Frederic had been faceless as well. His body found farther down the river where it had washed onto a sandy shoreline. The doctor trying his best to assure everyone it had been some wild dogs or wolves that had devoured his ruined features well before his body was discovered. Still, despite his attempts to persuade them otherwise, the unexpected death had nearly started a panic. Coming on the heels of the murder of the young farmhand in the woods near the circus, many villagers became convinced a human fiend now hunted them alongside the strange beasts of the forest.

Flipping the corpse over, Francois exclaimed loudly as discolored water suddenly ejected from the nose and mouth. Several slimy leeches twisting lethargically in the brownish puddle pooling near his feet. Grimacing, he stepped onto each until he felt them flatten and burst under his weight. The sight eerily similar to what he'd encountered helping Eve the year before. Nearly his first act as her physician had been to remove the many parasites feasting on her ruined flesh. All manner of vermin nesting in the folds of her tumor-laden body – leeches included. The tiny bloodsuckers, along with swarms of fleas and lice, competing with a host of bedbugs for meals.

After he'd disposed of Frederic's body, which came back to haunt him mere days later, he'd spent a lot of time attempting to communicate with Eve. Slowly gaining her confidence and explaining she was now a free woman. Talking with her about his interest in helping, and describing the possible causes and remedies of her affliction. Letting her know he was a doctor with the schooling and tools to potentially cure her. But insisting she must be completely honest with him. If Francois was to help her, he must have the truth. Pressing her about the two murders and threatening her with a return to the circus if he found out she lied to him.

Barely speaking, she'd nodded and reached one hand inside the robe she'd been wearing. Retrieving the murder weapon she'd used and somehow kept hidden on her person. Warm and damp, Eve placed the steel blade in Francois's outstretched hand.

An aged stiletto still mottled with blood.

Sighing, Francois recognized her silent confession to the crimes. There could be no doubt now that he had invited a murderess into his home. For the remainder of the day, he'd considered his alternatives. Deciding in the end to allow her to stay. Housing her in an unused sitting room near his own bedroom where the hunting dogs were kept and caged during the worst of the winter months. The room currently filled with unwanted furniture, mirrors, and art he no longer favored. Creating a place for her to sleep and purchasing supplies he felt would be needed for her treatment. Discreetly moving one of the two operating tables from his office into the home.

Treating her superficial wounds and providing Eve with comfortable shelter and regular meals had made an immediate impact. The doctor stunned at how quickly she healed. The bruising and lumps about her face and neck dissolving away, her blonde hair thickening and her tongue thinning. The ragged cough and cold she'd battled since arriving fading. Her labored breathing returning to normal and her speech steadily improving. Examining her physically, Francois became cautiously optimistic he truly could help her. Much of what appeared diseased and bloated were tumors of soft tissue. Cutting them away could free her body of the burden she carried. Perhaps, though he held out little hope, she might even appear normal.

Once Francois judged her strong enough, he explained the treatment. Assuming she would be scared and possibly refuse his services, he had told no one else of his plan. So, when Eve readily agreed without hesitation and all but leapt for the operating table, he'd first tried to backpedal. Explaining he wanted his assistant, Irene, to help with the procedure. But Eve had insisted he start that very night. Begging for relief, exonerating him of any blame should complications arise. With her beautiful eyes, instilling a faith in his talent that Francois wasn't sure he shared.

Giving in – refusing Eve slowly becoming an exception – Francois agreed to begin. Telling her the procedures he hoped would free her from the tortured body she labored under could take months to complete. He'd start with the smallest tumors until certain his diagnosis was accurate. If that went well, he'd gradually move onto bigger tumors until they were all cutaway.

Hours later, the operation began.

CHAPTER TWENTY-FIVE
FRANCE—MODERN DAY

THE SUBTERRANEAN TUNNEL THEY crept down was utterly black. A chasm of blind fear. Stander and Secrist, their unlit flashlights ready but dangling at their sides, skulked slowly forward in the darkness. Moving in tandem each time the mysterious light would briefly flash and show them a clear path. The erratic illumination helping to keep them cloaked as they silently closed the gap. The light they stalked accompanied by strange howls and wails. Both the periodic sights and eerie sounds unsettling in the oppressive and claustrophobic passageway they navigated.

Ahead of them, the shadow of a lone figure began to slowly take form. The sporadic flashes of light, they recognized, coming from what appeared to be a lantern held in the dark shape's hand. The familiar blueish-tinge from a halogen bulb near blinding each time it appeared. The earthen channel they traversed plunged into absolute darkness whenever the light vanished inside one of the tunnel's shallow, side chambers. The figure ahead of them, they now could see, was moving from one room to the other. Apparently searching each before walking over to the next. Yowling down the rock-lined chasm like a wolf every time it emerged from one of the rooms.

"Is that just some skinny-ass punk trying to scare us?" Stander whispered his question in Secrist's ear. Both men peering out of one of the voids tunneled into the wall where they'd momentarily stopped their advance. "Maybe we should hide in one of these little openings? Jump out and frighten the fuck out of him the same way he just did us."

"I don't think that would be very wise," murmured Secrist in reply. "What kind of a nutjob wanders around deserted, underground passageways howling like a wolf?" Secrist shook his head back and forth without taking his eyes from the flashing light. "Probably not the kind of person you want to freak out in the dark, wouldn't you say?" Beside him, Stander grunted noncommittedly. Both watching as the light and howling form drew close.

Soon, as the figure neared, more clarity and details emerged. Though slight in both height and weight, the outline was clearly masculine. When the man paused briefly in the center of the tunnel, the light he held lit up his haggard features. Nearly bald and hunched over, what they'd cowered from turned out to be a senior citizen of undeterminable age. The clothes he wore, plain and unremarkable, were modern but soiled. The cuffs of his oversized pants dragging in the dirt, the plain white t-shirt under his button-down flannel, more beige than white.

Stander sighed mightily. Under his breath saying, "You gotta be fucking kidding me." A few seconds later, stepping out of their hiding place, he confronted the elderly man. "You lose something?" Or, are you looking for..." Stander's jaw fell open. The rest of the sentence falling unspoken from his lips. Behind him, Secrist joined them in the passage. Stepping into the light of the lantern held by the old man.

The wrinkled elder was severely disfigured. A wet, and weeping gash splitting his features into two. Stander and Secrist's sudden appearance had clearly startled him, but the old man quickly recovered. Though his eyes were shadowed and unreadable, his marred mouth did its best imitation of a smile. Cracking wide before the man began to howl softly. He seemed pleased to have found them. Neither intimidated nor trying to intimidate, he stared dumbly across at them.

"Christ almighty, Russ." Though Secrist was whispering, there was no way to have a clandestine conversation in the still of the underground chamber. His hushed words echoing down the rounded walls. "A faceless man! Just like in my grandfather's diary."

Stander turned his head and squinted doubtfully Secrist's way. "You said those guys did it to themselves. Shooting their noses off or whatever. This," nodding slightly the old man's way, "is God's handiwork, not man's. Look closer. That is a cleft lip."

Though the geriatric oldster seemed unafraid, Stander held his arms out to his side passively as he stepped to him. "Friend," he started with, "we are going that way." He pointed back the way the old man had just walked. "You aren't going to try and stop us, are you?" Smiling but not speaking, the disfigured man simply turned to one side to allow them both to pass.

Turning on their flashlights, Secrist and Stander thanked the strange old man. Stander only got a few steps before he turned back around. "There are people... doctors who could help you, you know. Maybe there aren't any around here, but I could have someone travel down this way. Meet you and see what could still be done about that birth defect. Maybe with the..."

"Lordy, lordy," began the man. His thick European accent, wrapped in nasally tones, difficult to make out. "Defect!" He looked up at both Stander and Secrist. His face contorting. An aged scar of white now visible in such close proximity. The zigzagging trail of the blemish running from the ruin of his mouth up through his forehead. Shockingly dark hair, no longer than wispy eyelashes, visible in the valley of the scar. "I am the living embodiment of Mithras, the faceless one. And I couldn't be more cherished. My hide and my seek is for him, not others." He laughed hoarsely, an obnoxious guffaw that ended in a coughing fit. "When the time is finally right, you'll see. Despite the darkness, you will still see."

"Right, uh...okay." Stander turned back to Secrist and gestured they should continue on their way. "Bye, now," he added over his shoulder. The look in his eye and quick shake of his head showing Secrist he didn't think it was worth their time continuing the conversation. But, as he stepped forward, Secrist stayed rooted and spoke to the old man.

"I've heard of Mithras before. Heard the name." Nothing registered on the split face, so he continued. "My grandfather knew men, back in the First World War, that were followers of the religion. Prayed and made sacrifices to him. I've often wondered what caused those men to change… change what they'd believed…" But, wordlessly, the old man with the divided and valleyed features turned from the questions. Resuming his wandering and slipping inside one of the tunneled hallway's shallow chambers. His only reply a sorrowful howl.

"Forget it, Tommy. I'm not sure the guy is all there, if you know what I mean." Stander started walking again once he saw Secrist had given up getting any answers from the old man. "You saw that old scar. Must have been a hell of a shot to the head that did that. Maybe he was in a car wreck or something when he was younger?" Ahead of them, their flashlights made a halo of light that they walked through. Passing the last of the side chambers as the floor of the tunnel began to gradually incline.

"Yeah, I agree. It was worth a shot, though." Secrist looked behind him, the light of the lantern the old man held visible in the yawning black of the passageway. "I'd love to understand more about the cult, or whatever you want to call it, that follows this Mithras entity."

"Face it," Stander smirked as he made quotation marks in the air, "that has to be some obscure faith slowly fading with every new generation. That crazy old coot," he gestured towards the lantern light behind them, "was probably the last altar boy in the very last church. Faithful until the end."

"Wonder what would be on a Mithras altar?"

"Apparently, sacrificing good looks and beauty are what appeals to him." Stander laughed, the noises sharp in the rounded channel they walked. "Guess we don't need to worry. Neither of us have anything to offer him."

Walking steadily, both men soon reached the cave-in they'd used to access the hidden passageway. "Thank God!" Stander exclaiming loudly as the sunlight from the crack in the earth streamed through the opening. He scrambled up the side of the fallen debris and squeezed past the opening. Freed from the tunnel, he turned and offered his hand to Secrist who gladly took it.

"I glanced behind me before you pulled me up." Secrist talking as they both walked toward the chateau where they'd spent the previous night. "I'm pretty sure the old guy below turned around and started to follow us." He glanced over at Stander, "Doesn't that strike you as strange?"

"No, not really," he replied. "The other end was locked tight and it seems we, or Lucas anyway, has the key. Where else could he go? Besides, it seemed more like he was looking for something in those little side rooms or chambers. By the time he caught up to us, he was about at the end of them." Though he didn't say anything to Secrist, his eyes were sweeping back and forth across the meadow they walked and the forest that rimmed it. Looking for any sign of who he thought he'd seen watching them from afar. Had it been the old man with the disfigured face? Was he following them as Secrist insinuated? Perhaps the poor guy was homeless and using the chateau's crumbling outer buildings for shelter.

"I'm still anxious to search the rest of these grounds," Stander gesturing at the chateau. "Unless you are starving and can't hold out, how about we stick around here while it is still light out? Do some more exploring? When we finish, we can grab some food from that gas station where we filled up last night. Eat it on the way back to the hotel in Caen."

"That sounds good to me. But," Secrist stopped walking and grabbed Stander's arm, "you still need to call the police station and let..."

"I know, I know." Stander pulled out his phone, Secrist following suit. Same as that morning, neither had service. "Man, this must be a dead area." He repocketed the nearly worthless device. "Remind me once we start driving. I can put the call on speaker phone so you can listen in. Now that I remember exactly what happened to Beth, I may need your help explaining things."

"How in the hell are you going to explain?" Secrist gave Stander a quick look. "No one, especially a detective paid to solve murders, is going to believe she was possessed or whatever you think that was. I wouldn't bring any of that shit up if I were you. Admit to being there and what happened between the two of you. But, just stick with her going crazy and killing herself. Leave it at that."

"Sure, but you said earlier my DNA is likely all over the place. They'll just assume I'm lying, won't they?" Both men slowed as they approached the chateau. "I'm so fucking screwed."

"That's why I said to tell the truth. No matter what you believe you saw and heard coming out of her, they'll find the evidence needed to put you in the same location. Don't lie about anything, just omit all that Liz stuff." Secrist leaned against the rental car. The hood warm under the heat of the sun beating down from the clear sky above. "Beth just went psycho, that's all you know. She killed herself in front of you and you freaked out. Forensics should be able to recreate each wound. The trajectory and angle of each incision should show the stabbing was done from below. Hopefully, that she clearly did it herself. Exonerating you."

Secrist smiled with confidence that he didn't feel. Though all he'd said was true, he had no idea how motivated and proficient local law enforcement would be in Caen. Would they be more interested in solving her death quickly or accurately? Stander leaving the scene – accident, suicide, or murder – is what really muddies the water. That, plus waiting days before reporting what he'd seen.

Chapter Twenty-Six
Germany-18th Century

The steel sliced into the coarse flesh. Blood seeping around the edges of the scalpel as he worked. Francois carving away another superficial tumor and letting it slide off Eve's body. The wound left behind barely bleeding despite the density of the mass. The growth, just like the others he'd already removed, merely a bloodless sack of near-dead tissue. Stunned at the ease at which he relieved Eve of her physical deformities, Francois had worked straight through the entire night. Stopping only when he'd separated the last offending mark from her body. The results far better than he'd dared hope.

A successful operation.

Francois turned down the oil lamps he'd brightened for the duration of his work. Pushing away the standing mirrors he'd positioned to reflect and focus the artificial light. The multiple reflections illuminating the sitting room nearly bright as day. Verifying Eve's breathing remained regular and routine, he stashed the alcohol and opium combination he'd mixed. The concoction had seemed to help with the pain, though Eve did still cry out at times. His plunging blade merciless as he'd reshaped the burdened carnival freak into something more human. Ideally, he hoped she would be able to sleep away the coming hours. The bandaged and seeping wounds he'd stitched closed with catgut – string made from the intestines of animals – needing time to settle and bind.

Alone with his patient, Francois lifted the sheet and exposed the nude body beneath. Though partially swathed in the bandages he'd applied after each tumor was removed, there were less of them than he'd expected when he'd first began the procedure. As terrible as the affliction that caused the massive growths had been, once they were removed, Francois had been surprised by what he'd found beneath. The unblemished skin supple and youthful. He brushed the blonde hair away from her face. Though swollen and bruised from his work, there was an undeniable beauty that had been hidden within. Eve, as it turned out, was a relatively young and attractive woman.

Shamelessly, Francois let his eyes drift lower. Her slight breasts, no longer obscured by the growths and lumps he'd removed, drew his attentive gaze. Telling himself he was checking the bandages at her shoulders and stomach, his fingertips brushed for long moments against both. Stopping only when a slight moan escaped her puffy lips and her legs fell open. Francois briefly enjoying the view of the fair hair bunched between her thighs as he ran his hands along the remaining bandages. An enlarging growth of his own rising pleasantly between his legs.

Embarrassed by the carnal thoughts running rampant through his mind, the doctor slowly wound strips of clean linen around each of her arms and legs. Swathing her in white from head to toe. Only her eyes, mouth, and nose left exposed. Finishing, the tight wrappings hugged her body snuggly while covering the bruised, carved, and stitched flesh. The form shapely and curved. Leaving the room and locking the door behind him, he never saw the quick opening of Eve's eyes.

The weeks that followed were a blur. It didn't take the staff of the house long to realize Francois was harboring a secret guest. The doctor finally admitting he'd taken in the accused carnival freak. Telling the servants the poor thing was too ashamed of its appearance to be seen. Explaining they would both soon be leaving for the Swiss Confederacy where he'd found a progressive clinic that specialized in treating the affliction. The lies, prompted by Eve, falling easily from his lips.

For her part, Eve healed remarkably quickly. The portions of her body where the tumors had grown healing up nicely. Though the scars left behind remained prominent, none of the growths returned. Even her speech seemed to improve almost daily. Francois was soon looking forward to their time together. Their conversations and her thoughts about the opera, literature, and the arts, sur-prisingly astute. Despite her appearance and years in captivity, Eve proved to be cultured and intelligent.

It didn't take long for Francois to fall in love.

Soon, with Eve's help and flair for storytelling, the couple came up with a plan. Francois telling staff he would be leaving that very week to travel north to the Swiss Confederacy. Explaining the clinic he'd found had agreed to treat the circus sideshow attraction he'd rescued. But, unable to travel alone with such taxing deformities, the doctor would need to accompany the poor creature. Saying he would likely take advantage of the unexpected trip and stay on several more weeks to enjoy the beauty of the snowy alps.

The extended time away, the doctor figured, would give Eve's surgical wounds time to heal. Later, when they returned home from the trip, Francois would announce a surprise engagement! Telling everyone he'd met his new bride-to-be during his travels. Immediately smitten by her, Francois would say, he'd proposed and asked her to return with him to live at The House of Chanet. Figuring as long as Eve wore a long skirt, long sleeves, and kept her blouse buttoned to the chin to keep her healing scars covered, no one would be the wiser. Her head and face having already healed enough to pull off the deception.

Francois was overjoyed with the plan and thrilled by the sudden turn of events. Never having much luck with women, the doctor had a hard time containing his glee. Before the spring had turned to summer, he'd went from hoping he could help a tortured soul live a more normal life to finding out she would be helping him live a more normal life. Francois's extended bachelorhood already sprouting whispered talk among the villagers. He was certain the unexpected engagement (and bit of deception) would be happily embraced by staff and the nearby townspeople alike.

Ironically, the ruse, planned primarily to give Eve time to heal, had largely turned out to be unnecessary. Her recuperative powers astounding the doctor. The wounds from Eve's surgery healing incredibly quickly. Scars, as if months old, developed in mere weeks. The transformation startling. The couple's room, and soft feathered bed at the Inn where they lodged, quickly becoming a nest they rarely left. Their lovemaking fast and furious as if both were trying to make up for lost time.

Once they'd returned home – the happy news of their engagement well-received – Francois put the knife to Eve several more times. Initially, only doing small procedures she requested. Removing flaps of hanging skin and tightening loose areas that still troubled her. But later, Francois's physician's curiosity led him to look for more imperfections. Often, in the aftermath of their heated sex, exploring her body slick with sweat. Probing her flesh. Searching for more lumps, discolored patches, and pinching rolls of excess fat with distaste and telling her he could rid her body of the waste. "Let me cut this away, retighten everything up again. Make you..."

"Make me your bride," she would say. Giving herself submissively to the doctor to whittle and sculpt as he pleased. Letting him create his version of a perfect woman from out of the ruin she'd once been. Each time, pulling the velvet curtain closed behind her as she mounted the operating table and waited for his pain-filled touch. The cloth veil wavering as Francois donned the frock he wore to protect his clothing. Pulling and setting out the sharpened tools he preferred. The long wait and subtle clinking of the instruments becoming a purgatory between the hell of the pain and heaven the doctor longed for her to be. Carving away, bit by bit, the last of Eve. Letting the new *her* burst forth from the shambling mess she'd once been.

Francois creating woman out of ruined flesh.

Zorrie trembled as more and more lost memories crashed into her. A whirlwind of sights, sounds, smells, and images flooding her taxed mind. The tortured soul the butcher sliced apart had wailed in agony atop the surgery table. Blood dripping from the wounds; the green eyes beseeching her. The message easily read upon the tortured features.

Make him stop!

Stop the pain, stop the slashing knife, stop the bleeding. Stop trying to change her. Accept her as she was. Love her, not the flesh that sprouted from her bones.

Paralyzed by the horror, Zorrie had been unable to move. Even as one gore-streaked arm reached out to her, desperation now the message behind the eyes, Zorrie cowered from the touch. Unwilling to engage even as the faceless man behind the cloth mask wiped his dripping hands across his chest and vanished behind the curtain. The wavering velvet ominous as it gradually stilled. Most of all, Zorrie feared what lay beyond the veil. The unknown. The drape a twin for what clouded her mind. Shrouding her past from her present.

Finally daring his return, Zorrie stretched out one hand. The bloody fingers of the two touching. Cold and smooth as glass, her hand jolted out of fright and she quickly snatched her hand back.

The mirror shattering.

All it had framed within its wooden boundaries falling apart. The illusion it reflected stripped away, the shards of the looking glass crashing onto the floor. The fantastic delusion she had lived splintering into a thousand pieces and caving all around her.

Zorrie had been the tortured soul atop the surgery table. Her mind fracturing as she'd watched her transformation. The multitude of mirrors giving her an unfettered view of the reconstruction her body went through. Nearly overnight, an evolution from a bloated, despised, and revolting creature of pity to a slim and shapely woman of desire. Yet, no matter how many times Francois continually altered her form, he'd never been satisfied with the result. With her. The doctor studiously looking for more imperfections and faults. His love contingent upon what she presented to the world, not who, inside, she really was.

Stunned at the unfathomable revelation, Zorrie turned from the window of the empty room and sank to the ground. Her legs gone weak. The shutter she'd pried open settling back into place. Her mind racing to catch up with the memories she'd abandoned. The void in her mind slowly filling as she recalled her desperate escape.

It had been weeks and weeks of painful procedures and surgeries after they'd returned. Just when she thought Francois was finally satisfied with her transformation, he would find another flaw to amend. Something else about her he didn't like and thought could be improved upon. Her gratitude and happiness slowly dwindling much like the shape of her body. Eventually, she began to fear his inquisitive touch. Their lovemaking always ending with talk of the next operation. Days of dreading the pain to come following close behind.

As fall turned to winter and the snow began to fall, she'd made up her mind to leave. Grateful for all he'd done, she knew she couldn't face Francois. Couldn't bear witness to the breaking of his heart. Deciding instead that it would be best for her to slip away quietly rather than confront him with the truth. Determining it would be prudent to wait for the spring thaw before departing. Using a generous helping of the mixture used for blackening shoes to change the color of her blonde hair to avoid being recognized. Taking only the clothes on her back and her most cherished memento. The sharpened stiletto she'd carry eternally. The blade a gift from a long-departed friend and lover.

After dying her hair a deep black, she snuck out of The House of Chanet on one of the first warm nights of the season. Heading toward the nearby village but not making it into the town itself that night. The road taking her past the local cemetery where she'd been attacked by a foul ghoul.

Murdered, had that been possible.

The creature had been rail-thin and appeared sickly despite its impressive strength. It was awkwardly lanky with spindly legs and long, bony fingers topped by filthy nails. Dressed all in black, the suit of clothes it wore flowed as it moved. The dreadfully pale skin of the hairless wraith bright and shiny under the rising moon. Iridescent.

As if the monster had known she was coming, it leered hideously at her approach. The eyes of hypnotic green a match of her own. She withered under its glare. Exposed on the open road, the piercing orbs seemed to harvest with impunity from her secret garden. The briefest flash of recognition before it swarmed.

Gnashing at her neck with sharpened teeth of lust. Tearing her throat open in the night and feasting on the warm blood that flowed freely from the mortal wound.

When it was sated, or perhaps when the blood finally ran dry, it had unceremoniously dragged her unmoving body into the nearby woods. Tossing it carelessly into a deep ravine where it laid unmoving for days. Dead to the world. But inside, her immortal body was slowly repairing itself and replenishing the fluids the thing had stolen.

Rising after three days, she was hardly herself. Plagued by horrific pain that constantly tore apart her reason before it had time to bloom. Her head full of only agony and confusion; the mind wiped clean. Starving and ravenously thirsty, she had blindly stumbled into town. A priest pulling the corpse-like woman into the sanctuary of his church and tending to her until she had regained more of her strength. Helping her fight through the nearly debilitating headaches she was suddenly suffering and counseling her on how the other homeless migrants banded together to help one another. Asking a simpleton he called Jean-Baptiste that was begging outside his church, to escort and introduce the strange woman to the other homeless of the town.

Jean-Baptiste! She'd left him waiting for her near the woods!

Pushing herself away from the House of Chanet, Zorrie ran across the field and headed straight for the stand of trees they'd hidden behind earlier. Hopeful she'd find him snoring contently among the wavering grass. Instead, she found him talking with the one who had murdered her. The vampire sitting upon what was left of a rotten tree trunk. Both turned at her frenzied approach. The vampire licking his lips salaciously. Jean-Baptiste standing as she reached them, a smile of wonderment on his face.

"Zorrie, Zorrie, I just heard a new Bible story…"

CHAPTER TWENTY-SEVEN
FRANCE-MODERN DAY

STANDER AND SECRIST SPENT much of the day exploring the grounds and various structures that made up the Chateau Chanet. Finding the buildings that ran alongside the main part of the home and castle deserted and mostly empty. What still stood more ruin than edifice. The stone arches and pillars, unprotected and crumbling into decay, supporting nothing but themselves. The stables and barns, though still structurally sound, were missing sections of roof and portions of wall. The interiors, exposed to the elements, scattered with barely recognizable piles of junk. Unused materials from previous building repairs and remodeling left moldering in sagging piles. Sections of fallen iron fences and splintered siding dragged under the drooping roofs. A stack of nearly bald tires and several pieces of unrecognizable farm equipment rotting in the corners.

Pushing their way past a door blocked by stone planters filled only with barren dirt, both men peered cautiously inside what was left of the servant's quarters. The modest dwelling sharing a wall with the castle. Shining their flashlights around the biggest room on the first floor, they looked for anything intriguing. Finding the staircase running along the wall nearest to them had collapsed into a pile of cracked banisters, short rails, and wooden steps. Much of the second floor roofing had caved-in sometime in the past and now only covered the floor of the upper rooms. Avoiding the potential deathtrap, they circled around the perimeter and peered through the mostly glassless windows. Outside of some broken furniture and a crumbling fireplace, nothing caught their eye. The long-dead remains of a few unfortunate birds the only tenants.

With nothing but the main house left to explore, Stander and Secrist began investigating what was behind each door of the once magnificent castle. Systematically going through each room on both the first and second floors. "I feel a little weird rummaging around Lucas's home," Stander commenting after he shut the door of yet another empty closet. "I know he last lived here as a child, but still."

"Get over it," replied Secrist without glancing up. The longtime cop experienced in searching homes and personal belongings with impunity. "He told us we were free to explore and look around the place. I got the sense he didn't come here much anymore. Or really care for the property. Besides," he added with a sigh, "there doesn't seem to be much of anything here." He looked out the second floor window beside him. The view nearly the same on all four sides. Hills of green pocked by grey boulders with occasional stands of great trees smothered in moss. The chateau perched atop a peak overlooking the sprawling meadows and the valley below.

With Secrist right behind him, Stander walked back downstairs. The heels of his boots loud as he crossed a dusty marble floor and headed down the one long hallway they'd yet to explore. Nearly every room so far empty, save a few pieces of random furniture here and there; most covered by cloth sheets. He pushed a set of intricately carved doors that opened into what was once the chateau's weapons hall. The dark wood covering all the walls crowded with detailed images whittled directly into them. One side dominated by yet another stained bedsheet that clearly covered a large frame. Pulling it aside, Stander found it had hid a massive, gold crowned mirror. Secrist, reflected in the looking glass, glanced up at Stander as he spoke and gestured. "That reminds me, I wanted to show you something in here I noticed earlier when I was hunting for you this morning." He waved him over to the far side. Both of them strolling past a series of sculpted busts of serious looking men. "Check it out," he said, pointing.

Though faded and frayed at the ends, a coat-of-arms banner of mostly blue and gold was one of the few decorations that still graced the aged chateau. As Secrist had anticipated, the unexpected find captured all of Stander's attention. "What the fuck, Tommy."

"You tell me," Secrist joining him under the obscure symbol and looking up. "I've been thinking about it off and on all day. I doubt shields and swords are particularly unique when it comes to medieval crests and coats of arms. And I suppose I could be misinterpreting the shape underneath as well. But, doesn't that look like it is supposed to represent a glowing or powerful stone?" He traced the squarish, rectangular form in the air with his finger. "Plus, the four swords all have little squiggly lines coming off of them."

"So," Stander turned and looked over at Secrist. "Why do you think that matters?"

"Well, in both my granddad's diary and when that vampire was fighting you..."

"Fighting? You mean, kicking my ass." Stander looked sideways at his best friend. He'd been no match for the creature. The foul contagion had mocked and toyed with him. It still felt like luck that he'd even escaped the clutches of that hungry thing.

"Whatever, your words not mine," Secrist said, shrugging. "Anyway, in both cases it was the vibration or tone of the blade that debilitated the bloodsucking freak."

"Hmmm... OK... maybe," Stander responded doubtfully. "But, what about the little 'squiggly' lines coming off the rectangle? More vibrations?" Stander had made quotation marks in the air when he'd said the word squiggly.

"Or power. I suppose that could be true of the little swords on there as well." Secrist's expression grew uncertain. "I don't know. I mean, maybe that rectangle-looking thing is meant to be a treasure chest full of shiny gold." Once again, he shrugged as he pulled his phone out. "I'm going to take a picture and do some research. Some academic out there should be able to tell us."

"Lucas must know the symbolism behind his own family crest." Stander watched Secrist take several shots before he repocketed the device. "When we get back, we'll see what he says." Both men exiting the weapons hall and closing the door behind them. "Since we can't safely get up to the top of those two ramparts,

I think we are done here. I'm just disappointed none of the keys Lucas gave us opens that basement door. I'm dying to know if that winding catacomb of stone we walked earlier actually originates here or someplace else."

"It's hard to imagine it doesn't. As I understand it, tons of medieval castles and chateaus had hidden, underground escape tunnels for the nobility that occupied them." Secrist pursed his lips together in thought. "But, I suppose if this was all bombed during the First World War like the diary alludes, it might all be collapsed. I guess it wouldn't be a surprise if way back then they sealed the basement off completely. I'm sure Lucas can tell us."

Secrist and Stander grabbed their belongings and headed for the front door. Relocking the entrance and piling into the rental car. After stopping to grab some food, they retraced their route back to Caen. Heading down the same roads they had driven just the day before. Chasing after the setting sun as their vehicle was slowly engulfed by the long shadows left by its retreat. The mountain range they entered throwing up walls of rock on both sides of the two-lane highway. The tunes in Stander's phone the soundtrack for their travel.

And I have been a slave to the Judas in my mind

Is there something left for me to save

In the wreckage of my life, my life...

Less than an hour after leaving Chateau Chanet behind, as Stander sung along with the group *Fozzy*, he could tell something was on Secrist's mind. The former detective uncharacteristically mum on his music selections. Though Stander kept singing until the very end, as the song faded, he turned the volume down.

I'm becom-, I'm becom-, I'm becoming

I'm becom-, I'm becom-, I'm becoming

Judas in, Judas in my mind

"Can I ask you something? For real?" Intuitively, Secrist began to ask the same questions Stander had been silently contemplating most of the day. "Do you believe what Beth told you? I mean, about Liz and her temporarily borrowing bodies. Kind of keeping tabs on you over the years."

Sighing, Stander slowly shook his head back and forth. Lifting both hands off the steering wheel briefly and shrugging. "Tommy, I don't know what to believe anymore." He glanced over at Secrist. "I've seen some strange things over the years. I guess, recently, you have as well."

"We both saw what crawled out of your boyhood friend when you went back and rescued Chris a few months ago. If you believe what Beth said, how do you know whatever you saw in that room wasn't another one of those things? Warring for control over Beth's body?" Secrist still had nightmares about the oozing black creature they'd torched. What it had told them and its terrible, otherworldly screech at the end. Not to mention what his grandfather had revealed in his diary from the war. How he'd witnessed a bloodsucking wraith toying with the suits of flesh pulled from its victim. Wearing the gore as if it was the latest fashion. Secrist had begun to wonder if he'd ever be able to trust strangers again. What was that old cliche? *Never judge a book by its cover?* The saying now taking on a whole different meaning for him.

"You believe me, right? What I told you I saw and heard in that janitor's closet? That Beth did that to herself. That it wasn't me." Secrist held his stare. Stander's blue eyes beseeching his own.

"Honestly? That's why all of this keeps going round and round in my head." He turned and stared out of the passenger window. "If I didn't know you the way I do, would I believe you? Had I not seen Liz use that strange stone," he turned back toward Stander, pausing before continuing. "Which we later discovered is the eyeball or whatever out of the monolith Lucas is uncovering, for Christ's sake!" It was Secrist's turn to shake his head. Falling silent for long seconds as he tried unsuccessfully to make sense of it all. "Anyway, had I not seen her vanish with my own eyes, would I believe you?"

Stander waited for the expected affirmation. Did Secrist truly trust him or not? Though he longed for his friend's acceptance and approval, the mercy he yearned to be shown and hear never came. Secrist speaking abstractly about investigators Stander would soon need to face. "These are important questions to consider before you try to explain any of this to the local authorities. They won't have seen or heard what you have. Or, even witnessed the little bit of all this that I have. Which leads me back to my original question. If I was them, would I believe you?" Stander nodded agreeably. But, inside, he felt let down. Though a reasonable conversation, and helpful, it felt like Secrist had purposefully avoided answering Stander's own question.

Both men stared out of the windshield in silence.

"You gotta be kidding me..." Stander slowed the car, the road ahead blocked and impassable. The headlights revealing a flock of misled sheep milling mindlessly across an unfenced meadow and spilling onto the blacktop.

"Jesus! There has to be a hundred of them." Secrist glanced out all four sides of the vehicle. "Why would they be outside grazing at night? Did they escape their pen or pasture? Shouldn't a shepherd or farmer be keeping watch over them?"

"Must only be ninety nine then." Stander grinned at Secrist but, in return, all he got was a blank stare. "You know, like in the parable," he added as he pulled over and killed the engine just beyond a wall of timber. A finger of the dark woods they'd driven through extending nearly to the pavement as if pointing the way. Stander stepping out of the car and walking around to lean on the hood as the sheep gradually made their way across the road. A few stopping to *baa* and stare before Secrist joined him at the front of the vehicle. The constant bleating of the lambs echoing all around them as the road seemed to grow even more crowded with the lost flock.

"Good thing it isn't cloudy tonight or you might not have seen them." Secrist gesturing at the full moon shining brightly above them. "What's with the spray paint? You see that? Each one has the same kind of marking painted right onto their wool"

"Maybe it's for identification?"

"That makes sense. Probably hard to tell one farmer's sheep from another's." Secrist looked across the meadow. More of the flock seemed headed their way. "What do you think? Should we try and shoo these closest to the road away so we can keep going? Maybe we can herd them over to the side?"

Stander straightened and stretched. "Good thinking. Otherwise, at this rate," he pointed to the directionless grazing, "we'll be waiting all night." Both men made their way across the trafficless pavement and waved off the sheep not yet crowding the road, keeping them on one side. "All right, when I give the signal, let's walk back toward the car and, I guess, holler and wave our arms or something. Clear us a... Wait! I'm not ready yet!" All around them, the bleating grew high-pitched and frantic. The docile roaming becoming a panicked flight that instantly emptied the road.

"I didn't do anything." Secrist threw his hands up, "Something must have startled them."

Both men noticed the wolf at the same time. It had taken Stander's place on the hood of the rental car. Hackles raised, the white of its fangs seemed almost luminescent in the glow of the moon. Soon, a second wolf appeared beside the car. Then a third. Moments later, the vehicle was surrounded. In the distance, back the way they'd driven, a single, mournful yowl rang out. In response, the pack returned the howl. Each wolf raising their head briefly before their stare returned to the two men.

"I don't like this at all. I've stumbled upon a wolf or two fishing in the most northernly parts of the yoop on occasion, but up there, they always run from man. These guys," Secrist nodded slightly, "don't seem worried about our presence one bit."

"If it was just one or two, we could probably grab some rocks and sticks and charge them. At least scare them enough that we could get back into the car. But, what are there? Seven? Eight?" Stander kept trying to count, but the pack seemed to swell. Then, as quickly and silently as they'd arrived, the wolves jumped from the vehicle. Dissolving into the field and racing up a slight knoll before vanishing completely.

Stander and Secrist exchanged a troubled look. Moments later, what had spooked the pack of wild wolves erupted out of the forest. Roaring, it charged. Both men, without enough time to scream, sprinted as fast as they could the opposite way. Racing across the open meadow blindly. A small cluster of tall trees the only visible shelter. Stander, far faster than the hobbled ex-cop, headed straight for the stand of trees. Secrist falling farther behind him with each step. The monstrous behemoth of fur, claws, and teeth gaining. Its jaws snapping open and shut as it closed the gap.

Leaping for the first tree he thought could hold his weight, Stander pulled himself from the ground. Securing himself atop a thick branch some eight feet in the air. Turning back, he reached down for Secrist. The men locking grips as he helped haul him up the side of the tree. Pulling Secrist by the scruff of his shirt collar just as what chased them crashed into the thicket.

Snarling with fury, it tore at the bark as it scrambled to reach them. Stander and Secrist climbing higher to put more distance between them and the ground it leapt from. Scaling the tree until the branches grew too thin to risk. The pair stranded in the middle of a field of weeds and hidden within the grove. Below them, a buzzsaw of ferocity with hungry eyes and a gaping maw of barbed and tusked teeth.

Chapter Twenty-Eight
Germany-18th Century

ZORRIE RAISED THE STILETTO she kept secreted on her person. Jean-Baptiste's eyes growing wide as she rushed past him. The knife in her hand slashing desperately at the leering face of the vampire without success. Moments later, finding herself pinned to the ground of the meadow. Her impotent blade knocked aside and the pale wraith astride her. The rank smell of rot and decay filling the air. The taste of disease and death filling her mouth and nostrils as she struggled to free herself.

"I find you, much like myself, a curiosity." The vampire's cold tongue of black slithering sensuously up one side of her face. A creeping familiarity in the cold touch. "Your episodes, as you've come to call them, like a siren demanding my attention. Compelled to learn more, I followed and laid beside you just to swim in the exquisite taste of your pain. Physical, emotional, the guilt you carry, and the distress over your homicidal ravings." The green eyes raking her body up and down as it spoke. "Slurp, slurp, slurp. I drank all of it up." The vampire grinning as he mocked her. "Indeed, after our time together under the bridge, I walked home utterly intoxicated. Drunk on your insecurity and fear even as you so cunningly crept after me."

"You! You've been following... Why me?" Unsure what may happen next, Zorrie tried to keep the fiend talking by asking a question. Daring a quick glance over at Jean standing motionless nearby. Wishing to herself that he was smart enough to run.

"I recognize your eyes, same as my own. Eternal. You were born of the stone like me. Both of us walking around in these decaying and drab bodies. It will take me centuries of clandestine feasting to become who I must. While you," the tone patronizing, "got the good doctor, Francois, to hack all your warts away. Hoping to make yourself more... ah... palatable to the masses, shall we say? But, we both know the pestilence you carry inside, don't we? What a vengeful little witch you truly are."

Abruptly, the voice changed. "We'll always have Paris," it mocked. "Your pathetic husband Hans...tsk, tsk, tsk. I guess the best one can say about Hans is that someone will always get the best of him. You certainly did." The raucous laughter that followed fading into melody. *Mozart's* ballet *Les Petits Riens* rising from the lips of grey. The popular song from the opera *Le Finte Gemelle* hummed in perfect key. Zorrie knew this both because it was among her favorite songs and because the voice singing was her own. The vampire able to mimic both her and Hans's voices perfectly.

"Weeping, weeping, that's the song you sing sleeping!" Jean's voice cutting off the tune. "You sing like an angel, Zorrie."

"Not I?" The creature rose with an emotionless smile, freeing the attacker from his grip. "After all, it is said I am supposed to be a fallen angel."

"You?" Zorrie sat up and snatched the nearby stiletto. Placing her favorite memento back in its hiding place under her clothing. "Why? Are you the devil?"

"There is no devil, you flockless sheep. No Satan, no Beelzebub, no Belial. Only me. I am the well of fear man drinks from once his lips quit suckling their momma's teat."

"Lucifer." The single word a whisper that Jean could barely get out.

"Lucifer? The light-bringer?" Again, laughter poured from the mouth of barbs. "You flatter me! But, no. That's just a word once used to describe the Kings of Babylon. Some lazy scribe mistranslated it later on when he was either adding to the stories or cutting away the parts he didn't agree with. Probably the same genius who decided Jonah should be swallowed by a whale instead of a fish. Writers are a soulless lot that only care about snagging more readers. After all, King James had his own books to peddle about sorcery, witchcraft, and his devil. Why else do you think he had all those demons added into his version of the gospels? Who would dare dispute his own ravings once he'd twisted and plagiarized what the disciples originally wrote?"

"Who are you then?" Her question tapered off to a whisper as well. By the time she asked, Zorrie was no longer sure she wanted to know the answer.

"I've been known by three names since Mithras first entrusted me with his eternal kiss. The last, and the only one you would recognize, was Judas." He cocked his head as his eyes found Jean-Baptiste. "Though much of what I did was later cut from the scriptures, at least they got that name right."

Now it was Zorrie shaking her head dismissively. "That doesn't make any sense. How could you have been a disciple of Jesus yet say the very idea of the devil was based off you?"

"Simple. Isn't your devil supposed to be the father of lies? The great deceiver? Wouldn't the deceiver of the whole world as your infallible Bible calls me, be able to trick eleven guys desperate for something to give their otherwise meaningless lives purpose? Where's your faith?" Again, the creature laughed haughtily before continuing. "Jesus was too busy changing all the water into wine for himself to really pay attention to much else. Especially once Mary Magdalene finally revealed her real self to him. Trust me, he had plenty of other things to decide after that. Worrying about what I was doing after she laid that load on the poor guy was the farthest thing from his mind."

Zorrie couldn't disguise the expression on her face. Though what spoke was intelligent and strong, it most closely resembled a walking corpse. As if understanding the unspoken question, he continued.

"You must forgive the form I use now. This flesh mirrors the greatest fears of the nearby locals and villages. Keeps them from prying. Most stay huddled and afraid in their own beds the nights I feed. Dress for the job you want, indeed?" Once again, the creature cackled with delight. "But, back then, I looked no differently than any other man. I lied to get close to the Nazarene, and when the time was right, I overtook one of the four in his circle of trust. Sliding the flesh I stole over my frame and taking his place. Sure as the kiss of…"

"Four? I thought there were, including you as Judas I guess, twelve apostles?" Zorrie knew little of the Bible, but she was sure of that much.

"There were twelve, but that matters little. There are always only four of true importance, and three of them must be misled. When the right time finally arrives, Mithras will show me the way. Mithras is good and, once more, I have been born anew. Glory to Mithras!"

"Judas, Judas, what is a Mithras?" Jean had remained rooted in one spot during the entire telling. Transfixed by the fantastic tale and hanging on every word. Instead of immediately replying, the resurrected being drew close to him as if to impart a vital message.

"I'm pleased you asked, Jean-Baptiste. I've explained much in hopes what I tell might, shall we say, tempt you?" A deep chuckle followed as one spindly arm was thrown across the manchild's shoulders. "I can see by your face that Mithras would accept you." Once more the tongue of black extended from out of the cadaver-like face. Intimate as a lover, the tip of it lightly teased the malformed split of his upper lip. Spittle stretching between the two as Jean recoiled.

"You see, this glorious mark from your birth already makes you his. It is all anyone ever sees when they look at you, Jean-Baptiste. Is that not true? You are the living embodiment of a faceless man." Tears welled within the simple eyes, a quiver cueing the overflow as he began to weep and nod. "Who wants to live forever?" The question asked in the same manner one would speak to a dog. And, much like a dog eager to please, Jean-Baptiste readily agreed.

"No!" Zorrie screaming at the two as she rushed to separate her friend from the sickly sweet contagion being spread. "He knows not what he is doing!"

With one arm, the fiend held her at bay. "That matters not. Does a child born to parents of any faith understand what is forced upon them? Are they able to make an informed decision? How about the infant sprinkled with water? But, Jean-Baptiste can know and claim his prize. Meet his maker. I suspect Mithras has need for a new lapdog, and Jean will be his eternally."

Pointing a frightfully thin finger at him before turning to face Zorrie, the vampire spoke one final word to Jean-Baptiste. "Stay."

"Now, my dear, I'll ask the same of you. Do you want to *live* forever? Or merely exist as you have these centuries since Herbert first brought you back? Wallowing in self-pity as those you grew to love withered and died. Betrayed by the corruption within your own body once more until none can bear the sight of you? Going from the adulation of the opera crowds to the scorn of the lowest of mankind. Moving from city to city to avoid capture when your rage overcomes your senses. Splitting the faces of those men who mistreat you. Fearing the itch you just can never quite scratch."

Silently, just as Jean had earlier, Zorrie began to weep. Every word true. Her endless life aimless and directionless. Her undead existence all performance art. Hans had forced her back into this world. But the rage that drove her to end her own life came back as well. All of these last two hundred years she'd been mostly alone and miserable. Betrayed by the repulsive rot of her own body, she'd all but quit caring. Allowing herself to be caged, mocked, and taunted as the freak she'd always felt she'd been. Could this Mithras give her purpose?

"I have been brought back one final time to serve Mithras. Soon, whether it be another hundred years or five hundred, Mithras will direct my purpose. But, he also has need for ones such as yourself." Judas paused then, letting his words marinate. "As the rot inside you festers, the growths will return. You might be able to prostitute yourself for another hapless doctor's butchery in the future. Perhaps snatch some semblance of normalcy. Perhaps." Again, Judas grew silent. Allowing his words, and the *who* in the details, to sink in.

"But, I know of a place not far from here. A place where you could belong. A home of infinite possibilities if you do his bidding. In return, he will cure the sickness within. Even heal the pain you feel inside. Help you focus it." He paused to let the grounding gravity of his words weigh in. "Give yourself to Mithras and let him guide you. If we can stop the fourth and final sacrifice, nothing will change. We can live forever in this paradise. A king and queen ruling all that is humankind eternally. Imagine the possibilities!"

"What of Francois? I owe him this body, regardless the pain it cost me. He is a kind and true man that I would loathe to hurt. What will happen to him and The House of Chanet?" Zorrie spoke in a hushed whisper as her head slowly turned. Both eyes locking on the darkened windows of the grand home.

"I have plans for this place." Judas waving his arms to include the village, countryside, and the House of Chanet. "Eventually, I'll need him gone. I'll use my influence to ensure the big home keeps a fresh supply of tenants I can drop in on as needed. I'm sure Mary," he paused and pressed one finger to his lips with a grimace. "I guess she goes by Madeleine now, will keep her fingers in my business as always. The sanctimonious bitch! But I'm sure the other side of the Chanet family will remain nearby. Afterall, the Chateau is only just across the border. I'll show it to you on the way."

"Where are we headed?" Zorrie took the hand of Jean and squeezed it.

"No place special. Just a hole in the ground. Think of it, if you will, as a shrine of sorts..."

I

The deeply forested land was well-hidden from prying eyes. A near jungle of thick foliage, soaring trees, and massive ferns waving wildly in the wind. The marshland, a place where only the hardiest fauna could settle roots and thrive. The warm temperatures and ever-present humidity aided by the tropical rains that often lasted days. Yet, this desolate location high above the body of water had seemed to call to the man who now trod unceremoniously across it. Welcoming him once he'd abandoned the small vessel he'd sailed upon to reach the shores.

The man shuffled his bare feet as he ascended the mountain. On one side of him, a torrent of water cascading across a riverbed of polished stones. The dark dirt he trekked over near the shoreline showing each footfall. A trail of the steps he'd taken to reach this point. He glanced up at the rise that had caught his eye as suitable. Towering trees huddled so close together their branches had become hopelessly intertwined. Each limb thick and sturdy. He laid his dark hand on the surface of the tree. His fingers absentmindedly exploring the rutted bark as his eyes scrutinized each limb. Satisfied with the choice, he began to wind the corded slack he'd let drag on the ground behind him. Coiling the rope in his hand before tossing the opposite end over one branch. Grabbing the dangling lead and hunching over it with the setting sun at his back, he worked the thick, rough-textured line. Periodically wiping at the sweat that stung his eyes when it dripped into them. Tying and twisting the end until he was satisfied with the result.

A noose.

When he was done, the man hurried to secure the opposite end of the rope. Winding it several times around the thickest part of the tree trunk behind him before tying it off. He tugged and pulled hard until he was sure the knot would hold. When he was finished, he cast his eyes back the direction he'd come. His hands began to tremble as he spied the outline of two stationary figures observing his actions from the shoreline below. The man all but leapt for the tree beside him, quickly shinning up until he sat on the thick branch where his rope swayed in the wind. Without a second backward glance, he fitted the crafted noose over his own head.

Mumbling to himself with a wry smile, the man pulled a handful of silver from the hidden pouch he'd secreted on his person. "I want to live forever," said the man before softly closing his eyes as he slipped off the top of the branch. Plummeting headlong towards the ground below before the rope snapped tight. The force of the long drop instantly severing the head from his body. As the decapitated torso hit the hardened, rocky earth under the tree, it burst asunder and all of his bowels gushed out. The gore and splatter mixing with the clinking nuggets.

A bounty of blood.

The moon had risen a deep red, and the ominous sky above suddenly seemed awash in blood. A forbidding crimson hue that pricked the eyes and bruised the hearts of all those bearing witness to the executions. The three crucified men – framed against this prematurely darkening sky – each hung limply. Only one figure yet stirred, and he labored painfully through the last of his agonizing breaths. Beneath him, as he sagged one final time, the ground underfoot began to rumble and shake. The two crude and misshapen tree limbs he'd been barbarically fastened to swayed slightly in the emerging chaos, but remained upright.

Below the crucifixions, staring stoically across the increasingly panicked and scattering masses, a lone woman stood apart from the commotion. Her features and expression unreadable. Though her piercing eyes never wavered from the scene of the crucifixions, she didn't move against the guardians tasked with the grim retrieval of the bodies. The gangly youths stripping the corpses and casting lots for the clothing and meager belongings of the three.

Behind her, struggling gamely to crest the top of what was known locally as Skull Mountain, a badly hobbled and disfigured leper girl slowly approached the woman. A tightly folded package of cloth held reverently in her hands. They both wore similar garments of the highest quality and, though the young newcomer's speech was marred by her deformed mouth, she greeted the woman with obvious familiarity. "I've brought what you asked, Inanna. Do you want me to take it over?" The girl's claw-like fingers pointing to a small group of weeping men who stood nearby.

Pursing her lips together, the woman replied in a hushed tone. "Remember, you need to keep calling me Ishtar until we leave this place," she said, frowning in mild reproach. "But, no. I want to have a word with Lugal before I give him the shroud." The girl handed the woman the thick, iridescent cloth. The neatly folded material at first appearing grey, or perhaps silver, before slowly becoming more beige and brown as it was passed. The color undeterminable in the strange scarlet glow of the blood moon above.

After conversing briefly with them, the peculiar cloth was passed to the men and Inanna strode back. Muttering to herself with a wan smile, "One down, three to go." The girl, nearly a young woman, asked shyly if everything had went as hoped and expected.

Inanna turned with a wink. "Certainly," she replied. "Sure as the kiss of Mithras."

Chapter Twenty-Nine
France-Modern Day

The end of the workday nearing, both of the weary men stepped back to admire their handiwork. The strange monolith nearly freed from the last of the rock and dirt it had been buried in. Though well below the earth's surface and still hidden within the vast underground labyrinth, nearly the entire surface of the massive stone effigy had now been exposed. Dr. Lucas Chanet, formerly the professor of archeology at the nearby University of Caen, looked across the dig site with satisfaction.

"I have to say that I'm amazed at how much we got cleared over these last two days." Lucas reached over and patted the sweat-drenched man beside him across his soaked back. "Granted, the little team of archeologists and graduate students I had working on this over the last few months did the bulk of the heavy lifting, as they say. But, still, I never expected just the two of us to get so much done. You are like a machine, Chris. Working as if possessed. Relentless!"

With a smile, Lucas wiped the perspiration away from his own brow. Like his coworker, the only other person working alongside him in the underground chamber, he was dripping wet and exhausted. Both men spending the bulk of the previous two days peeling back the last layers of sediment that had encased the enigmatic find. Back-to-back 14-hour days spent scraping, brushing, and hauling away the dirt. One carefully screened bucket at a time.

"As strange as it sounds, I've actually been enjoying myself." Chris grinned at the compliment. "Right after the accident, I thought I was a goner for sure."

"Accident? You were bitten and nearly bled out!" Lucas, when he'd first seen Chris after the attack, was certain he'd been killed. "You were all hunched over and walking like you had a broken collarbone just a week or so ago."

Chris nodded in agreement. "I really think my strength is finally coming back. All this physical labor is exactly what I needed. I feel amazing right now." He lifted the collar of his soiled t-shirt. "Reborn even," he added as he wiped at the dampness crowning his thinning red hair. "Besides, it has been fun seeing what the big guy looks like," Chris added, pointing at the carved figure of stone. "I think you were right to hold off sending Stander and Secrist any pictures of our progress. I can't wait to see the look on their faces when they finally see the whole thing." He gazed up at the figure. The artificial light that flooded the chamber bright and cheery. The rounded, chipped walls they worked in carved out sometime in the far distant past. Like the strange artifact itself, no written record of when the work was started nor completed.

"But, before we wrap up for the day, finish your story. You said your family has always been here in France? Why didn't any of them ever leave? You'd think at least a few would have been tempted to move away." Chris helped Lucas return the various tools, brushes, and buckets to the rack where they were stored each night. Locking the equipment, along with the sword, inside a metal cabinet. The men, finished for the day, packing up all of their things as they talked.

"I can't say for sure whether any of this is true or not. But, it has been said that the site of my ancestral home was originally a fortress. Allegedly, some ancient order my family was connected with built a fortified tower – a 'keep' as they are sometimes called – to protect and defend an ancient wonder. My family supposedly inherited all the responsibility, as well as all the land, associated with whatever started the rumors." Lucas shrugged nonchalantly as he spoke.

Though the majestic tale sounded intriguing and fantastic, he'd never put much stock in any of it. As a small child, he'd only lived briefly at what was once part of the grand estate. His father's premature death ending Lucas's time in the rural community on the border of Germany and France. The farm where his dad had been raised and worked far too much of a burden for a single mom raising a toddler all alone. His mother retreating back to Caen where her parents had still lived to find more suitable housing and employment. The farmland, worked and watched over by contracted neighbors, barely made enough for the upkeep and the taxes.

"So, 'once upon a time' as they say, the Chanets may have been a powerful and wealthy family with ties to royalty in both Scotland and Egypt. But, somewhere along the line, I guess our fortunes must have changed. I can tell you this much for sure though, the land around the farm, Chateau Chanet as it is known locally, is pretty much worthless. You wouldn't believe all the lore and rumors about it being haunted. The forest next to the property, even in this day and age, considered cursed as well. Half of the locals still believe it harbors all sorts of weird creatures and monsters. That France's own werewolf, The Beast of Gévaudan, was birthed within those same dark woods." Lucas, with everything they'd used stored and locked away, started up the tunnel that led to the surface. Trailing just behind him, Chris asked more questions.

"You said half of the locals still believe all that folklore. How about the other half?" Chris scratched at the wound near his shoulder. The itching always worsening at night. "What do they believe?"

"Oh!" Lucas unlocked the door that led outside. His hand resting on the handle as he chuckled. "The other half believe it was the Chanets that really slayed the beast, not the King's men." Lucas opened the door. The setting sun streaming into the underground chasm. Chris shielded his eyes as they both stepped outside. "In fact, though the location was lost over the centuries..."

"Centuries?" Chris was squinting as he followed Lucas to where his car was parked. The lot empty except for the lone vehicle. "When was this Beast of Gévaudan running loose?"

"Depends who you ask. Officially, it was sometime in the 18th century. Not long before the French Revolution. But," Lucas hit his key fob and the automobile chirped, "you can find plenty of older legends about werewolves in that area of the country." Though both car doors were opened, Lucas continued talking as Chris soberly eyed him from across the roof. "For that matter, even today there are those who say they've seen the beast. That they still see the oversized immortal wolf roaming the timber and fields near Chateau Chanet." Lucas shrugged in a way that conveyed, *what can you do...*

"Where did your ancestor supposedly battle and kill this werewolf?" Chris paused, his eyes drawn to the last rays of the sun as it dipped below the shadowed trees in the distance. "For that matter, how did he kill the thing?"

"Yeah, that part, after all I've seen since working with Stander, does give me pause." Lucas's eyes narrowed and his brow furrowed momentarily. "The legends say our family possessed a magic sword that somehow sang and soothed the savage beast. Using the songs to lull the creature to sleep before plunging the enchanted blade deep into the heart of the monster."

Chris seemed to blanch, the color draining from his face. "Holy shit, man. A freaking sword! That sounds awfully familiar, huh? Do you have any idea where this happened? Or the location of the sword now?"

"Not a clue. I don't think anyone does. I never paid much attention, nor really believed the local folklore and legends. I always thought the tale was hyperbole at best. But," Lucas slowly sunk into the seat of his car, "even if I did believe, it wouldn't matter."

"What are you talking about? Almost nothing could matter more. You saw how Stander used the blade we found buried down in the quarry." Chris sat beside Lucas, both men shutting their doors as the automobile was started. "What if that sword of your family's is also wrapped up in all this?"

"If you are willing to believe that part of the legend, you have to believe all of it." Lucas dropped the transmission in drive and began to make his way out of the abandoned lot. Turning onto the blacktop lane that led back to Caen. Meadows of wild, yellow flowers swaying in the breeze on both sides of the car.

"Believe me, I'll believe after all I've seen." Chris grinned at his choice of words. "What is the rest of the story?"

"Well, for starters, the blade is supposed to be made of pure silver. That alone makes it different than the one we found in the quarry. Plus, there is no mention of any symbols or anything like that stamped into it like the sword Stander used." Lucas gave Chris another shrug of his shoulders.

"I see what you mean." Chris flipped down the sun visor, shading himself from the rays. "Did blacksmiths really make swords out of silver?" Lucas shook his head no. Silver, he knew, was way too soft of a metal to be used as weaponry. "Thought so. And if that part is bullshit, who knows about any symbols that may or may not be present."

The short drive from the dig site to Caen only took about twenty minutes. Lucas dropping Chris off at the same hotel where Stander and Secrist also had rooms. "Sorry I have to leave you to fend for yourself tonight. I made plans with some friends awhile back that I don't dare break. You alright with grabbing dinner for yourself from the hotel's restaurant?"

"Yeah, sure. No problem. Don't worry about me," Chris replied as he exited the vehicle. "I think I'll hit the shower first though. I must smell something awful." Chris lifted one arm and scrunched his face up in mock disgust. "Besides, I don't have much of an appetite at the moment. As exhausted as I feel, I may turn in early anyway." Chris stepped back to close the car door. "Have a good time tonight," he added cheerily before slamming it shut. "See you in the morning."

Entering the hotel, Chris nodded and smiled at the staff manning the front desk. Each face familiar after spending the past several weeks, along with Stander, living out of his suitcase on the premises. Using a keycard, he unlocked his room and headed straight to the bathroom. Peeling off his soiled clothes and jumping into the spray that cascaded down from the showerhead. The warm water soothing on his tired and aching arms.

After washing and putting on clean clothes, he sat on the edge of his bed contemplatively. With Stander and Secrist not expected back in town until late that night, Chris was all alone. It wasn't lost on him that it was the first time he'd been left to his own devices since leaving rehab. "Not that I ever had a moment to myself while I was in there," he mumbled to himself as he stretched out across the bed. He'd told Lucas that he didn't have an appetite. Technically, he hadn't lied. Even after showering, his appetite and desire for food never rose. But, that didn't mean he had no hunger.

Rolling onto his side, his gaze fell on the curtained window of his hotel room. The city of Caen and its bright lights were just a short walk away. Chris, his eyes wavering, closed them in shame. Silently cursing what he considered weakness. Every fiber in his body clamoring with need. Knowing it would be so easy to find what he wanted. It was right outside his window.

Vaulting to his feet, Chris grabbed a water bottle from out of his room's minifridge. Downing half the contents in one gulp. Walking back into the bathroom, he splashed a couple handfuls of water across his features before drying himself off. Unable to sit still, he yanked the room's curtains open. Staring for long minutes at the cars entering and exiting the hotel's parking lot. The busy street beyond a boulevard that led into the downtown area of Caen. His eyes briefly following the route before he slid the drapes shut. Pacing the room, he reached for his phone almost out of desperation. "I'll call Rusty. Maybe they left early and are almost back now." The phone ringing without answer before going to voicemail. Chris ending the call without leaving a message.

Sighing with frustration, his need filling and commandeering his every thought, Chris grabbed his jacket. Turning the handle of the room's door, he looked down at the colorful hotel carpeting that ran the length of the hallway as he walked it. His eyes welling with shame. Each step a little quicker than the previous one, Chris made his way outside. On one side of the sky, the last rays of the setting sun. On the opposite side, the brightening moon was rising just above the tallest buildings in Caen's downtown area. Turning toward the full moon, Chris began walking.

Chapter Thirty
France-Modern Day

"Do you have your phone? Mine is still plugged into the car." Stander, having to holler to be heard over the frenzy below them, questioning Secrist. The two men treed by a ferocious beast that had charged at them from the timber. Chasing both across a small, moonlit meadow before sending them scrambling up the side of a tree for safety.

"No," Secrist answered haltingly as he pulled himself up to a neighboring branch. "My phone is sitting on the dash." Winded, each word was accompanied by an exhale or intake of breath. "Who the hell would we call anyway?"

"I don't know. The fucking army maybe? Look at that thing!" Jumping at its prey, the claws on its forelegs scrabbled at the bark. Shredding the side of the tree and leaving deep grooves in the wood. "What in the name of God pissed it off so much?"

"It must have heard you singing," Secrist, despite the danger, throwing a little jab his way.

The snarling snout was coated in soppy drool. Each raving growl spraying the burdened tree with more slobber. The gnashing teeth clacking together with frightful force. The set of tusks protruding from its lower jaw yellowed and jagged. The bristling fur-covered body – its hide a mixture of black and dark brown – was the size of a small horse. Each paw the size of full grown man's hand and tipped with fearsome claws meant for digging in the dirt. The outlandish creature, a massive wild boar made up of mismatched parts that nearly doubled its natural size.

"Hakuna Matata, motherfucker! Hakuna Matata!" Stander hollered down at the enraged creature. Vulgar language and sharp-witted humor the only weapon he had. With each passing moment the absurdity of the predicament they were in dulling their initial fears.

"How in the hell does a pig get that big?" Secrist turned his scowling face Stander's way. "And if you say doughnuts, I'm pushing you right off of here."

"It must be one of the survivors. From what we saw earlier. All those twisted animal corpses down in the tunnels. Some of those experiments, or whatever was going on down there, must have been successful." Stander shrugged his shoulders as if to say your guess is as good as mine.

"Yeah, but what we saw was mostly just bones. No way this thing is that old." Secrist shifted his weight in the darkness. The full moon on the opposite side of the tree and casting long shadows.

"Must be generational." Stander pointed down at the enraged hog. "Any of those that survived whatever was going on down in those caverns must have bred. Or tried to, anyway. Who knows what that thing's ancestors looked like."

"Well," Secrist sighed, the breath he'd lost while running finally reclaimed, "what do we do now? Wait for it to get tired or the boar to get bored?"

"Do you think you can run? I mean, if I took off the opposite way and let it chase me." Stander couldn't see the rental car or the road from their perch, but he thought he could make it back to their vehicle.

"When pigs fly..." Secrist pointed down at his foot. As Stander knew, he'd had surgery on it almost a year earlier, but still suffered from complications. He could run, just not very fast.

"Don't fucking say that," Stander grimaced in the moonlight. "Height is the only thing saving our ass right now."

Careful where he stepped and contorting his body to keep at least one hand secured to the tree, Stander looked out across the wispy weeds and nearby woods. Though he wasn't positive where they had been stopped along the road, the little village and pub they'd eaten at the day before couldn't be far. Scouring the countryside, all he could see was a single light off in the distance. He pointed it out to Secrist but, before they could discuss the significance, a long baying howl rang out. The haunting, mournful yowl silencing the surrounding area. The animals of the forest all falling mute. The incessant drone of the insects fading to an eerie silence.

Below them, the ferocious hog briefly paused before returning to action. Paying little mind to the unsettling cry, its singular focus on the men it had chased. Downwind from the stand of trees, it never smelled nor saw the shadow emerge from the edge of the nearby timber. The creeping form stealthily stalking the wild boar. Silently advancing through the swaying weeds it parted like a shark cruising its favorite waters. Stander and Secrist, their mouths agape, watching the approach of the second beast.

Even larger than the outsized pig with tusks, there was no confusion about what was advancing on their position. It was a wolf of immense size. Monstrously shaped and covered in nearly all black fur, it crept forward until it got roughly twenty feet from its prey before it leapt. Landing on top of the startled boar and knocking it to the ground. Horrible squeals and shrill, human-like screams of death erupting in the darkened field. The enormous wolf ravaging and tearing into the wild hog. The barbed jaw pulling hunks of fur and flesh with every bite. Arterial spray gushing from the wounds. The boar fighting back with all it had, its long tusks sinking into the meat near the wolf's neck. Blood glistening on the hides of both beasts - long claws slashing and tearing.

"This might be our only chance! While they're distracted and fighting. Follow me! The light is this way." Stander quickly scrambled down the side of the tree. In his haste, slicing open one hand on a broken tree branch. Thick blood dripping onto the ground. Behind him, Secrist followed. Cursing and mumbling under his breath the entire time. "Move it, Tommy!" Stander imploring him from the ground.

"This is not some damn movie, Russ! When do you think I last climbed up and down tree? I'm old as shit." Landing on the ground with a stumble, Secrist didn't even look at the two fighting behemoths before he took off after Stander. Following him across the weedy field before bursting into the woods on the opposite side of the meadow. "If I so much as reach for a bag of sugar wrong, I feel it all day long." Slipping across some fallen branches, he fell silent as he pushed through the brush. "And you want me to run across this goddamn gulley in the dark?" Panting, he was huffing and puffing between sentences. "Through all these tick infested trees because you think you've seen a light? Jesus Christ..."

"Are you done raving, old man?" Stander half turned and was pleasantly surprised to see Secrist had mostly, despite his constant bitching, kept pace. "I was right. There is a house up ahead!"

Farther back, the huge wolf had gained the upper hand. The eyes of the infernal beast locked on Stander. Between its bloody teeth, the limp neck of the boar. The hog's legs flailing weakly as its throat was steadily crushed. Bone splitting bone. Thick crimson and gore – pouring from the fatal wound – slick and shiny in the moon's luminescence.

Secrist could read the troubled look on his friend's face. Redoubling his efforts, he thought of nothing but reaching the small house they were closing in on. The moonlight above revealing a clear path of cracked flagstones that led to the door of the smallish dwelling. Though his foot screamed with fiery pain, all he paid attention to was the shrinking distance between himself and the house.

"Help us! Please!" Stander, pounding at the entrance, screamed for the home-owners. "Open the fucking door! There is something out here with..." Swinging wide, yellow light bathed Stander and flooded the tiny deck he stood on. Turning once more, he waved desperately for Secrist. Waiting until he'd crossed the threshold before following, slamming the door and sliding the deadbolt in place.

The doorway they'd rushed through had deposited them into a small kitchen. The backdoor of the house glassless and made of solid wood. Secrist had collapsed onto the floor – panting like a dog – garish linoleum of oranges and greens under his knees and hands. Above him, an unturning ceiling fan sporting three dim lightbulbs. The soft glow of each revealing a room of outdated appliances in matching mustard color. The kitchen long overdue for a remodel.

"Thank you so much." Stander turned to the presumed homeowner as he tried to catch his breath. Squeezing the palm of his cut hand tightly shut to stem the flow of blood that began to drip onto the linoleum floor. "You wouldn't believe what we..." Abruptly, Stander fell silent. His eyes widening in shock.

"You!" Secrist, using one of the four wooden chairs that rimmed the kitchen table, slowly pulled himself to his feet. "You were at that tavern where we ate yesterday. You... you work in the back, right?"

The woman who had opened her door to the strangers nodded timidly. She stood in one corner of the kitchen, a rifle or shotgun leaning against the wall beside her. Though her placid gaze was neutral, she stood rooted beside the gun. Her English, heavily accented, was easy to understand. "What has happened? You sounded scared. Has someone been hurt?"

Stander took one step toward her. "Liz?" When he moved closer a second time, she retreated farther into the corner. Her green eyes narrowing as she brushed a strand of blonde hair away from her forehead.

"Perhaps you are confusing me with another? My name is Elsie." Though she turned to Secrist, she kept one eye on Stander. "And yes, my sister and I own the brasserie and bistro down the road. You two stopped there last night. I remember you both." Elsie looked from one man to the other. "What were you running from? What has happened?"

Secrist looked expectantly at Stander, assuming, as usual, that he would take the lead. When he failed to speak, the room grew awkward until Secrist finally replied. "Our car was stopped on the road by a bunch of crossing sheep." Secrist wanted to point but, in their panicked flight, he'd lost all sense of direction. "There were so many that we got out to try and shoo them along when some... something came after us. Came from the woods."

As if expecting as much, Elsie turned and grabbed the gun she stood beside. Expertly loading what turned out to be a shotgun. Smartly cracking open the empty chamber and inserting two shells she pulled out of a nearby drawer before closing and racking the bolt. "Did the wolf follow you to my door?"

"How did you know it was a wolf?" Stander was smiling like a smitten school-boy. "Seems like you were kind of expecting it." He nodded toward the cocked and loaded weapon in her steady hand.

"Around here, everyone always expects the wolf to be at their door. These mountains and woods are its home. We have all seen it at one time or another. But, rarely does it attack man." Elsie gave both men a quizzical look. "Unwarranted."

Stander threw his hands up in mock surrender. "It came after something else. We just happened to be in its way." Briefly, he explained the gargantuan wild boar, the tree, and how they'd run when the two monstrous entities had collided in combat. "All we want to do is to get back on the road and leave here. But, I'm not even sure which way the road is. Or, if that wolf..."

"Beast. The wolf you saw is no ordinary animal. It can't be killed. These dark woods are home to it. Home to the Beast of Gévaudan." Elsie pulled a set of keys off a hook hanging near the backdoor.

"Beast of Gévaudan? From the 18th century? I thought King Louis had it killed and stuffed?" Secrist had, just a few days prior, been reading about the local monster and its legend.

"So it was said," Elsie answered, but was busy looking out of the kitchen windows. Satisfied, she turned back. "Yet, here you are telling me it chased you to my home." She nodded at the backdoor, indicating they should leave. "I see nothing outside. Whatever it was, wolf or not, has gone now. The garage and my car is just to the left. I can drive you to the main road. I have a pretty good idea where your vehicle must be."

Moving as one, the three skirted the edge of the house and garage, each with their heads on a swivel. Jumping into Elsie's car and slowly driving the two-lane road. All three watching closely for the monstrous wolf and anything else unnerving until the bright green of the rental car finally came into view. The automobile no longer ensconced among woolen sheep and appearing to be untouched.

"You were asking about King Louis," Elsie, her car still running, rolled down the driver's side window as Stander and Secrist tentatively approached their vehicle. "He wanted to be credited with having the Beast killed by his royal hunters.

But, in this part of the country anyway, they knew what really happened. The noble who ruled over these lands set a trap for the monster. A trou de loup, which in English means wolf hole. He let the Beast come to his door and caught him in the giant collapse he'd rigged. Then, ran the wolf through with his sword. Leaving his family's sacred blade buried to the hilt."

Elsie's green eyes locked on Stander. "Like a knife to the chest, he tore a hole through its heart. Then sealed the collapse to ensure that beast could never rise again."

"How could that be true if the fucking thing just chased us through the woods?" Stander felt himself drawn to Elsie, shuffling a few steps back toward her car. Thinking to himself how, in the orange glow of her dashboard, she looked so very much like Liz. "Was there supposed to be a pack of them or something?"

"No. But the Beast was around long before the rein of King Louis. And we still catch sight of him even today. Some will tell you the Beast is more like a watchdog. A pet, even. If one gets put down, another is raised up to take its place. The Beast doing the bidding of something far more powerful. Far older..." Elsie reached down and put her car in drive. "I hope you gentlemen have better luck from here on out and make it safely back to Caen."

"Hey! Um..." Stander took another step and laid one hand on Elsie's car roof. "If I get back down this way, maybe I'll run into you again sometime." He gave her his best smile.

Grinning back at him, Elsie's laugh was warm and inviting. Her green eyes blazed briefly. The fire in them achingly familiar before she winked a single time. "Not if I see you coming first," she replied before driving off. Stander, abandoned by the side of the road, slowly climbed back into the driver's seat of the rental vehicle. Starting the car and pulling away, Secrist's fingers pattering the screen of his phone in the seat beside him. Both men lost in their thoughts.

Elsie turned into the driveway and parked her car where she always did. Opening her door, the dome light above illuminated where Stander had sat. Drops of drying blood left from the cut on his hand staining the floorboard carpet and seat in several places. She thought to herself, *If I don't clean that up tonight it will stain*. Groaning, Elsie grabbed the shotgun and retreated into her house. Minutes later reappearing with spray cleaner and a wet sponge. A scowl on her face. She'd found more of his blood spilt along her kitchen floor that she'd also need to clean up. Sighing, she pulled the passenger side door wide and began scrubbing. The entire time wondering why she'd opened her home to the strangers. Living alone and painfully shy, it had been completely out of character for her.

But moments later, behind her where the edge of the lawn met the timber, a thunderous crash disrupted all of her thoughts. Branches snapping and rotten logs crushed underfoot as a massive wolf galloped out of the shadowed woods. Spinning, Elsie found herself face to face with the same snarling monster that invaded the worst of her nightmares and had haunted her hometown for an eternity.

The dreaded Beast of Gévaudan.

Its ferocious charge hesitated just as the moonlight hit her. Trembling, Elsie felt tears stream down her face as the fearsome creature's long muzzle of rowed teeth scrutinized the air around her. Whiffing in and out heavily as if unsure what to make of her. The thing's hot breath on Elsie's cheek and neck. An aged scar running along one side of the snout. Though too scared to ponder the significance, what looked like human skin and teeth poking out from the bloodless slit.

Howling, barking, grunting or yipping, incredibly the mammoth wolf seemed to speak to her. Woofing out unintelligible sounds that made no sense to Elsie. Its baleful glare softening with what could pass for recognition. Seeming to say "sorry" or something similar sounding twice before the fearsome features turned cruel again. Whatever had given it pause apparently resolved.

Elsie screamed one time before the savagery of the attack tore away the tender flesh of her neck. The vice-like clamp of the muzzle shattering the windpipe and crushing the top of her spine. Alive but unable to speak and barely able to draw a breath, Elsie looked helplessly at the grass of her lawn as she was dragged across it. The massive brute carrying her by its gore smeared jaws into the thick fauna. Pulling her methodically into the deepest black of the woods. Trees rushing past her as the brush she was hauled through tore at her clothes and pricked her skin. The nightmarish ride only ending when she was tossed carelessly into a shallow pit of gleaming white bones. Long tailed rats scattering from the fall of her body. A dark cloud of buzzing flies rising up from the filth she landed in and obscuring the moonlight.

Elsie watched helplessly as scores of creepy crawlies pulled themselves out of the muck closest to her face. Hard-shelled cockroaches and beetles with clacking mandibles marched toward her weeping wounds even as a host of winged insects swarmed her eyes and mouth. Squeezing them tightly shut, she could only imagine what advanced on her. The sound of bone on bone as something padded across the pit of decay. Rancid breath, hot as sin nuzzling the ruin of her neck. The last sounds Elsie heard was the squelching of her own flesh as it was stripped piece by piece from her shuddering body.

Her green eyes, now opened but unseeing, filled with the brightness of the full moon above.

Chapter Thirty-One
France-Modern Day

The breaking of the day was warm and cheery. Lucas, though still a bit weary from his night out on the town, pulled into the hotel and parked near the main entrance. Strolling into the bustling lobby, he was surprised to find Chris was already waiting on him. His new friend and co-worker habitually late for everything, it seemed, by at least five minutes. Lucas, now used to the idiosyncrasy, had gotten in the habit of snagging a free cup of hotel coffee each morning while he waited for him to appear.

After grabbing his usual to-go cup of steaming caffeine, Lucas and Chris exited the hotel. Climbing into his vehicle, Lucas pointed at a small car painted a brash shade of green. "Is that Stander's? His rental, I mean."

"Where?" Chris barely turned in his seat to see what Lucas was questioning.

"There. See that ugly little green car? That must be theirs. Did they make it back last night?" Lucas had started the engine but left it idling in park.

"I think... maybe..." Chris sounding uncharacteristically distracted and annoyed before his demeanor softened. "Sorry. I mean yes. I got a text sometime in the night, but I didn't see it until this morning. They had some trouble on the road coming back and got in really late. Said they were going to sleep in but would see us later. At the site." Fidgeting with a tube of lip balm, he gave Lucas a quick smile. "Let's get going! I'm anxious to get started."

"Damn, Chris. You feeling okay?" Lucas chuckled as he dropped the transmission into drive. "Most mornings you're barely conscious until we start working.

You get up early today or something?" Easing out of the parking lot, he pulled onto the busy street. Retracing their usual route back to the dig site.

"What can I say? I just feel really great this morning." Chris unrolled his window and let the morning air tussle his red locks. "Guess I'm just excited to show Rusty and Tommy how much we got done."

Arriving onsite, both Lucas and Chris began their workday without incident. Spending the entire morning freeing more of the ancient monolith from the earth it had been buried in. Stopping only briefly to eat the lunch Lucas prepared each day for them. With the majority of the gigantic stone figure's front now exposed, they worked with small digging tools and bristled brushes to free more of the backside. Soon discovering a void that had been carved out of the back of the statue. A long, rectangular cavity emptied of whatever once resided within. Much like the missing adornments on the front, it appeared the hollow opening had been liberated of its sole possession.

"Although the timing doesn't make any sense, it sure looks like our massive friend here was robbed." Lucas, chugging water, pointed to the various concave indentations along the statue's face and neck. "We know that, however improbable, the missing pupil turned out to be the obsidian stone recovered from the cave where the Norseman was discovered back in Michigan. I believe the bowl-shaped depressions around the neck were meant to hold more decorative stones or jewels." He turned to Chris and handed him the bottle he drank from. "I found a couple in our initial digging that matched the 'good luck charm' you and Stander found as kids."

"It is kind of nuts to think a piece from him," Chris gestured as he shook his head back and forth, "is what saved my life back then."

"Believe me, everything about this dig has been nuts, as you say." Lucas sighed as he surveyed the site. "Everything I ever learned about dating relics and the ground they are recovered in turned upside down. It's like the rules don't apply to him." Lucas looked up at the massive face of the effigy. "All around him we find impactite, which is only formed by the fiery impact of a meteor. Yet, the dirt, rock, and soil above him is all in situ. Completely undisturbed." He reclaimed the bottle from Chris's outstretched hand. "So, unless the big guy landed here millions and millions of years ago, we have a scientific conundrum as well as an archeological one."

"Maybe this was the site of a meteorite crash and ancient man carved him to mark the spot?" Lucas nodded without speaking. His expression reflecting plenty of doubt.

"Like the Carnac stones, the Locmariaquer megalithic site, and the Gavrinis tumulus, France is home to some of the oldest and enigmatic stone formations in the world. Makes you kind of wonder if these things are all somehow related." He turned to Chris. "Did you know that if you draw a line on a map, our guy here aligns perfectly with the Carnac stones on the other side of France? There are various theories that link the Carnac stones with other known structures and alignments on a global scale. Seems preposterous to think he," Lucas nodded at the grim visage, "doesn't fit in with all that in some way."

"Maybe if we can find all the missing pieces to the guy, it'll become clear." Chris, no archeologist and with only a high school education, could only guess. "I bet whatever filled that opening in his back is the key."

"You could be right," Lucas shrugged. "Ready to get back at it? Hopefully Stander and Secrist will show up here pretty soon. Maybe they discovered something that will help figure all this out."

Both men labored throughout the remainder of the day. The tandem working in practiced synergy to clear the last of the debris from the back of the enigmatic monolith. Stander and Secrist finally arriving just as they'd begun to wind down their efforts for the day. The duo apologizing for their late arrival and recapping the previous night's adventure. The four men gathering around a split and broken boulder in one corner of the underground chasm. Stander regaling them with colorful descriptions of what he and Secrist had seen at the Chateau Chanet and what they'd learned along the way. Summarizing their harrowing journey and bringing both up to speed.

By the time he was done, Secrist had already begun inspecting the work Chris and Lucas had accomplished in their absence. Stander joining him as Lucas pointed out the various concave indentations on the front of the massive stone effigy and what he believed they once held. Showing each the huge hollowed-out opening in the center of its back. The cavity, now emptied of the debris it had collected, looked like a small elevator just big enough for one man to stand comfortably inside.

Carved as if from one single stone, Stander and Secrist circled the massive statue. Seeing the visage completely cleared of the dirt, rock, and earth it was buried in for the very first time. Lucas dragging over several of the electric lights and positioning them in such a way that the figure was brightly lit up. The features of the human-like face and various carvings adorning it fully exposed. The monolith dominating the subterranean cavern it was housed in.

From the bottom to the top of the head, Lucas reported, it measured just over 60 feet. The width of the body and face roughly 20 feet across, the thing's expressive mouth as long as an average sized man. On its forehead, the same odd symbol Stander had found carved into the fireplace hearth of his Great Aunt Madeleine's home in America. Circular and rounded, it was teardrop shaped much like, as Lucas had pointed out when first uncovered, the Egyptian Ankh. Inside the odd symbol was a series of markings that crowded the emblem from top to bottom and side to side. Though it looked much like an unknown script, Lucas and his network of archeologists confirmed it was not. The deeply carved marks only one symbol that was repeated. A series of bent crosses hooked together. Angled swastikas that mirrored how the symbol has been found in cave art going back more than 6,000 years. Most scholars agreeing it was a sacred symbol without borders or the boundary of time. The closest known match to what they'd found still revered in the far east where it represents divinity and spirituality.

"I had suspected the detail and adornment would be limited to the frontside of the statue." Lucas frowned as he spoke, most of his assumptions about the puzzling discovery later proven wrong. "But the intricacy of what we found on the backside is just as interesting. The back of the head is hooded for some reason. What looks like a cape falling down along the back. The way it is sculpted reminds me a little bit of a Greek statue I've seen many times in the Louvre Museum of

Paris called the Winged Victory of Samothrace." Lucas grabbed a flashlight to highlight what he described, using the beam like a laser pointer as he talked. "See how it was carved and molded along here? Stunning artisanship! The stone seems to flow as if caught in the wind. Gorgeous!"

"What does it mean?" Stander had followed Lucas as he'd circled the monument, absorbing the details he pointed out. "Do you think that hood and cape have any significance?"

"Hard to say." Lucas played his light along the stone surface. "It's a real quagmire, for sure."

"It's not a hood and cape." Secrist spoke placidly from where he'd remained rooted at the front of the statue. His eyes never leaving the face and head of the strange effigy.

"No?" Stander and Lucas walked toward him, arriving at the same time as Chris. All four men staring up at the enigmatic find. "What do you think it is, Tommy?"

"It's a shroud," Secrist's eyes found Stander, "covering the entire entity. That's no hood," he gestured at the massive head, "just excess cloth bunched up across its shoulders. And what you guys are calling a cape is just a covering. In proportion, it is even the same size as what we found in your Great Aunt Madeleine's home."

"So, what do you think it means then?" Stander dropped his eyes from Secrist's gaze.

"You're the one with the birthmark, Russ." Secrist's expression was unreadable. "That symbol carved into its forehead, as you've shown all of us in the past, is virtually identical to the mark on your arm. Right down to those weird-ass swastikas running all along it." All three men were facing Stander, different emotions rolling across their features.

"I don't know what the fuck you expect from me. I'm just as clueless about all this as you guys." Stander looked from one pair of eyes to another.

"Can we save this for later? I'm not feeling very well right now." Chris, clutching at his stomach, was the first to turn away. "Doesn't it seem hot in here?"

Secrist, ignoring him, pressed on. Speaking directly to Stander even as Chris stepped to the nearest wall and leaned against it. "You know, I've seen you at your worst more than once. I mean, we've been friends a really long time, right? Over the years I've helped you out of some pretty rough spots. More than just a time or two. But I'm just now realizing that with all your hair and that big old bushy moustache... hell, even all those tattoos running up and down both your arms, I doubt I'd recognize you without those trappings. I truly have no idea what you look like underneath all that. It's like all that hair and ink is a distraction meant to keep our eyes off the real you, Russ. Almost like a disguise. Keeps you a faceless man."

"Don't be ridiculous," began Lucas, coming to Stander's defense. "We all know..."

"I think underneath everything," Secrist turned from his friend and looked back up at the stoic face carved out of rock towering above them, "*that* is you."

"Sorry, guys. I... I'm going to be sick." Chris, slightly bent over began hurriedly walking from the group. "Can you let me outside real quick, Lucas?" He turned at the end of the cavern and headed up the underground passage that led to the surface. The automatic lights in the tunnel suddenly buzzing with life. Lucas, concern showing on his face, pulling out the key and jogging after him.

Stander and Secrist stood mere feet apart. Secrist's glance bouncing from the stone-faced effigy to his stone-eyed friend in the awkward silence. Just as Stander turned and began to open his mouth, the howl of a wolf echoed throughout the chamber. The chilling sound coming down from the passageway Chris and Lucas had just ascended. Without words, both men raced for the channel. Chasing after the same sound they'd run away from the night before. Just as they hit the outside door, the awful baying came a second time.

Chapter Thirty-Two
France-Modern Day

Bursting out of the unlocked door, Stander raced to locate Chris and Lucas. Nearly running straight into their retreating forms. Both scrambling back toward the safety of the subterranean passage and caverns below ground. Behind them, the same massive wolf Stander and Secrist had run from just a day earlier. The infernal beast somehow tracking them to the abyss.

Retreating – no time to close let alone lock the outside steel door – all four men sprinted back down the rock-lined passageway. The looming monster barking at their heels before slowing as it neared the entrance. The beast woofing deeply and growling with a menace each man heard as well as felt in their chest. The wolf pausing as if to savor their panicked flight. The flickering lights exposing the ravenous jaws that hungered after them. Frothy drool dripping onto the dirt as it entered the earthen shaft. A shiny pelt of grey smothered mostly in black that dominated the opening. Meat cleaving claws at the end of each thick limb, the thickly corded muscles of its hackles rippling with ferocity.

Once inside, the beast descended the tunnel rapidly. Overtaking a stumbling Chris without slowing. The redhead ending up cowering on his hands and knees as it thundered past. Moments later, sick and retching violently into the dirt between his hands. Ahead of him, the other three darted into the cavern where the unearthed monolith stood.

Lucas, Secrist, and Stander immediately split from each other as they raced into the room. Lucas turning sharply and quickly diving behind a cracked boulder near the entrance. Secrist, ahead of him and with frantic eyes, headed straight for the tables and equipment on the far side of the cavern. Stander, momentarily unsure, ended up behind the stone effigy. His eyes upturned, he scrabbled for a hand or foothold he could use to scale the massive statue. All three men falling silent and unmoving as the oversized wolf padded into the room.

Barely hesitating, its snout whiffing dramatically once, the black lips of the wolf parted to reveal the ferocious bite it offered. The growls, yips, and howls that poured from the frightening jaws sounding very much like a language of sorts. Staring at the gigantic form where Stander hid, it headed straight for him. It's lengthy stride closing the gap with frightening speed. Behind the beast, unseen, Secrist pulled the sword from the storage cabinet where it had been housed. Swinging it wildly toward the ground. The metal blade striking one of the chunks of rock that littered the floor of the cavity. The hum of the vibrating blade stopping the wolf in its tracks.

Incapacitated, the still form quivered as if in the throes of an awful palsy. The dark hide shimmering briefly before revealing the form within. The receding fur and diminishing claws and canine snout somehow absorbed back into the man left in its place. The guttural fury heard in its unintelligible growls evolving into English that he fairly spat out. "... baptize in gore and bathe in the crimson," the snarl becoming a roar of anguished words. "Wash myself in his blood..."

"You! A fucking werewolf!" Stander peered out from his hiding place, his astonished expression a mirror of Secrist's own. Both men recognizing the old man with the cleft lip they'd encountered just a day earlier. The *crazy coot*, as Stander had called him, who had trailed after them in the underground tunnels back at the chateau. "Chasing us all this way back to... back to... God, the quarry."

The old man who had arrived in the guise of a beast smiled at Stander. The gash of malformed teeth and split flesh weeping with clear saliva that dribbled down his chin. "Lordy, lordy, I'm finally facing the killer of Zorrie." As the resonance of the blade faded, the beast within began to reemerge. Dark fur sprouting, the eyes yellowing and filling with blind rage. Astonishingly, the disfigurement on the man's face became a perfect human smile as the features of the wolf gradually began to return. One side of its snout hairless and ripe with pink flesh and straight, white teeth.

Understanding how to capitalize on the sword's fantastic power, Secrist struck the blade again. The vibrations once more revealing the man within. The beast dormant once more.

"I can still smell her on you. Even now. I've tracked you. Waited for the right time. The time when my other half rises to the surface. Waiting to introduce myself." His smile broadening and his eyes brightening. "My, my, aren't you afraid of how Mithras will have you suffer and die?" Cackling, the old man laughed uproariously.

"Killer? Zorrie?" Stander advanced on the man paralyzed by the hum of the blade Secrist held. "Do you mean the blonde with green eyes? Beth? From the club?"

As the reverberating tone began to fade, the man nodded slightly. Answering in a hushed tone between his barely moving lips. "Death took Beth. Death took both. Death took Beth. In my story she was Zorrie. Zorrie, Zorrie, my only friend in the quarry."

Entranced by the shimmering man with the odd cadence and lulled by his simple likeability, Stander and Secrist exchanged a look. The old man obviously had known Beth and knew that she'd met Stander. Blaming him for her death and accusing him of her murder. Lost in their thoughts, neither man recognized the vibrating blade had stilled until it was too late. The man returning to form, howling as new fur swarmed over his body. Thick canines erupting inside his elongating muzzle.

"Take that!" Lucas speared the wolf and the man. The sword he'd liberated from Secrist's grip slicing through the hide and flesh. Rupturing and gouging the heart as it passed. The tip of the blade spraying reds and pinks as it burst from the old man's chest.

"Wait! What are you doing?" Secrist lunged for the weapon but it was too late. The wolf became all man as it died. A cascade of blood pouring out of the wound and soaking the ground under him. Kneeling, Secrist looked up at Lucas. "Why did you do that? I had questions I wanted to ask."

Lucas seemed stunned by his own actions. His stare going from the sword in his hand to the corpse lying on the ground. "He was changing. Changing again. I thought... thought he was going... He was going to kill you." He looked over at Stander, the color draining from his face. "My God. It happened just like in the legends. The family lore. Am I... was I...? Was this all a prophecy?" He took two backward steps before adding, "I've never killed anyone before."

Moments later, a near blinding flash of blue light forced each man to cover their eyes. As it faded, the source became evident. A lone woman stood apart from them. Her features and expression unreadable under the fine cloth covering she wore loosely about her face and head. Her piercing eyes never wavering from the bloody scene. In her hands, a shiny stone slowly fading to a dull black.

Just behind the new figure, stepping out from her shadow, a woman with blonde hair and green eyes. A tightly folded cloth package held reverently in her hands. The material at first appearing grey or perhaps silver before slowly becoming beige or brown under the artificial light of the underground cavern.

"Liz!" Stander took a step toward her before stopping. Abruptly, all the guises she'd used melded into one. He now recognized, as if a veil had been lifted from his eyes, she'd been with him all along. The reveal itself utterly staggering. She was Liz and she was Izzy. The last woman he'd fallen in love with and his very first love. Plus, a host of others between that had come in and out of his life over the years when he'd been adrift and lost. Trainloads of recollections arriving that tracked the deeply rutted lows and soaring summits of his life as it had dipped and turned along the route. The clarity suddenly blindingly obvious to him. Somewhere inside of each of them it had been her calling him on. And when she hadn't been near, his life had always seemed somehow broken. Just a walking carcass searching for a lost soul that could bring life to his bones.

Resurrect him.

Seeing Liz so near but not touching made every fiber inside him ache with loss. Like whispers riding the wind, faint memories he could barely catch glided past him. The scent of her hair, the tilt of her chin, the winks in her eyes, and the feel of the small of her back. Her unbridled laugh, the softness of her touch in his hair, and the taste of her mouth on his. Stander knew he would have charged and swept her off her feet had it not been for the other beside her. His bewildered and dumbfounded gaze slowly returning to the woman who'd arrived first. Incredibly, he recognized her as well. In many ways, though differently, he had just as much love for her.

"Madeleine? Aunt Madeleine, is that... can that really be you?"

"Hello, Russell." Bronze skinned, tall, imposingly lovely, and appearing middle aged, Stander had no doubt it was the same woman he'd spent his boyhood summers with. His Great Aunt Madeleine, an individual one could never forget. Yet despite his confidence, Stander wrestled with the impossible. He'd last seen her as a teenager back in the '80s. Back when she'd died as a nearly 100-year-old woman!

How could any of this be?

Stander opened his mouth. The questions he had feeling both urgent and desperate. But as he began to speak, Madeleine's voice drowned him out. "We have very little time before they arrive. So, I must be concise." Her blazing eyes boring into Stander's. "I commend you for enduring. You have done well. Each test, trial, and tribulation thrown your way handled. But, the worst is yet ahead. Elisabeth," she nodded toward Liz who was watching intently from behind, "can no longer assist you. Now, it all falls onto you four." Madeleine's gaze landing briefly on Chris, Lucas, and Secrist. Each face masked with their own version of baffled astonishment. "Each with a vital role if you are to succeed."

"Judas, as if by design, has already snaked his way inside this inner sanctum." Madeleine opened her arms wide to include the entirety of the underground cavern where they stood. "This sacred hallow. This shrine to the first stander on this world." Lifting her eyes to the recently unearthed monolith, she left no doubt she spoke of the enormous stone effigy that had been hidden deep within the catacombs of the quarry since time immemorial. "Yet, despite the nearly unfathomable efforts undertaken by the first stander, his works will be eclipsed by the last stander."

Madeleine turned to Stander. "Russell, my last stander, you must prevail. Noviodunum Suessiones is so much more than just the name of your family trust. Do what you know to be right and this world can truly live free. Unburdened of the artificial life that would swallow whole the very spark that ignites humankind."

Behind Madeleine, Liz stepped slowly forward and placed a hand on her shoulder. Weeping, her wounded emerald eyes sought out Stander's own. The hurt and loss within causing his own to pool with heavy tears as his breath began to hitch. Before he could react, the blinding blue flash that accompanied their arrival repeated. Without another word being uttered, the four men were once again alone. The crumbled form of the dead man with the hare lip vanishing along with the two women.

"No...no! W... wait!" Stander stumbled as he took a step, **"Wait!"** His legs giving out, he sank awkwardly to his knees. The welling tears falling to the ground. "Please don't leave me... leave me again." The shuddering breaths he took in full of more emotion than oxygen. His words hoarse before dropping to a whisper. "Izzy... you... we promised each other."

Sagging until nearly face down in the dirt, the support of his three friends all that kept him upright. Secrist and Lucas clutching at his arms and shoulders while Chris kneeled in front of him. The two boyhood friends embracing and bawling together like neither had done since they were kids. Not since they'd both been forced to watch Brian, their childhood best friend, cruelly slaughtered like cattle before their 14-year-old eyes.

Slowly, the two sobbing men stilled. Eventually being helped back to their feet by Secrist and Lucas. Long minutes of contemplative silence following until Stander eventually began to come back to life. Confusion and anger conspiring to snuff out the pain and sadness. His eyes dried, they began to fill with more fury than pain.

"What the fuck am I supposed to make out of all that?" Exasperated, Stander picked up the sword Lucas had hastily dropped earlier. Dejectedly swinging it back and forth as he paced back and forth across the floor of the cavern before jabbing it into the dirt at his feet. "And how can Judas be somewhere inside here with us?"

None of the men were able to answer his questions. They had no time. A pounding on the steel door sending Lucas up to the surface to investigate. The archeologist returning several minutes later with two men in suits flashing badges as they entered the subterranean chamber. Unhurried, they strolled casually across the dirt floor. Their fine leather shoes kicking up dust as they took in the entirety of the cavern.

"Russell Stander?" Though both ignored the others and walked directly to him, they waited for the nod of his head before continuing. Introducing themselves as police detectives working for the city of Caen. "The hotel staff told us you were likely to be here."

"What's this about?" Though Stander had been expecting to have this conversation, falling on the heels of all that had just transpired couldn't have been worse timing. His head still spinning from the revelations and cryptic conversation.

"We'd like to ask you a few questions. Forgive the intrusion into your work, but our calls and the messages we left for you at the hotel went unanswered." Both detectives seemed to be sizing Stander up. "Perhaps you have been out of town." With judgement reflected in their eyes, it was more statement than question.

As Stander opened his mouth and began replying, Secrist beat him to the punch. "Why can't this wait until tomorrow? We were about to head out and call it a day. Wouldn't the morning be a better time for this discussion?"

"Ah, yes. You are the American policeman, correct? Monsieur Thomas Secrist?" Nodding, Secrist held his tongue. How did these guys know about him? "You're not as offensive as I'd expected." The detective from Caen smiled, but there was no joy in his eyes. "We would be interested in speaking with you as well. I understand you two recently traveled together across our lovely country. Over to the border, yes?"

"If you know who I am, you know I'm also retired. But that doesn't mean I can't still smell bullshit from a mile away. What are you accusing him of?" Secrist worked hard to keep his tone even. He knew he needed to keep his cool if was going to be able to help his friend.

"Accuse?" The man pulled a small pad of paper from inside his suit jacket. "We would never just accuse him of being the last person to see Dr. Elizabeth Drexler of Michigan University alive before she disappeared. Or accuse him of suddenly flying overseas right after she vanished." The well-dressed detective began reading from the paper he held. "Nor would we accuse him of running from the Illinois town of Almore right after multiple citizens vanished or wound up dead." He paused, his eyes rising from the words he read. "Under very suspicious circumstances according to what we've been told."

The second detective thrust his phone in Stander's face. "We also wouldn't accuse Monsieur Russell Stander of losing a very expensive antique stiletto in the maintenance room of a bar." Stander barely glanced at the image he was being shown. It was the blade Beth, or Zorrie, or whatever her real name had once been, used to pulverize her own face.

"What you are insinuating is ridiculous. Had there been even a shred of truth, or any evidence of foul play at all, the local authorities would have been all over him." Secrist was steaming. He'd partnered with a few cops like these two in the past. They loved making even innocent people squirm. "The scenarios you are describing would be impossible."

"Agreed," the man said as he repocketed the little paper tablet. "Not without a local patsy. Maybe if he'd befriended someone working on the police force though? Get him his drinks for free at the bar he owned? Find something in common like, say, music or maybe fishing to keep him friendly? Have him keep his ear to the ground like a Native American scout. " The man snapped his fingers as if an idea had just popped into his head. "Or, if things get too dark, hand him a silver lining as he heads into retirement." The detective from Caen moved closer to Secrist, his nose inches from his face.

"How much is he paying you again, Judas?"

Watch for the apocalyptic, two-book conclusion to the Skulldiggery series.

The Remnant – Skulldiggery Book 7
The Ruin – Skulldiggery Book 8

ALSO BY DM GRITZMACHER

The Relict
SKULLDIGGERY BOOK 1

The Quarry
SKULLDIGGERY BOOK 2

The Lingering
SKULLDIGGERY BOOK 3

The Shroud
SKULLDIGGERY BOOK 4

The Trench
SKULLDIGGERY BOOK 5

The Shrine
SKULLDIGGERY BOOK 6

The Nazis Stole Christmas!